No
More
Drama

La Jill Hunt

URBAN BOOKS LLC
www.urbanbooks.net

Urban Books
6 Vanderbilt Parkway.
Dix Hills, NY 11746

Copyright © 2004 La Jill Hunt

ISBN 0-9747025-0-1

First printing November 2004

10 9 8 7 6 5 4 3 2 1

Distributed by Kensington Publishing
850 Third Ave
New York, NY 10022
For store orders call 1 (800) 221- 2647 ext 527

Printed in Canada

Dedication

This book is dedicated to my Detroit family —
Uncle Johnny, Helen, Bruiser (and the Detroit Ruff
Ryders), Rochelle, Tanika, Nita, and LaTonya. Thank
you for your love and support!
Lindsey for Life!!

Acknowledgements

First and foremost, I have to thank God. You have been so good and so merciful throughout this entire journey and I thank You for Your continual blessings.

Thanks to my family, the Hunt, Smith and Williams families, for being there and supporting me in all of my endeavors. I love each and every one of you.

Thanks to Pastor Kim W. Brown, Sis. Valerie K. Brown and the entire Mt. Lebanon Missionary Baptist Church family. There are no words to express my love and appreciation for all you have done for me. Pastor, thank you for your guidance, advice and encouragement and most of all for being the voice of reason as I try not to blow this. LOL!!!

To Carl Weber, my brother, who gave me the opportunity to show what I can do, thanks for believing in my talent and *Drama Queen* from the jump and always being there when I need you. My success is a reflection of your savvy.

To Martha, my editor, who taught me how to write, I will forever be indebted to you for all you have shown me. I love you for sharing your gifts and making me a better writer.

To Robilyn Heath and Yvette Lewis, two people I can always depend on whenever I need anything, thank you for being you.

To Dwayne S. Joseph, my brother, my friend and literary twin, you have been there for me from the beginning and this experience would not have been the same without you. I love you and thank you for your friendship. Wendy, you're the bomb too, girl...without you, there would be no Dwayne!!!

To my Urban Books family, thank you for making me laugh and being there for me. It takes a special kind of writer to be down with Urban Books, and I am proud of each of you.

To my big brothers in the big, bad world of writing: Roy Glenn, Thomas Green and K. Elliott, thank you soooo much for your insight, your time and your humor. Each of you has made this journey all the more fun for me.

To my friends until the end: Joy, Shan, Saundra, Cherie, Danita, Tomeica, Norell, Toye, Robin, Pam, Mechellene, Selena and Tomika, thanks for having a sister's back whenever she needed it. You are as true as they come and I love you for it!!!

To all the readers and book clubs everywhere who supported *Drama Queen*, I thank you for helping make it a success. I pray that you enjoy this endeavor just as much. LOL.

To Ju Joyner for hooking my site up, thank you. Now that the second book is out, I definitely got you! LOL!

Thanks to all the bookstores that supported me, especially Richard Holland of Sepia, Sand and Sable for making me laugh; Black Classics (Mobile, AL) for welcoming me home; all the Karibu stores; and Shrine of the Black Madonna (Detroit, MI)

Thanks to Meeko, Christine and Marvita for letting me slide so many times! And to Ernestine for hooking the hair up every week!!

Well, I think that's it. If I forgot anyone, please forgive me. I would thank the haters, but the last time I did, people I didn't even know were hating on me came out the woodworks because they got called out. So, I won't thank them this time in an effort not to offend anyone. I'll just leave you with a quote from my girl Stephanie Johnson, author of *She's Got Issues*: "I don't fight, I write! So make me. Please."

E-mail me at mslajaka@aol.com

www.lajillhunt.com

Prologue

Terrell rolled over and grabbed the ringing phone off the nightstand. He thought he was dreaming when it first rang, so he ignored it. Whoever was on the other end was persistent and determined to talk to him, so the ringing continued, letting him know that this was indeed reality.

"Yeah," he whispered into the receiver. He cleared his throat as he fought off the grogginess of sleep.

"Terrell," the small voice came through the phone, "I'm sorry it's late."

"It's a'ight. You have that dream again?"

"Yeah, they're getting worse. This time she killed herself and Craig showed up at the funeral." Terrell rolled onto his back, listening as she talked. "In the dream, he told Geno he slept with her too. You think that happened for real?"

"I doubt that seriously." He laughed.

"It's not funny, Terrell. Look, I know you're 'sleep. I got a little freaked out, that's all." Kayla sighed.

"Have you talked to her?"

"Who?"

"Your sister. Isn't that who we're talking about?"

"Hell no! What am I gonna talk to her about? The drama she's caused? I ain't got no words for her."

"You need to talk to her, Kay. The dreams ain't gonna stop until y'all squash this and you find out what happened. Why or *if* she even caused all that stuff."

"I told you I have no words for her," Kayla restated. He knew that she wasn't changing her mind and he didn't feel like arguing, so he decided not to press the issue.

"You home by yourself?"

"Yeah, I mean Day is here with me," she said, referring to Terrell's six-month-old goddaughter. "Is Nicole there with you?"

"Naw, she's at her own crib."

"You decide what you're gonna do yet?"

"No, not yet. I got something else I got to take care of first."

"I hope that something is named Darla. I can't believe you slept with that skank. Are you at least gonna tell Nicole?"

"Look, I thought you called to talk about your nightmare."

"Well, now the convo has turned to your nightmare," she replied, voice dripping with condescension. Terrell knew it was time to end this conversation. He was not in the mood to discuss his multitude of problems, especially at 3:00 in the morning.

"A'ight, Kay. I'm hanging up now."

"I'll talk to you tomorrow, Terrell."

Hanging up the phone, he folded his arms over his face. He loved Kayla to death, but sometimes she seemed like a thorn in his side when she tried to be all up in his business. He didn't need her reminding him about his issues; they were ever present in his mind. *Darla.* He didn't even want to think about the fact that he had ever slept with her, but now it was evident because she was pregnant.

Then there was Nicole. There was no doubt that he loved her. She was beautiful, intelligent, funny, and ambitious—everything he desired in a woman. Possibly, wife material. Now, he had jeopardized all of that in a stupid moment of weakness. He could kill himself every time he thought about that night when he left the club. It wasn't even that memorable, but he was drunk and Nicole wasn't up for company. Darla, on the other hand, welcomed him with open arms, breakfast on the table, some bomb-ass Kool-Aid and a warm bed. What more could a man ask for? *How about a condom, stupid? But you didn't use one, and now she's pregnant, pregnant, pregnant.* The words had seemed to echo when they came from her mouth. He thought she had to be joking. There was no way she could be pregnant, especially since Nicole had just told him the exact same thing three hours earlier.

It was amazing how differently he felt when both women told him the same news. With Nicole, it was unexpected but still came with a sense of joy. With Darla, he felt as if he had just been handed a death sentence for a crime he didn't commit. Darla was threatening him with suicide because according to her, he broke her heart. Nicole was hell bent on him committing to her, which he planned to do, but he wanted to be sure. The stress of both women carrying his seed began to take a toll on him and he became frustrated with everyone around him.

Last night, he needed some chill time by himself. Avoiding both women, he drove around until he found himself at Floyd's, a small jazz bar he frequented when he wanted to disappear. A couple rounds of drinks, a few turns on the dance floor, a little small talk and he was ready to leave. He hadn't left alone.

"Was that her?"

Terrell turned to face the woman who was stirring next to him. "Who?"

"Your soon-to-be fiancée."

"No." He reached over and touched the naked shoulder. The glow from the streetlight came streaming in, casting shadows on the wall.

"Who was it?"

"None of your business." He pulled on the thick covers, revealing the contour of the naked body, and snuggled closer.

"Well, then it must have been Ms. Kayla."

"Whatever," he said, caressing the smooth skin with his fingers.

"Come on. Tell me what's going on now."

Terrell felt the hand moving higher up his thigh. "Nothing. She's just having these nightmares."

"Aw, poor baby."

"Let it go," he groaned.

"Oh, so you want me to let it go?" The hands teased between his legs.

"You know what I mean."

"No, tell me what you mean."

"I mean you and your sister need to squash the nonsense." Terrell pulled the firm body onto his and kissed Anjelica full on the mouth before she could say anything else. He felt her placing the condom on and as she mounted him, all thoughts of Nicole, Darla, and Kayla immediately vanished. Moments like this made him realize maybe he wasn't ready to settle down. *So many women, not enough time.*

Chapter 1

Terrell sat in his Camry and watched as the rain fell on the windshield. As much as he loved the rain, he hated driving in it. He flipped the switch to turn on his wipers. For a moment, they swished back and forth to the same beat that Biggie was rapping to. He turned up the volume and nodded his head to the notorious one asking why she had to stick him for his paper. It was just the song he needed to put him in the right frame of mind for what he was about to do. He had told himself that no matter what, he would remain calm.

He pulled his cell phone out of his pocket and dialed the numbers as he pulled in front of the apartment building. She answered on the first ring.

"Yo, come out here for a minute. I need to talk to you." He knew he sounded cold, but he wanted to get this over with.

"Why can't you come in? It's raining."

"And what, you gon' melt? Come out here. And hurry up 'cause I gotta go to work." He hung up the phone and leaned back on the headrest. A few moments later, she came outside and walked to the car.

"Hey, baby." She smiled and tried to lean over to kiss him. He put his hand up to let her know that it wasn't happening. He noticed the look of disappointment on her face but disregarded it.

"Look, we gotta take care of this situation before it gets any further. You know what I'm saying?"

"I don't wanna handle it, Terry. I love you and I wanna have our baby."

"Darla, don't be crazy. There is no way that I can have a kid with you. I don't want a kid with you. It ain't happening."

"So, what do you want me to do, kill it? Kill our baby?"

"Be realistic. You already got two kids that you're barely taking care of now. You don't even have a steady job. Does it even make sense for you to have another kid? Come on. You and I aren't even all that tight." He looked over at the heavy woman with fair skin. Her long hair fell around her chubby face. "I mean, we cool and everything, but Darla, I don't love you."

"So, you do want me to kill our baby." She sighed.

He could tell that she was hurt, but Terrell didn't respond. They sat in silence with only the sound of the rubber blades whisking the raindrops off the heavy glass he was staring out of. He watched as the city bus stopped and an older woman with two small boys got off. They all held hands as they ran into the building next door. For some reason, it made him think of his own brother, Toby, and how their mom worked hard as a single parent.

"I'm telling you to be smart." He reached into his pocket and pulled out the card that he picked up earlier. "I made you an appointment for nine in the morning."

"Huh?" She looked up at him, confused.

"I'll pick you up at eight-fifteen. I'm sorry that this all happened the way it did. You're a sweet girl, and—" The sound of his cell phone interrupted him. He looked at the caller ID and saw that it was Nicole. He sent the call to his voicemail.

"I'll be ready." Darla wiped the tears from her eyes as she opened the door and got out.

Terrell breathed a sigh of relief as he watched her slowly walk back to the building. It had gone better than had expected. From the way Darla had been acting over the phone, he anticipated a teary-eyed, scream-filled temper tantrum.

He listened to the message that Nicole left, telling him that she loved him and asking him to call her later. He reached into the back seat and grabbed his CD case. Finding the disc he was looking for, he pumped the volume as Jodeci sang "Forever My Lady." *Things may work out after all,* he thought.

Chapter 2

"What are you trying to say, Roni?"

"I ain't trying to say nothing. What I'm saying is that your brother got set up. Darla couldn't get you, so she went after Terry. Now she's pregnant. That means she'll be tied to both of you," Veronica called out from the bedroom where she was getting dressed.

Toby checked the clock on the stove to make sure she wasn't running late for work. He knew she didn't intend on spending the night at his place last night, but as usual, he convinced her that it was too late for her to drive back to her apartment. He grabbed a dozen eggs out of the fridge and started preparing one of his famous omelets he knew she enjoyed. The sounds of his morning mix, which was aired on the local radio show, drifted from the other room.

"She ain't gonna be tied to me. It ain't my kid!"

"But it'll be your niece or nephew, Uncle Toby."

"If you think for one moment that Terry is gonna let her have his kid, then you're crazy. Hundred dollar bet it never happens. You want bacon or sausage?"

"Sausage. And it's not his decision; it's hers. Nasty, she's just nasty. I can't believe y'all slept with her. Both of y'all, at that."

He caught a glimpse of her as she walked past the kitchen and into the den. She had a way of being sexy without trying, and he loved that about her. He continued to spy on her through the breakfast bar which separated the two rooms. She casually sat on the edge of the sofa and placed her black high-heeled shoes on. He loved watching her dress. She stood and pulled her short, black skirt down, adjusting her white blouse. She caught him admiring her and licked her lips seductively then blew him a kiss. He remembered the food on the stove and focused on cooking.

"Hey, you wanna go to Jasper's tonight? They got a new band I wanna check out."

"You mean the infamous DJ Terror doesn't have to work?"

"Nope, not tonight, and I know you're not complaining about me working, Miss I-want-the-wedding-of-the-century."

"Baby, believe me. I ain't complaining about the work. I'm just surprised we can go out on a real date for a change," she said, hugging him from behind.

Toby understood that being engaged to a man who worked almost every night of the week might be a little difficult for Veronica Black. He knew that she was a diva in her own right and liked to be treated as such. Roni enjoyed being wined and dined and shown off by whoever was lucky enough to have her by his side, but between working at the club, radio station and private parties, Toby really didn't have the quality time that he wanted to spend with his fiancée. He had decided that he better start making time and gotten one of his boys to work his Thursday nights, starting tonight.

"So, does that mean you wanna go?" He flipped the eggs and sausage onto a plate and she grabbed the orange juice out of the fridge.

"Of course. Why wouldn't I?"

"You know how you and your crew make plans. I thought you may have had to call Kayla, Tia, Yvonne, Susie, Cheryl, Margaret . . . " He began counting on his fingers.

"Shut up, Toby. You know that's not true." She giggled. They sat across from each other and bowed their heads as he prayed over the food. They quickly began eating.

"It is true. How many times have I heard 'Me and the girls' or 'Well, the Lonely Hearts Club . . .'"

"They kicked me out the Lonely Hearts Club, thank you very much." She sighed, batting her eyes at him.

He faked a look of shock. "No. Whatever for?"

"I'm not lonely anymore, I guess."

"You don't sound like that's a good thing." His eyes fell on her empty ring finger and he thought about the black velvet box sitting on the shelf in his closet.

"Tobias Sims, you are the best thing that ever happened to me. Don't ever forget that. Now, I gotta go before I'm late. I love you and I'll call you during lunch." Roni jumped up and kissed him.

He walked her to the front door and helped her put on her blazer. She turned and he looked into her eyes. She was the most beautiful woman he had ever known, and she was perfect for him. He wanted nothing more than to make her happy.

"I love you, Roni Black."

"I love you too, DJ Terror."

She pulled him closer and kissed him full on the mouth. Her tongue teased his bottom lip and he opened wider and savored her taste. He ran his hands along the small of her back and he felt himself becoming aroused as a small moan escaped her throat.

"I gotta go," she said, pulling away.

"I know." He laid his chin on her forehead. "I'll pick you up at six-thirty. Be ready."

Roni waved as she backed out of the driveway. His eyes fell on a skateboard lying in the neighbor's yard and he smiled at himself. *Yeah, no doubt I love the hell outta that girl.*

Toby had finished cleaning the kitchen and was about to jump in the shower when the phone rang.

"Yo."

"He wants me to kill our baby," a loud voice wailed in his ear. He knew that Terrell was going to tell her to have an abortion. He also knew that she wouldn't take it very well. Darla wasn't the most mentally stable girl in the club. That was why he always dealt with her in a special manner.

Toby had only slept with Darla twice. The first time, he was in a drunken stupor and she actually had to drive him from a party they both happened to be at. The second was when he had bronchitis and was so doped up on antibiotics and amphetamines he didn't even remember it happening. Funny thing was that both times, Darla swore she was in love with him, like there was a chance in hell he would consider being with her permanently. She was a nice enough girl; she would often come by with groceries for his crib and would clean up if she saw a need, but she definitely wasn't his type. She was his STD—something to do. If he needed something done, he would call her, and she always came through. There were times his utilities would have been turned off if she wouldn't have been on hand to drop off a payment. For that, he was grateful.

His brother, on the other hand, should have known better. Toby couldn't even understand how Terry got himself in this situation. Darla was not the kind of girl you sleep with unprotected. He didn't even want to think about the fact that Terry didn't even care that his own brother had already slept with this girl. He pushed that thought completely out of his mind for fear that it would show that Terry had a lack of loyalty to him. But she wasn't that important, so he wasn't that worried.

He didn't know what to say to her at this point, though. Not that he supported abortion, but this time, one would make sense.

"So, you talked to him?"

"He just left. He made the appointment and everything. He says he's taking me in the morning." She sniffed.

"Damn," was all he could say. He began making up the king-sized bed that he and Roni had just gotten out of.

"What am I gonna do? I don't want to kill our baby."

"But Darla, he doesn't want the baby."

"I want it, though. I love him, Toby. This baby is a gift from God. Are you telling me you don't believe that?"

That question made Toby uncomfortable and he decided that maybe he shouldn't be talking to her about this. "Look, this is a decision between you and my brother. I don't have anything to do with it."

"Talk to him, Toby. This is your blood he's about to get rid of, your niece or nephew."

"I'm sorry. I don't have anything to do with it, Darla."

"The night I told you I was pregnant, you swore you would support me and I was your friend. You lied!" she screamed at him.

"Hold up. I am supporting you. I'm listening to what you got to say. For real, yo, this really ain't even my business. This shit is for you and Terry to figure out. He's a grown man and whatever he wants to do is on him."

"So that's it? That's all you got to say, Toby?"

"That's all I got to say. I wish you the best."

"Thanks for nothing. You ain't shit and neither is your brother. I'm glad I'm getting rid of it. I wouldn't want to be bothered with anything with your blood running through it, you bastard."

Instead of responding, Toby hung the phone up. He knew she was hurt and was speaking out of anger. There really was nothing he could do; the decision wasn't his. One thing he did know was that Terry did have a cursing out coming to him. He called his brother's cell.

"What up, dawg?"

"Man, I don't even wanna know why the hell you slept with her, man. That don't matter. But you ain't use a rubber? I thought I taught you better than that."

"I know, I know. But I got it under control. It'll be taken care of tomorrow."

"Now she blowing up my spot, crying and yelling at me like I'm the one that knocked her up."

"She called you? What she say? She's still going tomorrow, right? Man, tell me you told her to do this."

"I can't tell her what to do, Terry. You think I'ma tell a woman to get rid of a baby I ain't have nothing to do with creating?" Toby thought his brother truly was crazy. He began looking in his closet for something to wear.

"Well, what did you tell her?"

"I told her it was between you and her and I ain't have nothing to do with it."

"And?"

"And what?" Toby was wondering where Terry was going with this line of questioning.

"Did she say she was gonna go tomorrow?"

I should play with his head and make him sweat. "She said she ain't going nowhere except her doctor to get some prenatal vitamins."

"What? Yo, you gotta call her. I can't have no kid with that chick. Man, I'm thinking about asking Nicole to marry me. Look, I gotta tell you something."

"What?"

"Nicole's pregnant."

"Man, do you ever wear a rubber?" He was shocked. He knew that Terry could be out there sometimes, but two girls knocked up at the same time was ridiculous. "You better pray that this Darla thing gets taken care of with the quickness. So, what are you gonna do about Nicole? Same thing?"

"Hell no. You know Nicole ain't trying to have no abortion. And I don't want her to, to be honest. I love her, man. I think I wanna marry her."

"You sure about that, Terry? I don't think you know what you want to do. Marriage ain't nothing to play wit'. You know that. Before you go doing something you know you ain't ready for, you better think and make sure."

"I know I want to take care of this thing with Darla and I wanna marry Nicole and get on with my life. Simple as that."

"Handle your business then. Just be sure. That's all I'm saying."

"I will, Toby. And believe me, this is the last time I'ma get caught up in some drama like this."

"I hope so, Ter. I hope so."

"Man, don't act like you ain't have no drama of your own a little while back."

"It wasn't like this, though." Toby instantly knew that Terry was referring to the situation he found himself in when Roni arrived at his house unexpectedly, catching him in an innocent but compromising position with Darla. His girlfriend was so furious that she not only broke the bay window of his house, she attempted to demolish his truck with a skateboard that his neighbor had left in the yard. After all of the damage she caused that night, he still found himself in love with her and decided then he would marry her.

"A'ight, bro, I gotta take these calls. Unlike you, some of us have to work a regular gig. We all can't be living the glamorous life, DJ Terror." Terrell worked as a consultant at an insurance company along with Roni's best friend, Kayla. That was actually how they all met.

"Whateva. Don't forget what I told you. Handle your business."

"See you tonight."

With that being said, Toby showered and dressed quickly. He had a lot to do and only a few hours to get it done.

Chapter 3

Terrell called Nicole on his first break. She had left a message telling him she had to work a double shift at the hospital and wouldn't be getting off until late. He appreciated the fact that she was such a hard worker. Nicole was a nurse on the labor and delivery floor, and she was also studying to be a certified midwife. He loved an ambitious woman.

"Hi, baby. I got your message," he told her when she answered her phone.

"Hey, I tried to catch you before you got to work." He could hear the hustle and bustle of the nurses' station in the background. "You guys busy?"

"Not really. We got four patients in active labor and three already delivered. It's a regular day, I guess."

"How you feeling?"

"Okay, a little queasy, but that's to be expected. I'm just praying it doesn't get worse."

"I told Toby this morning," he told her.

"What did he say?" she asked after a pause.

"Nothing. He congratulated me," he lied. "So, what time you getting off?"

"I'm trying to leave by seven. Is that gonna be too late?"

"Naw, you should still be good. I'm not gonna be able to pick you up, though, because I gotta get there by eight. You good to drive?"

"Yes, Terry, I can drive." She laughed.

"I'm just making sure. I don't want you having to pull over on the side of the road, throwing up and stuff."

She laughed and told him she was being paged by a patient. "I'll see you later, Terry."

"I love you," he told her.

"Love you too."

He grabbed a drink for himself and Kayla on the way back to his desk.

"Aw, man, what's up with this tea stuff? Can't I get a Pepsi? I'm not pregnant anymore," she whined when he put the can in front of her.

"Did you pay for it?"

"What? You want your fifty-five cents? Now that I think about it, maybe I do need to pay you back. You might need to break off one of your baby mamas." She reached into her desk drawer and plopped three quarters on his desk. "Keep the change."

He rolled her eyes at her, picking up the quarters and putting them in his pocket. "I know you ain't joking, are you? Shall we start naming the issues you got going on right about now? Let's see, should we start with your married baby daddy or the psychotic ex-fiancée of your boyfriend?"

"Oh, so it's like that?" Kayla's eyes widened as she looked around to see if anyone overheard them. "I was just playing with your sensitive ass."

He had unintentionally hit a nerve and he regretted it. Kayla had been through a lot these past couple of months both physically and emotionally, and despite having her own issues, she was always there for him as a friend. She was the sister he never had.

"I'm sorry, dawg. That was uncalled for. I just got a lot on my mind right now. I got this thing tonight and then Darla is still tripping."

"Does she know about Nicole?"

"Hell no." He shook his head.

His cell began vibrating and he didn't recognize the number. Making sure no supervisors were around, he flipped the phone open and whispered into the receiver. "Hello."

"Hey, big sexy, I just wanted to thank you for a wonderful night."

"Uh, that's cool, man. You good," he answered.

"So, what's up?" Anjelica whispered.

"Chilling at work." He swiveled his chair, turning his back to Kayla, who he knew was eavesdropping. "Yo, look, I'ma hit you back later. Is that cool?"

"Yeah, that's cool. It's no big deal, really. I know you really can't talk. My sister the drama queen is probably right there in your ear anyway. Call me when you get the chance."

"A'ight. Peace."

"Who was that?" Kayla asked, startling him. He turned back around to face her and it was like déjà vu from this morning. It was amazing how much the two girls really did look alike. "I hope it wasn't one of your little tricks. You need to start telling them to stop calling. Cut them loose now, Terrell. I'm telling you."

"Can I help it if I'm a pimp?" he joked.

"I thought it was godpimp."

He laughed at the nickname he had given himself when Kayla asked him to be Day's godfather. She was his confidante and he could tell her anything. He even considered telling her about last night, but knowing the hatred the two sisters held for each other, he decided that it definitely wasn't a story to be shared with Kayla. *Not right now, anyway*, he thought. *Soon, but not right now.*

"You and Geno coming tonight?"

"I wouldn't miss this for the world. Roni already called and told me that she was going on a 'real date' for a change, just her and Toby. She has no idea that we're all invited too? How is that gonna work?"

"Toby says he has some kind of master plan. All I know is that everyone is supposed to be there by seven-thirty and wait in the lobby." Terrell had been working with his brother to concoct this event for a minute now. Everyone showing up in time seemed to be the only problem they could come up with. That was one of the reasons they told everyone 7:30. The moment wasn't scheduled to take place until after 8:00.

"Is he nervous?"

"About what? He loves that girl. Is she nervous?"

"Please, Roni's ready. You better hope Toby is. You know how his reputation precedes him." Kayla laughed.

"Don't front. Roni ain't nowhere near being Virgin Mary herself."

The two friends spent the remainder of the day going back and forth as they always did. Five-thirty came sooner than either one expected, and they headed to the parking lot.

"I'll see you tonight, Kay. I'm praying that y'all be on time."

"We'll be on time, Terrell. You need to be praying that she says yes." Kayla jumped into her car and honked the horn as she pulled out of the parking lot.

Chapter 4

Toby arrived at Roni's at 6:30 on the dot. He was surprised he hadn't thrown up because his stomach was a ball of knots and he thought he could pass out at any moment. Everything was going perfectly—a little too perfectly.

After leaving the house that morning, he dropped his car off to be detailed then walked two blocks up to get a haircut and a shave. He didn't have to wait to get into a chair and by the time he was finished, his truck was ready. He went to the radio station and mixed his tracks for the morning show, finishing in enough time to run his last minute errands. He accomplished all this without fainting. Now, hopefully the woman he was doing all of this for was ready and waiting like he told her to be.

"I'm almost ready, baby. I promise." She kissed him as she opened the door. "Damn, you look good. Maybe I should change."

"No!" he yelled. Toby knew that if Roni decided to change clothes, it would be a thirty minute wait, at least. He thought she looked wonderful anyway in a short black dress that exposed her shoulders. Her perfect neck was accentuated by a small gold chain with a diamond encrusted heart. "You look perfect."

"You just don't want me to look as GQ as you. That's okay. You look so nice. I love to see you dressed up." Roni ran her hands along the lapel of the dark suit he was wearing. Instead of a tie, he wore a wide-collar shirt with the top buttons undone. He put his hand in his pocket to make sure the ring was still secure.

"Oh, so I don't dress up?"

"You never wear a suit. I don't consider jeans, Timbs and a SeanJohn shirt dressed up, Toby. I gotta finish touching up my face and then I'll be ready." She disappeared down the hallway, leaving an anxious Toby standing in the living room.

"Are you sure you got permission from your girls to go out tonight?" he called, looking at a picture of Roni and her best friends sitting on the mantle. They were a tight bunch and he knew that tonight was just as important to them as it was her.

"Ha, ha, very funny. I don't need anyone's permission to go out. They were surprised that you didn't have to work tonight, though. Who's deejaying at the club tonight anyway?"

"Um, they're having Oldies but Goodies night on Thursdays now."

"Does that mean you're gonna be off *every* Thursday?"

He knew she would like that idea. He was going to wait and tell her later, but the present seemed as good a time as any. "For a little while, at least."

"And we can go on more dates, like regular people?" Before Toby could answer, her phone rang. "Hello. Hey. Good. Yeah, yeah, uh-huh. Um, sorry. I have plans. Yeah, nice talking to you too. Take care."

Toby fought the urge to ask who it was and what he wanted, although he was curious as hell. From the tone of her voice, he could tell it was a male. She used the throaty laugh that she would use when she was flirting. *Probably nobody. Somebody about work*, he told himself.

After a few moments, she emerged, looking perfect. "See, I told you I was almost ready."

Toby playfully looked at his watch and replied, "Yeah, but you're late and we missed our reservations. We may as well stay here and order pizza."

"Like hell. You'd better stop playing and come on," she said. She grabbed her purse and they were about to leave when the phone rang again.

"Don't answer it. Come on, Ron. We gotta go," he warned.

She checked the caller ID. "It's Ma."

Toby knew this was a call Roni was going to take. Ms. Ernestine could talk a hole in anyone's head and there was no doubt this was gonna take a while. He plopped down on the edge of the sofa. "Shit."

"What's your problem, Toby? It'll only be a minute. Don't get an attitude." She put the phone to her ear and began chatting. "Hey, Ma, what's up? For real? That's great. Well look, Toby and I are walking out the door. No, he got the night off and we're going to Jasper's. I don't know. Let me ask him. Toby, would you mind if Ma joined us?"

Toby looked at Roni without saying a word.

"Tell you what, Ma. How about I take you to Jasper's this weekend, just the two of us? I'll call you later. Love you too. Bye." She tossed the cordless phone on the sofa. "Happy? Now let's go, DJ Grumpy!"

Toby sat and stared at her for a few moments then stood. "You better watch it, girl. You never know when a DJ might change your life."

Jasper's was a premier supper club in the city. It was owned by JJ Sims, Terrell and Toby's uncle. Working there had been the first job that each of the boys had. Both started as busboys, then served as waiters at the restaurant. Toby had even tried his hand at bartending. They got their love of the nightlife from Uncle Jay. Jasper's was home. The large restaurant was open and airy so patrons could move around freely, yet the ambiance was romantic enough that couples felt as if they were the only ones in the place. The lighting was dim but inviting, and in addition to its fine jazz and cozy atmosphere, it was well known for its magnificent food, a combination of Creole and soul. It was the perfect spot for Toby's plan.

"You're late," Uncle Jay said when they arrived. He greeted Toby and Roni with a hug.

"Hey, Uncle Jay. Take that up with Ms. Black here. I told her be ready by six-thirty."

"I was ready, Uncle Jay. Don't listen to him. Besides, you think I haven't learned by now that Toby lies about what time I should be ready? It's ten after seven. I bet our reservations aren't until seven-thirty."

"Uh, seven-fifteen." The handsome older gentlemen looked at the hostess' book and corrected her.

"And since when do Toby and I need a reservation?" She tapped him on the shoulder.

"You must not've heard that Thursdays are our busiest night now. We got a new group called Liquid and they pack the place every week."

"I doubt if we need a reservation, though. I know if my mother doesn't need a reservation, then we don't." Roni winked.

Toby looked at his uncle, who was now insisting that they be seated. "What is she talking about, Uncle Jay?"

"Nothing, nothing. Come on. I got the best table waiting for you down front." He grabbed two menus and led them to the tables near the front of the stage.

Toby knew they made a stunning couple. As they walked, he placed his hand on the small of Roni's back. He saw people staring at them and he enjoyed the feel of being one of the beautiful people. The waiter had already been advised to take special care of them. They ordered drinks and Toby looked around nervously. The band hadn't started playing yet; a deejay in the corner was playing old school slow jams.

"What's wrong?" Roni frowned.

"Nothing. I'm just checking the place out. So, what's up with your mom and Uncle Jay?"

"I don't know. Every time I talk to Mom, she's always talking about eating here and what a good time she and *JJ* had. How long has he been single?"

"A little while. His wife died about five years ago." Toby sighed. "She was so nice and man, the most beautiful woman I had ever seen in my life. She looked like an angel."

"I thought I was the most beautiful woman you had ever seen. Or was that a lie?" Roni teased. "What happened?"

"She was killed by a drunk driver," Toby said sadly. "Jasper's was closed a long time after that. I was surprised he opened it back up, really. That's when I started deejaying at the club because Jasper's closed. I used to think I would own the place before she passed away. I was on a roll, too. Had worked my way from busboy to manager."

"That still may happen. You never know."

"Nah, Uncle Jay's having too much fun running the place right now, and I got my DJ Terror thing going on."

"That's right, you the man. I forgot." She noticed Toby checking his watch. "Why do you keep checking the time?"

"I thought the band was supposed to start their set at seven-thirty and they haven't."

The waiter brought their drinks and appetizers and they talked until their food arrived. Soon, Uncle Jay came to the stage and introduced Liquid. The band consisted of a small brass quartet, a bass player, a drummer and a talented guy who sang lead and played the keyboard. The evening was beginning to get even better as they enjoyed some of the best music they had heard in a while.

Toby loved being with Roni. She made him laugh and stimulated that part of his brain that he had to utilize in order to participate in intelligent conversations about politics and race relations, something he hadn't done in a while. As a special education teacher, Roni was concerned with the state of black students who had been mislabeled at an early age. She was a martyr for these kids who were clearly smarter and never should have been placed in her class. He smiled as she explained her position in between bites of crab cakes off her plate and steak off his own. She was the best thing that had happened to him.

The band announced that they would be taking a break as the waiter cleared their dessert plates from the table. The curtains closed around the semi-circular stage and the deejay began playing again.

"They were off the chain," Roni commented as she applauded.

"I told you I heard they were good. I'ma go backstage and holler at Uncle Jay. I think I saw him go back there," he told her as he stood up.

"Go ahead. I need to use the restroom myself."

Toby's heart began racing as she reached for his hand. Her going to the restroom was not in his plans. If she went through the lobby, everything would be ruined. He tried to think quick. "You may want to wait until after the band begins; looks like every woman in here has made a beeline for the bathroom. You know you don't do lines."

Roni nodded as she took her seat. "You're right. I'll wait."

"Be right back," he said with relief. He kissed her on the cheek and hurried toward the back of the stage. Terry was waiting when he got there.

"Everybody here?" he asked his brother, who was looking dapper as ever in a two-piece black linen outfit.

"As far as I know. I came through the back door, though. I saw Tia, Yvonne and Theo in the parking lot."

"What about Kayla and Geno?"

"I didn't see 'em. I saw a black Maxima, though, but I didn't look at the tag. That may've been her car."

"What time did you tell her to be here?"

"Everyone knew it was going down at eight-thirty. Don't worry; she's here. You ready?"

"Yeah, let's just hurry and get it over wit' before I shit on myself."

"I know the cool, calm, collected DJ Terror ain't nervous. Come on, man. You love this girl. She already knows you're gonna marry her. You already told her."

"That's right. Calm your scared ass down and go propose." A deep voice came from behind the two men, causing them to turn around.

"Jermaine! Man, you made it!" Toby ran and hugged him.

"I had to see if you really gonna go do it." The tall, athletic man gripped Toby's hand and smiled. "What's up, Terry? How you been?"

"I've been a'ight, Jermaine," Terry said. "You all moved in?" He was pleased to see his brother's best friend, who was relocating to the area. It would give him someone new to hang out with now that Toby was about to be tied down. Jermaine had always been a suave brother who attracted women like honey to flies. Funny thing was, although they were all dark brothers, growing up, they always teased Jermaine about being blue-black. Toby was the cute, athletic one; Terry was the chubby, smart one; and Jermaine was the quiet, dark one. Needless to say, Toby was always first choice, Jermaine got the second cuts and Terry got the leftovers. Sometimes, that was a good thing because they seemed to be the most flavorful.

"Well, both my best men are here, so let's go do this!" Toby put his am around both men and they set off to take their places.

The second time Uncle Jay took the stage to introduce Liquid, Jasper's was standing room only. Toby took several deep breaths and said a small prayer for courage and strength to do what he was about to do. He could see Roni looking around for him as the curtain opened. The audience got quiet as the lights dimmed. Toby began playing the piano softly as he spoke into the microphone.

"Good evening, ladies and gentlemen. Welcome to Jasper's. We certainly hope you're enjoying your evening so far. My name is Tobias Sims, and tonight I will be accompanied by Liquid, along with the help of a few other special people. I have a very special dedication for a very special woman in my life."

"Go on, boy!" someone screamed from the audience.

Toby looked down at Roni, who was sitting with her mouth hanging open. He had never told her he could play the piano or sing, so he knew this was a total shock to her. He licked his lips and winked at her then began to sing the first lines of "Let's Get Married" by Jagged Edge. He saw the tears forming in her eyes and almost didn't make it to the chorus. He was glad to hear Jermaine's and Terry's voices combining with his. The remaining band members soon joined them. Terry stood up from the piano and jumped from the stage, landing in front of their table.

Females began screaming throughout the place as he got down on one knee and took Roni's hand into his. When he reached into his pocket and pulled out the black velvet box and opened it to reveal the three-carat platinum engagement ring, someone yelled, "He got a ring, too!"

"Roni, I love you with all my heart and soul. You are my soul mate, and I want to spend eternity with you. I thank God continually for putting you in my life. I am begging you to be my wife. Will you marry me?"

Tears were streaming down his cheeks as he touched her face, which was drenched with tears as well.

"You go boy!" a male called out.

"Yes! Yes! Yes!" She was finally able to answer between heaves. She pulled him to her and they embraced. The restaurant erupted with applause and Toby pulled her up as the house lights came on. He turned her so she could see all of her friends, as well as her mother, standing around them, crying and clapping. The band began playing "Spend My Life with You" and Uncle Jay ordered a round of champagne for everyone.

"Oh, baby," Ms. Ernestine gushed, wiping her eyes. "I'm so happy for you."

Kayla, Tia, and Yvonne raced to Roni's side, pushing Toby out of the way. He spotted Geno, Jermaine, and Terry at the bar and went over to join them. People came over to congratulate him and wish him luck, and it pleased him that everything worked out exactly as planned.

"That was tight, player!" Terry handed him a drink.

"Tight ain't the word. You know how many numbers I got when I made it offstage? You get much props for this one, T. Next time you wanna propose, I'm definitely down for it." Jermaine smiled. "Know what I mean, Terry?"

"There won't be a next time. And Terry, you better shut up. You need to hurry up and do the same thing so your life can be drama-free like mine."

They were interrupted by the sound of a woman on stage. "Ahem. Good evening. I'd like to send this one out to the happy couple. Congratulations."

She began singing a version of "Inseparable" that would have made Natalie Cole shut up. No one moved as she belted out the powerful notes. They didn't know what was more stunning; her amazing voice or her striking looks. She wasn't very tall, about five-foot-three, but it was enough to carry her curvaceous figure. She sported a sleeveless black top that criss-crossed at her ample cleavage. Her shapely legs extended from her short black skirt, and she wore black strappy heels on her small feet. Her amber skin was flawless, and the wavy texture of her long hair made it apparent that she was of mixed race. She swayed to the music as she sang, and she touched the microphone so seductively that the men were mesmerized as the notes escaped her full, pouty lips. By the time the song ended, everyone was once again on their feet, applauding.

"Bro, looks to me like your drama is just beginning," Terry said, leaning on the bar.

"No doubt about that," Jermaine said as he watched someone help the gorgeous woman from the stage. "That's a definite."

Chapter 5

"Roni should definitely get that girl to sing at the wedding," Nicole said as she walked up to Terrell and put her arms around him.

"Hey, baby. You made it. How long you been here?"

"Long enough to see my baby daddy sing. That was awesome. Toby, that was the best proposal I have ever seen in my life."

"Thanks, Nicole. You know I tried to come up with something to impress Veronica Black."

"Well, I think you impressed everyone here. Between your proposal and that girl singing, you all are making Jasper's the spot to be tonight."

"Jasper's is the spot to be any night," Uncle Jay said, joining them. "Toby, that was wonderful."

"Uncle Jay," Toby hugged his uncle, "I appreciate you helping me set this up."

"Tobias, I am so proud of you," his uncle told him. "You Sims boys are something else, I tell you."

"That they are."

Everyone turned to see Darla standing before them. Terrell and Toby looked at each other, neither one saying a word. She walked past them then turned and gave Terrell an evil look, adding, "I'm sure you'll make a great husband and *father*, too, Toby."

"Uh, thanks, uh . . . Darla," Toby stuttered. She turned and walked away, relieving the stressed men. Toby rolled his eyes at his brother, who just shrugged and shook his head.

"And that was so nice of Isis to come and sing, too. When did she get to town?" Jermaine picked up the conversation where it left off.

"You know her? She was awesome. Isis, that's the perfect name for her," Nicole said.

"Yeah, she's an old friend." Jermaine smiled.

Toby didn't find anything funny about the situation. A million questions filled his mind as his eyes scanned the crowded club.

"You looking for me?"

"You know I was. I need my fiancée by my side at all times," he answered Roni and kissed her. "You happy?"

"Um, let me think." She pretended to be deep in thought, then she looked deep into his eyes and told him, "I am beyond happy. I was happy from the day we met at your house last Fourth of July. Tonight, I think I'm more like ecstatic. I love you."

"I love you too, Toby," Ms. Ernestine interrupted. "You like the way I called as y'all were walking out the door? I added that for dramatic element."

"Gee, thanks, Ms. Ernestine. I appreciate your help in adding to my nervousness," he replied to his future mother-in-law.

"You were nervous, baby?" Roni tilted her head as she smiled at him. "I couldn't tell."

"That's 'cause I'm cool like that."

Surrounded by his family and friends, Toby tried to laugh and enjoy himself, suppressing the urge to walk around the club and find the cause of his distraction. After a while, Jermaine came over and whispered, "She's gone, man. She sang and she's out."

That being said, Toby reached in his pocket, passed his keys to his best friend, and told him, "Crash at my crib. I won't be using it tonight."

"Cool."

Kayla gave him the signal and he announced, "Well, I just want to thank all of you for making tonight a success. Roni and I love and appreciate you. And on that note, we are outta here."

He grabbed Roni's hand and led her through the crowd, followed by their small entourage. She squealed when they walked outside and saw the black limousine waiting for them. Everyone clapped and waved goodbye as the driver opened the door for them.

"Congratulations, DJ T," the driver said as Toby gave him a pound with his fist.

"Thanks, man." Toby laughed.

Roni took in the opulence of the leather interior, smiling as she sat back in the soft seats. "Toby, now you know you didn't have to do this," she said as he took his place beside her and pulled her close.

"This is nothing," he said and reached behind the seat, pulling out a long box and placing it on her lap. She opened it and smiled at the dozen long-stemmed white roses inside.

"Thank you," she said, kissing him full on the mouth. She loved the way he would caress her tongue with his, gently sucking it. Toby always felt that you could tell a lot from the way a woman kissed. He believed that if she had skills in kissing, she usually had skills in other sensual areas, too. And Roni definitely had skills.

He stroked her neck as she helped him out of his jacket and leaned back onto the seat. He cupped her full, double-D breasts in his hands and heard her moan as his fingers brushed across her nipples. Then, out of nowhere, music started playing. Her eyes flicked open.

"It's just the radio." Toby smiled and began sucking on her neck. Roni ran her hands across his smooth, bald held, savoring the moment. "You like that?" Toby asked.

"Mm-hmm," Roni managed to murmur. He loved making her sound like that.

Her hands found their way under his shirt and she let her fingers play with his nipples. He groaned as she licked along his earlobe. Just as things were getting to the point that he knew she could take no more, the car came to a stop and they heard the front door open.

"I think we've arrived at our destination," Toby whispered.

"And where is that?" she asked, readjusting her dress as she looked out the window.

"We are at the royal palace," he answered, helping her out of the limousine. She realized that they were in front the Majestic, one of the largest, most lavish hotels in the city. The concierge held the door as they entered the massive archway leading to the lobby. She expected Toby to go the desk, but there was no need. He waved to the front clerk as they passed by.

"Toby," she started as they got into the glass elevator and he pushed the number twenty-two. He kissed her again, distracting her from any other thoughts she could have had regarding what was going on. When the car stopped on the designated floor, he bowed as he stepped off the elevator and reached for her hand. She decided to play along and curtseyed. They embraced each other as they proceeded down the empty hallway. When they got to the room, he asked her to wait a minute. "I'll be right back." She frowned but nodded.

He slipped into the room knowing she wondered what he was doing. After everything else that had gone on that night, she wouldn't know what to expect. He looked around the room and made sure everything was set. Kayla hooked the room up for him. *I owe her big time*, he thought as he made the final preparations. Turning the knob slowly and opening the door, he welcomed Roni in. She was hesitant.

"Come on," he told her. "I promise I won't bite."

"Promises, promises." She grinned.

Roni was dumbfounded when she walked in. Toby had not only reserved a room, but a full suite with a Jacuzzi in the center. There were white candles and rose petals arranged around the jetted tub. She spotted a bowl of fruit and a chilling bottle of wine along with a set of glasses on a tray near the steaming water. Prince was drifting from a nearby CD player.

"I love you, Veronica Black," he whispered and hugged her from behind. He kissed the ring she was now wearing then put her entire finger in his mouth, sucking gently. He guided her to the mirror hanging on the wall and he stared at their reflection. They made a perfect couple.

She turned and kissed him with such passion that it scared him. Toby could not remember a time when he had put so much thought and effort into planning anything. Between the passion of the moment and the alcohol they had already consumed, he was now drunk with happiness. Before he knew it, she was naked in his arms and he was carrying her to the hot tub. He removed his clothes with a quickness and lowered his body into the steaming water.

"You are so beautiful, do you know that?" he asked as he fed her a ripe strawberry. She bit into it, juice dribbling from the side of her mouth. Toby leaned over and licked it off, nibbling from her lips down to her collarbone. With a quick movement, he sat her in his lap, and she threw her head back as he kissed across her chest. He buried his head into her shoulder, moaning as the bubbles enticed both of them.

Roni reached for a glass of wine, pouring it over his head, then used her tongue to catch the cascading liquid as it made its way from his head to his chest. His strong hands searched between her legs, and she tensed as his fingers found the spot they were looking for. She closed her eyes and became lost in the moment. It was as if he had found a rhythm and was playing a melody. She looked at him as her hands now found the treasure she was looking for. Her fingers massaged him in the same cadence that he played. She stared into his dark eyes, letting him know that she was not going to lose control; she was too much of a woman for that. He could tell that the intensity aroused her, and they played the duet together until neither one could take it anymore.

He didn't say anything as he stood and reached for her once again. She stood and he helped her out. Lifting her once again, he carried her into the enormous bedroom of the suite. He laid her in the middle of the bed, and for a moment just looked at her. He pushed her legs open and began playing the tune again, this time using his tongue rather than his fingers. Roni bucked like she was losing her mind. Toby seemed determined to have her go crazy. She called his name over and over as her body shook with ecstasy. When he felt she was satisfied, he smiled.

"Having fun?" he asked. She nodded at him then began laughing uncontrollably. "What's so funny?"

She licked her lips seductively, smiling at him. "I'm just happy."

He joined in her laughter and she pulled him to her. He laid his head on her chest and began playing with her nipples. She knew what was next and she was more than ready.

"I know you came prepared," she whispered.

He nodded and reached for the condoms he had placed in the nightstand drawer. Roni was a stickler for safe sex, and he respected her for that. A lot of people, his brother included, didn't practice it very often. She took the plastic from his hand and tore it open with her mouth. Her eyes never left his as she rolled it on him. Then, like a graceful jockey, she straddled him and began to ride like he was a thoroughbred stallion. He buried his head into her ample breast as he thrust into her welcoming body. He gripped her strong thighs and his arms found their way to her firm behind. As if on cue, she leaned back and looked into his eyes, rocking faster and faster. She stared at him, his name escaping her mouth as she cried out.

"Toby . . . I . . . I . . . Yes, that's it!"

"Is that it?"

"God . . . yes . . . "

"Tell me."

"That's it," she moaned, rocking continually.

"And what is it?" He smiled at her, gripping her harder.

"It's . . . it's . . . " She could hardly talk.

"Huh?" He had her right where he wanted her. He was about to explode but was determined to make her talk.

"It's . . . yours. Toby . . . it's yours, baby!" she screamed, leaning forward and grabbing his shoulders.

"Show me, then." He reached up and pulled her so that her hair hung into his face. "Come for me, Roni! Now!"

He felt the tension that had built up in the moment release from deep within and explode from his body. Roni called his name over and over and he felt her legs begin shaking. Then, it was over. She collapsed on his sweat-covered chest and he kissed the top of her head.

"Damn, that was the best ever," she said as she panted.

"All that for putting a ring on your finger?" he teased, wrapping her hair around his finger.

"All that for being the love of my life." She kissed him.

Something about the way she said it bothered him. For a moment, it felt like déjà vu, only it wasn't with Roni in the dream he had, it was with another beautiful woman who in the end had run away, taking his heart with her. That was two years ago, and he hadn't even thought of her in months, until she showed up again tonight, singing on stage.

Chapter 6

"Where you going? I thought you were taking the day off," Nicole said sleepily.

Terrell leaned over and kissed her forehead. He had hoped she would still be asleep when he left, but that wasn't the case. "I got some stuff I gotta take care of this morning."

"What kind of stuff?"

"I'm taking my car to be serviced this morning."

"I can trail you and you can use my car if you want. That way you don't have to wait."

"That's okay. Stay in the bed."

"But you know we're supposed to—"

"I know. I'll be there at quarter to twelve. Promise."

He kissed her again and she reminded him to lock the door when he left. He hurried out to be sure he wasn't late picking up Darla. She was waiting when he got to her place and got into the car without saying a word.

"Hey," he told her.

"I'm moving and I need you to give me some money," she said, not looking at him.

He inhaled deeply, wondering where she was going with this. Her moving might be a good thing. That meant there was no way she could pull a stunt like she did last night or the several other times when she would just pop up at Toby's crib or the club.

"I feel you. When you trying to make this move?"

"Soon as possible. I already started packing. I need the loot, though."

He wanted to tell her that he was already paying for the abortion and didn't think he should have to pay her anything, but decided to chill for right now. "I don't have a problem helping you out."

It was a beautiful March morning and it seemed as if everyone was in a mellow mood. The weather was just about to break; not too cold, but not yet spring. Terrell noticed smiles on people's faces as he drove down the street, like they didn't have a care in the world. He, on the other hand, had the weight of the world on his shoulders, and was doing everything in his power to get rid of it, starting with Darla and this baby. *Which might not even be mine.* But he wasn't even taking the chance. The sooner he got rid of this baby, the better. *And now it looks like I'm gonna be getting rid of Darla, period. Hell, I betcha Toby will be glad to hear her whining ass will be long gone. She was always trying to pop up at his crib uninvited.*

Strangely enough, she didn't say anything the entire drive to the clinic. He was expecting an emotional temper tantrum, with her trying to convince him that this was a mistake, but she sat quietly looking out the window. He assumed she just didn't want to talk, so he turned the radio up and listened to Doug Banks. There was a radio advertisement promoting Dominic's nightclub featuring DJ Terror, and he smiled. He could remember a time when Toby would get in trouble for scratching up their parents' Kool and the Gang albums when they were little. After seeing *Beatstreet*, Toby was fascinated by deejays and determined to learn it like it was a science. Now, it seemed the beatings and practice had paid off because Toby's career was successful. Terrell was proud of his older brother; there was no doubt about that. He had the crib, the career and now, the girl. He looked over at Darla and decided, *I'm getting my life together too. I ain't going through this shit no more. She ain't even worth the gas I'm burning bringing her here.*

He pulled into the lot and parked on the side of the building rather than the front. It was then that Darla decided to speak.

"Good thinking. You wouldn't want anyone to spot your car outside the abortion clinic, right?"

He didn't respond verbally, but cut his eyes at her as he got out of his car. He walked ahead of her and went straight to the receptionist's desk, giving her Darla's name.

"Yes, sir, if you could just have her fill these forms out, someone will be with you in just a moment," the attractive woman told him in a sexy voice. She was a seductive blonde with an olive complexion, reminding him of one of the women from the TV show *Friends*. Terrell usually didn't go for women outside his race, but there was something charming about her that added to her appeal.

"Thanks. Do you know how long this is gonna take?" he asked.

"I'm not sure. It depends on a number of things." She shrugged.

"I understand. Look, can I go ahead and pay and then come back and get her?"

"We recommend you stay here with her, at least until after you speak with a counselor."

"Counselor? For what?" There was no way Terrell was going to talk to a counselor. This thing was getting more complicated than he anticipated. He had planned on dropping Darla off, paying, leaving, then picking her up and taking her ass home.

"So that you both understand your options."

"Is that really necessary? I mean, we've already discussed it and weighed our options. We've made our decision."

"Well, it's not a requirement or anything." She looked toward Darla sympathetically, then back to Terrell, who was pulling his wallet from his pocket. He had stopped at the ATM before he picked up Darla.

"Good. The lady I talked to yesterday said it was gonna be three-fifty. This should take care of it."

She took the money from him and gave him a receipt. "Come back around two."

"Cool," he said, thanking her. He turned and walked over to Darla, handing her the papers to complete. "Yo, you need to fill these out and they'll call your name. I'll be back to get you."

She took the papers without a word. He turned back and waved to the receptionist.

He began driving around, thinking of what he could do to waste time. He had taken the day off but didn't feel like going to his own home. Instead, he decided to go to Kayla's for a minute.

"What's up?" she asked, opening the door with one hand, holding Day in the other.

"Chilling. I came by to get some breakfast."

"You mean you came by to *cook* breakfast? Because you know I ain't cooking jack," she said matter-of-factly. He followed her into the living room where she was obviously packing Day's diaper bag and getting dressed for work at the same time. He took the baby from her arms.

"Hey there, princess. You been breaking any hearts lately?" he asked the vibrant infant. She cooed back at him, causing him to laugh. He sat on the sofa and bounced her on his knee.

"Well, I'm glad you stopped by. I can save my gas and ride with you," Kayla called out as she walked down the hall toward the bedroom.

"No can do. I got the day off."

"Huh? Then what are you doing out this early in the morning?"

"Your mama is nosey, you know that?" he whispered to the baby. "I had some stuff to do early this morning. Is that a'ight with you?"

"I don't care what you gotta do as long as it involves dropping Day off at the sitter."

"That definitely wasn't on my agenda this morning."

"Come on. You know I'm running late today, Terrell."

"You run late every day."

"Please. You're her godfather. You need to bond with her."

"We're bonding right now."

Kayla came back dressed in jeans and a sweater, carrying a pair of sneakers. Her long hair was held off her face with a headband. He shook his head at her.

"What? It's dress down Friday, Terrell. Don't even try it. Besides, I don't see where you look all that great either."

He looked down at his own jeans and Iverson jersey. "Whatever, yo, and I ain't talking about your clothes. I'm talking about that headband."

"I don't even have time to deal with you and your so-called fashion criticisms. Are you gonna take Day for me or what?"

"Don't even try to start making this a habit. You need to start getting up an hour earlier."

"Yeah, yeah, yeah. Thanks, Terrell. I appreciate it." She smiled as she kissed the baby. Grabbing her purse off the coffee table, she called out, "Her car seat is by the door. Don't forget the diaper bag. I'll call you later."

Terrell put Day into her swing and clicked on the television. After channel surfing for a few minutes, he settled on the news. He checked his watch and was disappointed that it was only 10:15. Time seemed to be creeping by. Day was beginning to drift to sleep so he decided he'd better put her into her seat and take her to the sitter. He gently took her into his arms and placed her into the carrier, buckling her in and covering her with the fuzzy pink blanket, which was lying in the chair. He noticed she was looking at him with her big, bright eyes like he was crazy.

"I know. Uncle Terry needs the practice, though, okay? Go back to sleep." He grinned. He made sure the door was locked and headed out to the driveway. Day must have understood what he told her because before he could even put her into the car, she was knocked out. He made sure the seat was fastened in and locked the door. His cell phone began vibrating in his pocket and he answered. "Yeah."

"What's up? You busy?"

"Naw, what's up with you?" he asked, walking to the driver's side and getting in the car.

"Nothing really. You drop your first baby mama off at the clinic?"

"Yep. Already took care of that. And quit calling her that."

"She is your first baby mama. And now you gotta go and meet your fiancée, right?"

"You know what, Anjelica? You're getting to be as much up in my business as your sister. Must be something in the blood."

"Don't ever compare me to her. I told you about that. Keep on and our friendship will end right here and now. I'm surprised she's not in your face right now."

"She's gone to work already. I'm dropping Day off at the sitter for her."

"How is my gorgeous niece?" she asked. He could hear the hurt in her voice. Over the past few days, he had learned that although Anjelica tried her best to be a bitch, she still had a love for her sister and niece. "I bought her some cute outfits and a new diaper bag last weekend, but Kay thinks they're from my mother."

"Damn!" Terrell said loudly, slamming on the brakes.

"What's wrong?"

"I forgot the diaper bag, and I locked the door. Dammit!" He looked at the clock and saw that he only had thirty minutes to drop Day off and make it to meet Nicole. "I don't have time to deal with this."

"Calm down. Look under the flower pot on Kayla's porch and get the spare key," Anjelica told him. He wondered how she knew this and began to question whether or not the rumors that Anjelica was the mastermind behind the attack on Kayla a few months back were true. Janice, Geno's ex, broke into Kayla's home and assaulted her, nearly killing her. There was talk that since Janice and Anjelica knew each other, she had set her sister up to be attacked.

"I don't even wanna know how you know where her extra key is," he said as he turned around in the middle of the street and headed back toward Kayla's house. He left the car running as he quickly dashed to the porch and lifted the large flower pot sitting there. To his horror, there was no key. "Ain't no key here!"

"Look under the mat that it's sitting on, retarded! And stop yelling at me!"

He lifted the green mat under the plant and sure enough, a bronze key was there. He breathed a sigh of relief and proceeded to reenter the house. His phone began beeping and he saw that it was Kayla calling. He told Anjelica to hold then answered the other line. "Yo."

"Hey, everything okay when you dropped her off?"

"I ain't made it there yet. I forgot the diaper bag and now I gotta go back in and get it."

"And lock my door when you come out!"

"I know to lock the door behind me."

"Obviously you don't. It was open for you to go back in and get her bag."

"Look, I gotta go. I'm supposed to meet Nicole in a minute," he said, grabbing the bag and leaving once again.

"A'ight, I'll talk to you later."

He clicked back over and heard Anjelica singing along with Maxwell.

"Yo, chill with all that," he told her.

"Shut up. Did you get the bag?"

"Yeah, I got it. Thanks, I gotta go."

"A'ight, player. Call me when you get the chance. And don't forget to put that key back!"

"I already did," he lied and took the key out of his pocket, laying it back under the mat and replacing the plant on top. He got back into the car and checked on the baby. She was still sleeping. *Must be nice*, he thought as he sped off.

"Ms. Rogers, this young man is looking for you."

"Tell him he's late," he heard Nicole say. The women laughed and then he was told to come in.

"I'm sorry," he said as he entered the small room. She was giving him a fake evil eye.

"You're late," she repeated.

"I know. They took longer than expected with my car and then Kayla called and asked me to drop Day off so she wouldn't be late. I left the diaper bag and had to go back for it."

"Okay, okay. Kiss me and you're forgiven." She smiled. He leaned over and kissed her tenderly on the lips.

"Hey, that's how you two got like this in the first place," a deep voice interrupted them. "How you doing, young man? I'm Dr. Fisher."

Terrell looked up and shook the hand that was extended toward him. The man looked just like James Earl Jones. "Terrell Sims. I'm great."

"Well, it's nice to meet you, Terrell. I take it you've come to see your child's first picture?" The doctor walked over to the tiny sink and began washing his hands.

"Huh?" Terrell asked, looking at Nicole who had lay back on the examining table.

"He means the ultrasound, Terry." She shook her head at him.

"Oh, yeah." He laughed nervously. He wasn't really prepared for all this. He was under the impression that he would just be meeting with Nicole's doctor.

Dr. Fisher sat on the stool near the table and pulled over a cart holding what looked like a portable DVD player. He advised Nicole to lift her shirt then put some gel on her flat stomach. Terrell stood in silence as the doctor clicked on the machine and the dark screen lit up.

"There we go. Right there, Nicole. See?" the doctor said.

"Oh my God. That's my baby's heart beating," she whispered. "Look, Terrell."

Terrell leaned to see what they were talking about, but all he saw was a grey screen. Then, ever so faintly in the corner, he saw something moving fast. He put his finger on it. "Is that it?"

"That's it. That's your child. Tiny as a pea, but that's it." Dr. Fisher laughed.

"Wow, it's small all right."

"Terry, I'm only nine weeks pregnant."

Nine weeks. Darla was twelve weeks. A little further along than Nicole. It was strange that as he was watching the heartbeat of one child, across town the heartbeat of another was being stopped. He wondered how that baby would look on this monitor, but then told himself not to be stupid. *That probably ain't even your kid. Besides, that fetus is long gone, and after this weekend you won't ever have to deal with that trick again.*

He looked down at Nicole and took her hand into his. She looked up at him and he told her, "I love you."

"I love you too."

"Well, everything looks fine. I don't have to give you the specifics, Nicole. You know to eat right, take your vitamins and get lots of exercise. No smoking or drinking, and I'll see you next month for your next appointment. Call my office if you need anything. Terrell, this young lady is one of the best nurses this hospital has. You get a gem and you need to treat her like one. You take care of her."

"I will, Dr. Fisher," he assured the doctor.

He helped Nicole get cleaned up with the doctor's words ringing in his ears. Nicole was a gem and he really cared about her. He had to get himself together if not for her, then for their baby that she was carrying. For the first time in his life, Terrell was ready to be a father.

After making an appointment for the following month, they walked to the parking lot. He saw that it was ten minutes before 1:00 and he had to go back and pick up Darla.

"You wanna go and get something to eat?" Nicole asked.

"I got a meeting at one, but we can meet up later." He pulled her to him.

"Well, I have some studying I really need to get done, especially since I didn't get anything done last night."

"Oh, you ain't get nothing done?" He looked at her provocatively.

"You know what I mean, silly." She blushed and put her arms around his neck. "We got more than enough done."

"I don't think we finished, either. We only went three rounds."

"We finshed. Believe me, we finished."

He felt the vibration of the phone in his pocket and knew without looking at it that it was Darla. He walked Nicole to her car and hurriedly kissed her, promising to call after his meeting. He smiled as he thought about the image of his child on the monitor and the beautiful woman carrying it. He was definitely about to make some serious changes in his life. He would give Darla the money to get the hell outta dodge then make things work with Nicole.

By the time he made it to the clinic, he was damn near on cloud nine. The fact that Darla was already waiting outside the clinic made it even better. He figured he would have to push her in a wheelchair and help her to the car or something, and he just knew she would be putting on the performance of a lifetime, moaning and groaning as if she was dying. However, none of that took place. *Thank God,* he thought as he get out and opened the door for her.

"You a'ight, yo?" he asked her softly.

"I'm cool," was her response. He saw the folded up pieces of paper in her hand and asked if she needed to stop anywhere. "No. I just wanna go home."

He looked over at her and saw the tears streaming down her face. She rolled her eyes at him. He pretended not to notice and turned the radio up, nodding his head to the beat of Jay-Z. She turned and looked out the window, sniffling. As he turned his car into the parking lot in front of her building, he noticed a guy leaning against her black Neon. He was a grungy-looking older man wearing a baggy sweat suit and a pair of run-over Reeboks.

"Shit," Darla whispered as she saw the man, who was now scowling at Terrell.

"Who the hell is that?" He frowned, turning down the music.

"Turk," she said barely above a whisper, looking shocked.

"Who the hell is Turk? Man, I'm telling you I ain't for no shit, Darla. Who the hell is he?"

"Nobody."

"A'ight, *nobody.*" He pulled into the empty spot on the other side of her car and the guy began walking toward them. "You better tell him something quick because I will knock him the hell out if he start acting crazy."

"I said it was nobody," she answered as she opened the door to get out.

"Where the hell you been?" Turk demanded as Darla stepped out of the car. "And who is *this* nigga?"

"Don't trip, Turk. He just gave me a ride from work, that's all."

"Don't lie, Darla. Your ass ain't even go to work. I went by there and they said you took the day off. And when I got here, Pooh told me you left wit' some dude. I'm guessing that would be this nigga here," he said, pointing toward Terrell, who was watching him, deciding whether to get out of the car. "Now, where the hell you been? Is this that nigga from the club?"

Ignoring him, Terrell rolled the window down and asked, "Yo, you gonna be a'ight?"

"What do you care? I'm sick of all y'all! Both of you need to leave me alone!" she screamed and rushed into the house. Neighbors began peeking out of windows, curious to see what was going on.

"I advise you to get the hell away from here, chump!" Turk growled at him.

Terrell was tempted to respond but thought better of it. *Forget it. She ain't my problem no more.* He kicked his car into gear and blazed out of the parking lot. For a quick second, he even tried to figure out who the loser was waiting for her at her house, but stopped himself. Relieved that the situation was now taken care of, he smiled to himself and decided to go to the mall and get his shop on. After all, he did have a new baby to buy for.

Chapter 7

Toby flipped through the crates filled with albums, searching for some old school LL Cool J. It was only 9:00, but Dominic's was already crowded. It usually didn't get packed until after 11:00 on a Saturday night, but since spring finally seemed to be in the air, he figured people were ready to get their party on. Females were showing off flat abs and pedicured feet as they bounced to the base pumping from the speakers. He loved this time of year; it gave him a new appreciation for the female physique.

"What's up, DJ T?" a voice yelled from the side of the booth. "A little bird told me you got married."

He peeked over to see who it was and a grin spread across his face. "Whatever, girl. What's been up with you, Meeko? You been hibernating or something?"

He opened the small door and let her into the booth, giving her a big hug. He inhaled the scent that he recognized as Miracle, one of his favorites.

"So, why didn't I get an invite to the big occasion?" she asked, folding her arms.

"Stop playing. You know I didn't get married."

"The rumors are coming from somewhere, and this one came from a reliable source. It all went down last month at Jasper's. You sang to Roni and then asked her to marry you, then you all jumped in a limo and headed to Vegas where you tied the knot. She must be pregnant . . . Is she?"

"No, she ain't pregnant!"

"Don't lie to me, Toby. Remember, I was almost your sister-in-law until your can't-keep-it-in-his-pants brother messed that up!" She laughed and Toby had to agree. A few years ago, Meeko was head over heels for Terry and everyone knew it, but he wasn't ready to settle down and she wasn't about to be strung along. Toby admired that about her.

She began flipping through his music and passing albums for him to mix.

"Something wrong with what I'm playing?" he asked.

"Whatever. Somebody gotta hype this crowd up!"

Sure enough, when he began to pump Mary J. Blige's "Real Love" mixed with Special Ed's "I Got it Made" the already crowded dance floor became flooded with people. She remained in the booth, helping him mix and shouting into the microphone until it was time to slow it down. He put on a slow jams mix CD he made and they exited the booth, heading for the bar.

"You look good, Meeko. I'm glad to see you," he said as they sat down. "You still drinking Long Island Ice Teas?"

"Naw, that was in my younger days. I can't take them anymore. Let me get some Stoli, straight."

"You can't handle Long Islands but you can handle Stoli? Go figure." He ordered their drinks then turned to look at her. It had been over a year since he had seen her and she hadn't changed a bit. She wore a fitted denim dress on her medium frame and her chin-length bob was tinted a color between burgundy and damn near pink. She wore red frames on her face the same color as her hair. Anyone could look at her and tell she was a firecracker.

"I ain't never been no punk, remember? So, how you been, Toby?"

"I been good, Meeko. What's been up with you?"

"You know how I do. I've just been working. That's pretty much it."

"You still writing?" Meeko could write songs like no one else Toby had ever met, and he had met some of the best.

"Not really. Guess I kinda been in a slump. Writing really hasn't been on my mind." She sighed. She looked over at him and took a deep breath. "I heard she sang for you that night after you proposed."

He swallowed the remainder of his Whiskey Sour and looked down into the empty glass. Meeko was the first one to bring up Isis since that night. He fought thoughts about her, but in the back of his mind he knew he wanted to see her, to talk to her, make sure she was all right.

"She sang for us." He nodded, not looking up.

"How did she look . . . I mean, did she seem okay?" Meeko asked, her voice full of concern.

"She seemed good. She sounded great—better than great. She was awesome. Blew everyone away, including Roni." He laughed. "I haven't seen or heard from her since that night. Have you heard from her?"

"I haven't seen or heard from her in two years. All I do is pray that she's okay and trust that God is taking care of her. She knows that if she needs me, I'm there. She's my best friend. Always has been, always will be," Meeko told him.

"Same here. It was just weird, though, Meeko. At first I thought I was dreaming. Everyone was clapping and congratulating us and then she was on stage. She looked and sounded perfect. Did you hear what song she sang?"

"Nope, but I bet you twenty dollars to a dozen doughnuts that it was 'Inseparable,' wasn't it?" She gave him a knowing look.

"How'd you guess?" He laughed. He could tell by the song that was playing that it was time for him to get back in the booth. Plus, the crowd was getting antsy and standing near the dance floor.

"Well, at least we know she's alive, so that's a good thing, right?" Meeko sounded like she was trying to convince herself as she said it. "She coulda called me, though. I wanted to see her. That's how *friends* do, though, huh?"

"True, but she'll call. She showed up, didn't she?" He stood up and stretched.

"Oh, yeah. I heard Jermaine was at Jasper's too. How is he doing?"

"Same old Jermaine. He's moved back here. You know he opened his own business and he's doing really well. I'm proud of him."

"You, Jermaine and Terry. The Three Anegroes reunited." She smiled, referring to the nickname they gave themselves. "Hey, isn't that Terry over there?"

Toby looked over to where Meeko was pointing at a guy hugging and laughing with a familiar girl in the corner of the club. Although it looked like his brother, he didn't want to believe it was, not after all the bragging he had been doing about changing his ways and being in love with Nicole.

"I don't think so," he answered as they made their way back to the deejay booth.

"Well, it was nice hanging with you, Toby."

"You leaving?"

"Yeah, I told you I can't hang like I used to. I'm getting old."

"A'ight, Meeko. Call me some time, girl." He wrote his numbers down and passed them to her. She put them into her pocket.

"I will," she assured him. She hugged him and turned to walk away.

"Hey," he called after her. "When she calls, tell her I asked about her."

Giving him a knowing look, she nodded. "I will. Bye, Toby."

"Meeko!" Terell was headed toward her smiling like a kid on Christmas morning.

She looked back at Toby and shook her head. "I told you that was him."

Toby didn't respond. He watched them walk away then focused his attention on mixing music and refilling the near empty dance floor. He combined current hits and old school jams until it seemed like everyone in the club was grooving. He became engrossed in his work, filling requests and sending shout-outs so that time seemed to fly by. He was surprised when the bartender signaled him that it was last call. *One more hour, then I can bounce,* he thought.

He scanned the crowd, hoping to see Roni or one of her friends. She told him she was coming tonight, but she hadn't shown up. They'd only been engaged a month, but she was already full swing into planning the wedding, which was probably the reason she didn't make it. Still, he thought she would have at least called and left a message.

"Man, Meeko looks good as hell, huh?" Toby didn't answer Terry, who was entering the booth. "I forgot how fine she was."

Toby began repacking his crates in preparation to leave. He was tempted to ask Terry about the girl he saw him hugged up with earlier, but didn't. Instead, he asked, "Hey, did you talk to Kayla tonight?"

"Nope. What, you were looking for Roni?" Terry waved at a group of women who were leaving the club.

"She said they were coming to hang out but I ain't see 'em. I was wondering if Kayla was with you."

"Sorry, bruh. I ain't talked to her." He shrugged as he helped his brother pack up. It was nearing 3:00 a.m. and the crowd was thinning. "You want me to take these out to your truck?"

"Yeah, grab those for me." Toby nodded toward the crates stacked in the corner of the booth.

"Where are your keys?"

Toby reached in his pocket and tossed him the keys. "Be sure to lock it when you come back in."

"Yeah, yeah, yeah. I know."

Finally, the last few stragglers had vacated the club and the wait staff began cleaning. He put on another CD for them to enjoy then went into the owner's office to get his check. He got his schedule for the next week and told everyone good-bye as he exited the back door. As he entered the parking lot, he could hear shouting.

"You are a trifling, no-good, nasty whore! That's what you are!"

"You're one to talk! How many men that come in this club haven't you slept with? So don't even come off at me like that, yo. I ain't even trying to hear that. Now, I'm warning you, you'd better get in your car and leave!"

"I ain't going nowhere. You ain't even call to check on me!

"See, that's where you're confused. You're not my woman. I don't have to call and check on you. For what?"

"You just dropped me off like I was a hitchhiker or something! Like I hadn't just left the abortion clinic getting rid of *our* baby!"

"You had another one of your niggas waiting on you when you got home, remember? He shoulda checked on you. It was probably his kid you got rid of anyway!"

Toby noticed people stopping in the parking lot to see what was going on. He walked over to his brother, who was two feet away from Darla. She was yelling at the top of her lungs.

"Hey, what the hell is wrong with you two?" Toby asked.

"Your brother is a fool and he's trying to play me like I'm one! You think I don't know about Nicole being pregnant and you going around bragging about it?"

"I don't give a damn what you know. That's my business and I advise you to stay out of it!" Terrell turned to walk away when she reached out and grabbed his shoulder. Toby quickly intervened, jumping between them before Terry had a chance to react.

"Darla, you're out of line. Don't put your hands on him," he told her.

"Or what? What's he gonna do to me?" she growled.

"I ain't gonna do shit because you ain't worth it. What? You think that because you out here clowning that's supposed to make me scared of you? Yeah, right. You'd better get real." Terrell turned around and spat at her.

A white Acura Legend pulled up and the horn blew, causing all of them to turn around. The familiar girl who was with Terrell earlier was driving. He smiled and threw Toby his keys. "I'll holler at you later, T!"

"I want my money, you fat bastard!" Darla screamed. "You better get real and pay up. Believe that!"

"Imagine that! You gon' try and carry me in public and then think I'ma give you something. You played yourself, trick!" Terrell laughed in her face as he opened the car door.

Toby knew his brother hated to be embarrassed, especially in public, and Darla was making it harder on herself by clowning outside the club, even though he knew she was angry and hurt.

As Terrell got into the girl's car, it dawned on Toby who she was. He just could not believe that his brother was getting into the car with Kayla's sister, Anjelica Hopkins, of all people. "Terry. Terry! Man, hold up!"

"Face it, Toby. Your brother is nothing but a whore, a club hopping whore," Darla huffed. "But he's gonna pay. Believe that!"

"Leave it alone, Darla. Just go home," he told her and ran over to Anjelica's car.

"What's up?" Terry asked.

"Hey, Toby. How you been? Congratulations on your engagement." The pretty girl smiled at him. He looked at her like she was crazy because he had heard about how conniving and wicked this girl had been in the past, even from Terry. That was why he was confused as to why his brother would be caught dead with her.

"Uh, thanks," he told her. "Can I see you for a minute?"

"Hey, let me holler at him and then we can roll," Terrell told her. She shrugged as he got out of the car. He watched her pull into a nearby parking space to give them some privacy then walked over to his brother, making sure he was far enough out of range that she couldn't hear them.

"What the hell are you doing, Terry? I ain't even gonna talk about your acting a fool with Darla in the parking lot. But what the hell—"

"Man, I ain't thinking about her," Terry started.

"Naw, what the hell are you doing with that chick? Do you even think about what you're doing these days?"

"What? Toby, she's cool. I promise it ain't even like that."

"Like what? Kayla's supposed to be your best friend, man, and that's her worst enemy. That's just wrong."

"No, you're wrong, T. She's nothing like you think she is. I've talked to the girl and I know what's up with her. Kayla is my best friend, but her sister is not as bad as you think she is," Terrell told him. There was something in his voice that made Toby question his brother's sanity.

"And what about Nicole, man? You say you wanna marry her, but you're leaving with another female from the club. You think that ain't gonna get back to her? Come on now, Terry. You're not thinking."

"It's cool. I rode to the club wit' Jermaine. Anjelica's just gonna take me to get my car, that's it. I got it under control, bruh. I know what I'm doing."

"Man, it's your life. You do what you want. But you'd better start thinking about the repercussions of your actions."

"I will, T. I will."

The two men gave each other a brotherly hug that was interrupted by the sound of screeching tires. A low-rider truck came barreling into the parking lot, music blasting and headlights shaking. As it neared the two men, it slowed and the driver's side window rolled down. Panic filled Toby's body as he saw the hand holding the dull, metal pistol aimed at them. *God, help us*, he thought as he reached out and pulled his brother down. They fell to the ground just as the shots rang out. People began screaming and Toby watched Terrell lifting his head and cursing as the truck careened past them.

"Stay down, fool!" he yelled to his brother. *Thank you, Jesus*, he prayed silently as he remained low.

"Hell naw!" Terrell huffed as he maneuvered his large body off the ground. "I don't believe this! That bitch had him come after me!"

"Who? What are you talking about?" Sweat was pouring from both of them and Toby's heart was beating a mile a minute.

"Darla! The guy driving the truck was some dude Turk I seen at her house! I know it was him! I'ma fuck him up. Believe that!"

Sirens could be heard in the distance and Toby looked around to make sure everyone was all right. "Calm down, Terry."

"Are you two okay?" one of the security guards ran over and asked. They assured him that they were and Toby continued to try to calm his brother. Terry was walking back and forth like a panther ready to pounce. The police soon arrived and they each gave a statement. Terry continued accusing someone named Turk.

"Let's go, Terry. Get in the truck."

"I'm cool, T. Besides, I already got a ride," he replied, waving toward Anjelica, who sat across the parking lot, still looking stunned.

"Man, don't you have enough going on in your life right now? Come on. Get in and leave that girl alone. You're asking for trouble, you know that?"

"I told you I can handle mine," he said, walking toward the car.

Toby reached out and grabbed his brother by the shoulder. His brother was acting so stupid he couldn't believe it. There was no way he could stand by and let him ruin his life. It wasn't happening.

"Don't be damn stupid, Terry! Leave that girl alone and go home to Nicole."

"Get off me! What's your problem, T?" Terrell snatched away from him, surprised that Toby put his hands on him like that. He looked at his brother, enraged that he would even go there.

Toby's eyes widened in anger and he squared off against his brother. Terrell was clearly bigger in size, but Toby's body was as cut as LL Cool J in the movie *SWAT*. Toby could feel his heart thumping in his chest and perspiration began to form on his brow. He hadn't fought his brother since they were in high school, and even then it wasn't serious. He was surprised at Terrell's actions.

"Hold the hell up, Terry. I'm just trying to get you to look at what you're doing!"

"I don't need you to get me to do nothing! That's your problem; you always trying to get me to do shit. I ain't you!" he snarled. Moments passed as they stared silently at each other. The few remaining people in the parking lot crowded around the two men, waiting for the fight to jump off.

Toby stared at his brother, confused by what was going on. There was so much animosity in Terry's voice and he didn't know where it was coming from. He frowned at him as he took a step back and told his brother, "You know what? You're right. It ain't my problem. You go and do what the hell you wanna do."

Terrell didn't say anything as he turned and got in the waiting car. Anjelica rolled down her window and began to say something. She must have thought better of it because she just shrugged at Toby instead and waved briefly was they pulled off.

All this over a piece of ass. I don't believe this, Toby thought as he got into his truck and headed home. *That brother was about to fight me over a piece of ass. Thank you, God, for looking out for him, because he almost got killed twice tonight.*

Chapter 8

"What the hell was that all about?" Anjelica asked as they drove down the street.

"Man, I don't even know," Terrell answered. He leaned the seat all the way back and closed his eyes. He had a million thoughts running through his mind at one time, and didn't feel like thinking about anything. He couldn't believe that punk-ass scrub, Turk, had actually tried to take him out—over Darla's fat ass, at that. But he had a trick for her ho ass too. She wanted to play those kinds of games, he would play them and win. Then there was Toby. He could not believe his brother tried to buck up like he wanted to swing on him. Over the years, he had taken a lot from Toby, but at this point in his life, he was tired.

"When that fool started shooting, I was like 'What the hell?' I'm glad no one was hurt," Anjelica said, trying to make small talk.

"Yeah," he responded. He rolled down his window and enjoyed the air. Anjelica must've sensed his mood because she fumbled with the disc changer and Maxwell began playing. She leaned back into her seat and remained silent.

When they were in the club, Terrell told her his car was at Jermaine's crib, about a mile and a half from the club. Now he noticed she was getting on the Interstate instead. He didn't ask where she was going; he just decided to ride. He felt his phone vibrating in his pocket and didn't even look to see who it was. He figured it was Nicole calling to see where he was, and he didn't feel like talking to her right now. There was too much on his mind to even attempt to explain to her what had just happened. All he wanted to do was relax.

The sound of waves crashing caused Terrell to wake up. He hadn't even realized he had drifted off to sleep. He looked around, unsure of where he was, and then he saw the sand sprawled before him. They were at the beach. Maxwell was still singing, but there was no one in the car with him. He opened the door and got out, stretching his arms. He looked at his watch and saw that it was almost 4:00 in the morning. The sky was blanketed in darkness with the exception of a faint, twinkling star here or there, and the shape of a dull crescent moon. He inhaled, taking in the scent of the warm, salty air. He scanned the scenery until he spotted a shadow in the distance, sitting on the ground. He took his phone out of his pocket, turned it off without ever checking the call log and tossed it into the back seat. Grabbing the keys from the ignition and locking the doors, he walked over.

"What's up?" he asked, sitting next to her.

"Nothing. Just chilling, enjoying the night . . . Or should I say morning?" She shrugged.

"Yeah, this is nice. I ain't been out here in a minute." He looked around.

"I come out here a lot. It's peaceful. I don't have a lot of peace in my life, but I'm sure you know all about that, huh?"

"What, not having peace in my life?"

"No, me not having peace in mine, Terrell," she told him. Her hands began playing in the sand, moving back and forth as she looked down. "You think I don't know what people say about me? How I'm the most hated person in my family?"

"I wouldn't say you were hated, yo. I'd say it was more like misunderstood."

"Misunderstood, huh? Let me ask you something. Why do you hang out with me? I mean, Kayla's your best friend, I'm her wicked sister, the one that has caused all this drama n her life. Why would you of all people want to be around me?" she asked without looking at him.

"Because I think you put up this front like you want to be this hardcore female that really doesn't care, but you do. Let me ask you this: why do you cause so much drama in your sister's life? Do you hate her that much?"

"See, that's where everyone has it all wrong. I don't hate her at all. She's not my favorite person in the world, but I don't hate her. I love her."

Terrell couldn't help laughing. "You what? Love her? Come on. You slept with her fiancé, in her house, in her bed! What? That was done out of love?"

"No, now *that* was a mistake. I went to a party and I was so drunk and high that it was unreal. I swear I've never been that blazed before in my life. The girl I rode with was drunk too, but she was gonna stay with her boyfriend. I told them to drop me off at Kayla's; I let myself in with the key. I knew it was Geno's bachelor party and Kayla was having her own li'l set at Roni's. I ain't think either one of them was coming home, I swear. I don't even remember much of what happened except that hot-ass water coming across my back."

"Damn." Terrell recalled how Kayla told him about tossing hot water on Anjelica and Geno when she caught them in her bed, but he thought she was exaggerating. His best friend was telling the truth after all.

"You know the saddest part about that whole situation? My friend's boyfriend found out later that this guy that had been trying to get with me all night had put something in my drink. They were gonna tell Kayla the whole thing, but what would've been the point? She called the wedding off. That was the last time I got high." She sighed as she reflected on the whole situation.

"Okay, then what about the whole Janice thing? Did you set that up?" Even he suspected her of having something to do with Kayla's attack, although he doubted that she meant for her sister to be hurt as badly as she was. He began asking questions that he wanted answered for the longest, and now Anjelica seemed to be in the mood to talk.

"Yeah, I had something to do with that too, right? I supposedly gave her Kayla's telephone number and address, right? I don't even *know* Kayla's telephone number. How about Janice followed Kayla from work and got her number from directory assistance?"

"But isn't Janice's sister your friend?"

"No, okay, I did lie about that. We work together, that's it. She ain't my friend."

"A'ight, a'ight, but what about when you pushed up on Theo at the baby shower?"

Kayla had walked in on Anjelica and Theo, her friend Tia's boyfriend, about to get it on during Kayla's baby shower. Terrell had even gotten confrontational with Anjelica that night, amazed at how nonchalant she was at the entire situation. To him, it seemed like she was doing everything in her power to make her sister miserable.

"I ain't push up on him. I was in his face, cussing him out because he had been blowing my friend, Yasmine's phone up trying to get with her. I was about to call him out when everyone came in the room hollering about me trying to push up on him. So, since no one wanted to hear my side of the story, I left it alone. If Tia gets played, it's on her. It ain't my problem."

"You really think you're hard, huh?" He laughed.

"I'm not trying to be hard. Do you really think I care about what they say about me? No, that's what Kayla does. She has low self-esteem and needs to be accepted. She cares about what everyone is gonna think or what they're gonna say. I don't give a damn. She was a grown woman who hid her pregnancy from her father because she was scared of what he was gonna say. She went to school to be a teacher because that's what my mother wanted her to do. Kayla doesn't even like kids; she wanted to major in marketing, but she did what everyone wanted her to do. I wasn't about to go to school; I like working. I ain't about to move out until I can afford to build the house I wanna live in, but that makes me a bum. I'm not Kayla. She has to have everyone like her and be friends with everyone. I don't need a whole bunch of friends. That's where all the drama comes from," she said loudly.

"I feel you on that one. But you and your sister need to get this worked out."

"There's nothing to work out, Terrell. I'm cool with it like it is. I like being the villainess, the bad girl. Let me ask you this, since we're being all open and honest all of a sudden. Why did you sleep with me that night? I know you couldn't stand me just as much as the others, but you still had sex with me. Why?"

Terrell didn't have an answer. He tried and tried to think of one, but couldn't. She was right; he did have as much hatred for her as everyone else, but he was still deeply attracted to her for some reason.

"I know what it is, Terrell." She winked at him.

"You don't know nothing." He looked at her from the corner of his eye. She was so sexy. He tried not to stare at her full bust, which was very much inviting through the provocative, sleeveless fuchsia top she wore. Instead, his eyes fell on her thick hips wearing black fitted pants, and continued to her feet—even they were sexy. She had taken off her racy, stiletto heels, the same color as her shirt, and they were lying in the sand. He picked one up and examined it.

"What, your hooker shoes got too tight for you? How tall are these things anyway, four inches?"

"Four and a half, and don't change the subject. I know why you slept with me. Kayla is your best friend, right? You two been thick as thieves for what, at least a year now?"

"Yep, that's my dawg." He reached over, pulled her feet in his lap and began rubbing them. They were soft, just like he thought they'd be.

"You were there for her when she needed you the most. You shared a lot, and had each other's back."

"Yeah." He continued massaging the arch of her right foot as she talked.

"But nothing ever jumped off between you and her." She leaned back on her elbows and continued. He began to wonder where she was going with this. "Knowing you, it was probably because she was pregnant. Plus, she was all caught up in the Geno/Craig, Craig/Geno, who's-the-daddy, who-do-I-love drama. That right there, I guess, would have been a turn off, of course. But you stuck by her, no doubt. You were her friend. I've seen how you operate, Terrell. Had that not been the case, you probably would have tried to get with her."

He looked at her like she had just fallen from the sky. No female had ever tried to go there with him. She just lay there, smiling at him.

"Funny, I look just like my sister. People even say we could pass for twins."

"Obviously, you have lost your freaking mind, Anjelica." He pushed her feet out of his lap and frowned at her.

"What? It's cool, Terrell. Why are you mad?"

"I ain't mad, you're crazy! I don't believe what you just said. You're trying to make it seem like the only reason I got wit' you is 'cause you look like Kayla. That's sick. She's like my little sister! I don't even think of her that way!" Terrell shook his head, appalled at what Anjelica had even suggested. He had never thought about Kayla like that. The one reason that their friendship had gotten to the level that it had was because he had never thought about that. Granted, she was probably the *only* female that he had befriended that he had *never* thought of sleeping with, *and* it was due partly due to the fact that she was pregnant and her life was drama-filled, but it definitely wasn't the reason he had slept with Anjelica. He was offended by her even suggesting it. She, on the other hand, was amused at his reaction, unable to suppress her laughter.

"Well, if I'm wrong, I apologize, Terrell. I just thought you had a subliminal desire to sleep with my sister. Come on, she's a beautiful girl, smart and funny. A lot of guys try to get with her. There is nothing wrong with Kayla."

"I didn't say there was. I have no interest in getting with her."

"You don't have an interest in getting with me, but that doesn't stop you from sleeping with me," she pointed out. She put her feet back into his lap and he resumed his position as foot masseuse.

"How do you know I don't wanna get with you?"

"Terrell, you're not ready to get with anyone. Not even Nicole."

"That's not true. I love Nicole."

"I didn't say you didn't love her. You probably do, but you shouldn't settle down with her. Not yet, anyway."

"Okay, why shouldn't I settle down with her? She's got a great job, a future, she's wonderful." His hands began moving under her pants leg, along her strong calves, kneading into her muscles.

"That's why you shouldn't settle down with her until you're ready; because she's a good person. If you know you still want to be out there, then don't lie to her. In the end, she's gonna wind up hurt and she'll hate you. You don't want that. Being hated is not a good feeling. Trust me, I know."

"She's having my baby, remember?"

"According to—what was old girl at the club's name? Darlene?"

"Darla." He cringed at the thought of her.

"Whatever. She was having your baby, too, but you ain't make no rash decisions to settle down and be a family with her."

"She's a ho!" His hands crept further and further up her leg and he enjoyed the feel of her firm thighs. His manhood began to rise with thoughts of making love on the beach.

"So are you, Terrell. You slept with her knowing she was sleeping with Toby—unprotected on top of that. That's nasty."

"Since when did you become Ms. Morality all of a sudden? Don't go there with me, Anjelica."

"I ain't going nowhere, Terrell. See, you and I, we're cut from the same cloth. We have more in common than we'll ever know. I understand you and you understand me on a whole other level. That's why the sex between us was the bomb."

"Was?" He stopped caressing her leg.

"Was. I made the mistake of sleeping with one engaged man. I ain't making it again," she told him. He could see the seriousness in her face and knew she meant it. "You say you're with Nicole, then that's cool. I commend you for that. But don't think I'ma be Darla's replacement. Despite what you and everyone else thinks about me, I ain't a ho, and more importantly, I ain't stupid. You ready?"

She stood up and brushed the sand from her behind. He looked up at her, his arousal suddenly disappearing. This was definitely not how he thought this would be ending when he realized they were on the beach. She reached out her arm and helped him get to his feet.

"Thanks," he said and brushed himself off as well. Instead of heading back to the car, she bent down, rolled her pants legs up and began walking down the beach. He walked beside her and they continued talking until the dark sky brightened and they could see the amber golden hues of the rising sun.

Chapter 9

"I guess you didn't have as much fun as you expected at the beach, huh?" she asked when she pulled up behind his car, still parked in the driveway behind Jermaine's Range Rover. It was just after 7:00 in the morning and he was contemplating asking her to breakfast.

"Naw, it was cool. You know I like chilling with you anyway."

"I guess that's something us Hopkins women have in common, right?" she teased.

"Shut up, girl. Oh, let me get my phone out the back seat. I wouldn't want you going through my numbers. Nosy as hell, that's another thing you Hopkins women have in common." He laughed, reaching into the back seat and retrieving his phone. He clicked the power on and the phone instantly vibrated. The screen alerted him that he had new messages. He decided to check them.

"You have eight new messages," the voice prompt announced.

"Damn, I got eight messages," he said aloud.

"Somebody been cussing you out repeatedly." Anjelica laughed.

"You're probably right." He sighed and listened to the first three, which were from Nicole, telling him to call her. By the third message, he could tell that she was pissed. The next three messages were from stupid-ass Darla, crying about how he ruined her life and she wanted her money so she could move. The next two messages were from Kayla, telling him to call her immediately. She sounded upset, as if she had been crying, and both messages were left after 4:00 in the morning, the same time that he was at the beach. He wondered if maybe someone had told her about him being with Anjelica at the club or leaving with her. *Naw, she just had those nightmares again,* he told himself.

"Something wrong?" Anjelica asked.

"Naw, Kayla called me twice around four this morning," he said.

"Oh no, not drama first thing in the morning." Anjelica faked a moan, but the sound of his phone interrupted them.

"It's her again. Something must be wrong," he said, answering it before it could ring again. "Yo."

"T-Terrell," Kayla said quietly.

"Yeah, what's wrong?" he asked. Anjelica was making faces at him as he talked into the phone.

"I . . . I . . . We're at the h-hos-hospital," she sniffed.

"Hospital? For what? What hospital, Kay? What happened?" Thoughts of the shootout at the club came flooding back and he wondered if Turk had come back and shot Toby. Anjelica's face now wore a look of concern.

"M-my father . . . he . . . he . . . "

"What? Tell me what happened."

"He had a heart attack. I'm here with Mama. We . . . we . . . "

He could hear the sound of the phone as it fell, then someone else picked up.

"Terrell, its Yvonne. We're here at Mercy Hospital. Mr. John had a heart attack around three-thirty this morning." Yvonne was another one of Kayla's buddies who he had gotten to know over the past year. There were four of them all together including her, Roni, Kayla and Tia. The Lonely Hearts Club was what they called each other when they were living the single life and hanging out.

"Damn." He sighed and looked over at Anjelica. "How is he?"

"What?" Anjelica whispered. "Who?"

"He's in critical condition. I'm here with Kayla and her mom. Geno is here too. I don't know where the hell Anjelica is. We've been trying to find her all morning."

"Who has Day?"

"Geno's mom has her. Where are you?"

The front door opened and Jermaine stepped out, looking at the car. Terrell opened the car door and got out, making sure he closed the door behind him. He waved at Jermaine, who took notice of Anjelica. He gave Terrell a nod of approval as he walked over to his truck. "What's up, Terry?"

"Chilling," Terrell told him then went back to talking to Yvonne. "Uh, I'm at my boy Jermaine's house. I stayed here last night. Tell Kay to give me a few minutes and I'll be right there." He sighed.

"Thanks, Terrell. I'll let her know," Yvonne said and hung up the phone.

Terrell leaned against the car and tried to think of what to do next. He knew he was going to have to tell Anjelica. She was already getting out of the car.

"What the hell is going on? Who's in the hospital?"

He walked around and stood in front of her, pausing before he let the words come from his mouth. "Anjelica, it's your dad."

"My dad? What about him?" Her face became clouded with confusion as she listened to what he was saying.

"He had a heart attack this morning, Anjelica."

For a moment, she just stared at him and he wondered if she heard what he told her. Her head leaned to the side and her stare was blank. Then, as if someone had slapped her, she straightened up. He saw her eyes quickly fill with tears and she began to shake, almost falling into his arms. Jermaine must have been looking because suddenly he was right there beside them.

"Yo, what's wrong with her? Is she sick?" he questioned. "Do I need to call 911?"

"Naw, man. She just found out her dad had a heart attack. I need to get her to the hospital," Terrell replied. He put his arm around Anjelica, who was now weeping quietly.

"Aw, man," Jermaine said. "I'm sorry."

"Is . . . is he—?" Anjelica started to ask, but she broke down before she could finish.

"He's in critical condition, Anjelica. That's all I know. Come on. We need to get going," he told her.

"I'll ride with you," Jermaine said suddenly.

"You don't have to do that, man. I got it," Terrell told him, leading a wobbling Anjelica back to the car. Just as he opened the door for her, she leaned over and began to heave. Vomit came from her mouth and he jumped back. "Shit."

"Sorry," she whined, still shaking. She looked down and noticed that she had soiled her shirt.

"It's okay. Come on. You can clean up inside before we leave," Jermaine told her, suddenly in charge.

Anjelica didn't resist when he reached out and put his arm around her. Terrell followed as his friend led her up the driveway. Jermaine was easily six-foot-five and practically had to lean to support her five-five frame. Her face was buried into his chest as they entered the house. For some reason, Terrell felt a slight twinge of jealousy, but brushed it off as he waited for them to return. He silently said a prayer for his friends' father as he leaned against the car.

A few minutes later, they emerged from the house. Anjelica was wearing a green-and-white T-shirt promoting Jermaine's security surveillance company, We Secure U. Terrell had about ten of the exact same shirts in multiple colors because every time he came over, Jermaine gave him one.

"You okay?" he walked over and asked. Anjelica barely nodded.

"Wait a minute," she said suddenly.

"What's wrong?" Terrell asked. He watched her as she looked down. He hoped she wasn't about to faint.

"I gotta get something out of my car."

"I'll get it for you. What is it?" Terrell asked, reaching for her keys.

"Grab my sneakers out the trunk."

"What?"

"Huh?"

He and Jermaine looked at her and shook their heads. Terrell walked to her car and opened the trunk. There were four different shoeboxes lying there. He grabbed the blue-and-white Reebok box and took out a pair of white classics.

"Are these good?" he asked.

She nodded her head and placed her arm on Jermaine's shoulder as she balanced herself, taking off her stilettos. She slipped her feet into the sneakers and handed him the pumps to put back into her car.

"You want me to drive, Terry?" Jermaine asked as he helped Anjelica steady herself.

"I can drive. Thanks for offering, though," Terrell answered, walking over to his car and hitting the alarm. He went to reach for Anjelica, but she clung to Jermaine's arm. Terrell realized that she was in shock. He looked at Jermaine and shrugged.

"We can just sit in the back." Jermaine opened the rear door and eased Anjelica inside the car. Terrell got behind the wheel and reached over to pull the passenger seat all the way forward so that Jermaine's legs wouldn't be in his chest. He couldn't help but smile as he watched Jermaine maneuver his long body into the back seat.

"You want me to try to call Kayla and check on your dad?"

Anjelica shook her head and the tears started flowing once again. "Just . . . just get to the hospital."

"We'll be there in no time," Jermaine assured her, looking in the rearview mirror at Terrell.

Terrell floored the car, maneuvering it with ease through the modish neighborhood, and merged onto the fairly empty highway. Even with no traffic, he knew the ride to Mercy Hospital would take at least thirty minutes. He turned the radio on and let the soothing sounds of Sunday morning gospel fill the car, praying that it would bring some comfort to Anjelica. He continually looked back to make sure she was okay. Jermaine still had his arm around her and her head was buried into her hands. Every now and then Terrell would see him whisper something to her and she would nod.

It was exactly twenty-one minutes later when he pulled into the parking lot of the hospital. He found an empty space and parked the car. Jermaine wasted no time hopping out and was opening Anjelica's door before Terrell even had a chance to get his seatbelt off.

"Do you know what floor he's on?" Jermaine asked as they entered the hospital lobby. "Is he in emergency or what?"

Terrell shook his head. "Yvonne didn't say. I'll ask the receptionist." He went to the desk and asked for any info on John Hopkins. The receptionist advised Terrell that Mr. Hopkins was in surgery on the seventh floor. She pointed them in the direction of the elevator, and they rode in silence. Anjelica hesitated when the doors slid open; Terrell and Jermaine stepped off.

"Come on, yo," he told her. She looked like she was about to throw up again and he couldn't blame her. The smell of the hospital almost caused him to be nauseous himself. He didn't understand how Nicole could stand working as a nurse. "It's gonna be a'ight, but you need to come on."

"I got her, Terry." Jermaine reached out and led her into the wide hallway. They proceeded under the sign pointing to the surgical waiting area.

Terrell could see Kayla sitting alongside her mother as he opened the heavy glass door encasing the waiting room. Her eyes were swollen and she looked as if she was barely holding it together. His heart went out to his friend and he knew there wasn't much more she could take. Her boyfriend, Geno, noticed him in the hallway and came out to meet him. Kayla didn't even look up.

"Hey, G. How is he?"

"He's still in surgery. They haven't told us anything yet." Geno sighed. His eyes went beyond Terrell and he realized Anjelica was there as well. "Anjelica, we've been looking all over for you. Your mom was worried."

"I'm okay," she said barely above a whisper. Geno took a step toward her, but she didn't move. Terrell saw her slip her hand into Jermaine's. The door opened again and Yvonne joined them in the hall. She spoke to Terrell then stood staring at Anjelica and Jermaine as Geno did.

"Oh," was the only thing she said. Terrell could tell she was lost for words.

"How're you doing?" Jermaine said to Yvonne. "Anjelica, your mom must be in here. Come on, so she'll know you're okay."

"Okay," Anjelica said. "Thanks for being here, Yvonne. You too, Geno."

Terrell opened the door and Kayla's mother rushed toward them. She reached past him and put her arms around her daughter. He eased past the two women and walked over to his friend. She stood and he took her into his arms, rubbing her back. For the second time that morning, a Hopkins woman cried on his shoulder. He searched his brain for the right words to say, but there were none. Kayla cried for a few moments longer then released herself from his grasp. Terrell moved his body so she could see her mother and sister.

"Your fam is here, Kay," he told her. The intensity in the room became apparent as the two sisters looked at each other. For what seemed like eternity, no one moved. The sound of the door opening once again caused everyone to turn as an older gentleman dressed in green hospital scrubs entered, a white surgical mask hanging between his chin and chest.

"Is he okay?" Mrs. Hopkins asked the doctor, her eyes wide with anticipation. Terrell felt Kayla reaching for his hand and he eased by her side, waiting for the doctor's response.

"Your husband suffered a massive heart attack, Mrs. Hopkins. We've stabilized him, but he's in critical condition," he told her.

Geno eased behind Kayla and put his hands on her shoulders. She closed her eyes and gripped Terrell's hands tighter. Terrell looked over at Anjelica, who was standing on the other side of her mother. Jermaine was still standing near, listening along with everyone else.

"What does that mean?" Anjelica asked. At the sound of her sister's voice, Kayla's eyes popped open. Terrell heard her inhale deeply as she glared at her sister. Her mother turned to the doctor for his reply.

"The damage to his heart was extensive, but we repaired it the best we could," the doctor said. Terrell could tell that there was forced optimism in his voice.

"And?" Anjelica stepped closer to the doctor and he seemed a bit disturbed.

"Anjelica, don't start," her mother said with a tone of caution. "I'm sorry."

"No, don't apologize for her. She's right."

They were all shocked to see Kayla step beside her sister. The two women stared at the man and waited for his response. Geno nudged Terrell, who just shrugged. Yvonne's mouth fell open.

"I know that you're upset, and we are doing all we can to take care of your father and make him as comfortable as possible."

"Look, don't try to blow smoke at us and sugar coat this situation, Dr. . . . what's your name?" Anjelica asked.

"Stevens. Clifford Stevens," he answered, looking nervous. He wasn't much taller than either one of them and he began stroking his salt-and-pepper beard.

"Dr. Stevens, it's not his comfort that we're worried about. We want you to save his life!" Kayla told him.

Terrell saw the color coming into the doctor's café au lait cheeks, and if he had been any race other than black, he probably would have been beet red by now. The sisters made a powerful united front, which took everyone in the room by surprise.

"Now, again, how is my father's condition?" Anjelica repeated.

"If he makes it through the next twenty-four hours, he'll have a fifty percent chance of recovery." He looked over at their mother, who was trying to keep her composure, but was slowly breaking down. Yvonne walked over and put her arms around her, leading her to the small sofa in the corner of the room.

The sound of Kayla's sniffling could be heard, but just as Terrell headed toward her, the two sisters turned toward each other. He looked from one to the other as they stared into each other's faces. His heart began beating rapidly as he tried to think of something to do or say. *God, please don't let them start fighting in here. They've been through too much already.*

"Thank you, Dr. Stevens," Anjelica told him, her eyes remaining on her sister. "When can we see my father?"

"I can take you to him now. He's still in recovery," the doctor told her. He moved toward the door and held it open, looking around to see who was coming. Yvonne slowly helped Mrs. Hopkins up and she turned toward her children, who continued to look eye to eye.

"Anjelica, Kayla?" she said aloud, wiping her eyes and running her fingers through her hair nervously.

Neither one answered their mother, nor did they move. Then, to everyone's surprise, including her own, Anjelica extended her hand to her sister. At first, Kayla just stared at it, then slowly, she took it into her own and the three women exited together behind the doctor.

"Man, that was intense," Jermaine finally said. Terrell had forgotten that his friend was there with them.

"That was nothing," Geno sighed and took his seat next to Yvonne. "I've seen worse when those two were together."

"Ain't that the truth?" Yvonne added.

Terrell introduced Jermaine to them then asked, "Where's Roni? Toby was looking for her at the club last night."

"Roni left a little while before you got here. She had been trying to call Toby but couldn't get in contact with him," Yvonne told him. "We got here a little after four."

"Man, he probably went home and fell into bed. We had major drama after the club closed last night." He went on to tell them about the shootout that occurred in the parking lot. He left out the part about Darla being the cause.

"I know Nicole probably fell out when you told her about it," Geno replied.

"Nicole. Damn, I need to call her!" With all that had gone on, he had forgotten. Yvonne told him that he had to go outside the hospital in order to use his phone. He hurried to the elevator, dialing her number as he walked.

"Hello."

"Hey, baby. I'm sorry. I just got a chance to call you," he said before he even got off the elevator. He knew she was probably pissed and tried to think of how to explain why he hadn't come over or at least called the night before.

"I've been calling you all night, Terrell! I don't know what kind of game you're—"

"Kayla's dad had a heart attack last night," he interrupted her before she could finish. He felt bad about using his best friend's sick father as his alibi, but he had no other choice. He hoped Nicole would assume he had been at the hospital with Kayla the entire time.

"How is he? How's Kayla?" she asked, her tone quickly changing from irritated to concerned.

"He's still in surgery and we're waiting," he answered.

"Do you need anything? Is there anything I can do?"

"I'm good. Thanks for asking. You getting ready for church?" He knew she was. Nicole was a faithful member of Shepherd's Heart Memorial Chapel. Terrell rarely attended with her because it was boring. Needless to say, it was one of the things that he and Nicole didn't see eye to eye on. As he stood outside the hospital, he forced himself not to admire two nurses who were walking by.

"Yeah, I have to usher this morning. I'll ride over to the hospital after service."

"Okay. Say a prayer for Mr. John, will you, baby? Hey, you feeling all right this morning? No morning sickness?"

"A little, but nothing I can't handle. I gotta get outta here. I love you."

"Love you too," he told her and ended the call. He thought about calling his brother but changed his mind. *I don't have the energy to deal with Toby's judgmental behind or his double standards this morning. I got my own problems.*

Chapter 10

Toby tossed the keys on the coffee table and flopped down on the sofa. He took his cell from the pocket of his jeans, but it was dead. He picked up his cordless phone and dialed Roni's cell. Her voicemail picked up instantly, so he knew that either her battery was dead or she had it turned off. He had already driven by her house and found out that she wasn't at home, so he decided against calling there. He was tired both mentally and physically, and contemplated just staying on the sofa. He convinced himself that his bed would be much more comfortable and slowly got up.

As he climbed the stairs and entered his bedroom, he heard a noise. Someone was in the bathroom. He slowly pushed the cracked door open and heard the sound of the shower. He entered to the scent of jasmine and saw the silhouette of a woman's naked body through the frosted glass. Her back was to him, and she hadn't realized he was there. He watched her for a while, admiring her beauty and listening to her sing about finding love on a two-way street and losing it on a lonely highway. He meticulously removed his own clothes, making sure he didn't make any noise. His soldier was at full attention as he carefully opened the door and stepped behind her.

"About time you came home," she told him without turning around. His eyes took in her perfect body from head to toe. The drops of water clinging to her caramel shoulder were an open invitation for his tongue to lick, and he obliged. She arched her back and he pushed her long, black hair out of the way as he kissed her neck. His hand reached around her small waist and rested on her hips as he pulled her to him. His rock hard penis rested on her firm buttocks. "Mmm, seems like someone is happy to see me."

Slowly, she turned and put her arms around him, smiling. He felt his heart melt as his eyes met hers. He wasted no time covering her mouth with his. He taunted her tongue and ran his hands through her thick hair, the steam of the shower surrounding them. She balanced herself on one leg as she wrapped the other one around him. His hands found their way to her center and he rubbed back and forth against her openness, causing her to gasp. Releasing the grip he had on her head, he lifted her into his arms and she wrapped her body around his. It amazed him that she was able to maneuver herself perfectly in one swift movement, and he smiled as he entered her.

She rocked back and forth, never missing a beat as he nudged the shower doors open and stepped out. She felt so good, her breasts crushed against his chest as she continued to ride. His eyes took in the sexiness of her hard nipples. He could feel her muscles contracting against his hardness, arousing him even more.

He quickly made his way to the countertop and sat her down, making sure they weren't near the candles she had burning near the sink. He continued plunging into her as she clawed at his back and bit into his shoulder. Their lovemaking was ferocious and he loved it. The glow of the candles reflecting in the mirror seemed to cause her image to glow as she looked at him seductively. He was determined to control himself, but before he knew it, she had leaned all the way back and wrapped her legs around his neck. She tightened around him and he closed his eyes as he felt himself about to explode.

"Oh, God! Ice!"

"Toby! Toby!"

Suddenly, his eyes flew open. He quickly looked around and realized he was still on the sofa. He rubbed his eyes and saw that Roni was standing over him, looking at him like he was a stranger.

"Toby, are you all right?" she asked, frowning.

"Huh?" he asked.

"That must have been a hell of a dream."

She was right; the dream had been vivid. He hadn't had one like that in over a year. He sat up and stretched. "Yeah. It was crazy."

"You're all sweaty, baby." She ran her hand along his forehead and showed him the perspiration that was apparent on her palm. "And you were calling for ice."

His head snapped around and he stared at her. "What?"

"You were calling out for some ice. Let me get you a wet washcloth," she said and disappeared down the hallway.

As he sat on the edge of the sofa, he tried to get his thoughts together. He couldn't believe the dream he had just experienced. *Isis Adams.* When she had first disappeared, he had them all the time, almost every night. But as time went on, they had become more and more infrequent. He laughed at himself nervously and stood up. *Man, you are really tripping.*

"Here you go, baby." Roni gently wiped his face with the cool washcloth. Her touch was tender and he turned his head and kissed the inside of her wrist as she wiped.

"I looked for you last night. I called you too," he told her. "What happened?"

"I was at the hospital all night." She sighed and sat down.

"Hospital? For what?" he asked, sitting next to her.

"Mr. John had a heart attack. I was there with Kayla and her mom."

"How is he?"

"He was still in surgery when I left. Yvonne is there with them now and so is Geno. Anjelica is nowhere to be found."

He remembered Terrell leaving the club with Anjelica last night and reached for the phone to call him. He knew that the chances of them still being together were strong. He had begun dialing the number as Roni continued talking.

"Kayla was able to locate Terrell and he was on his way. Even he was M.I.A. last night. The club must've been off the chain."

Toby clicked the phone off, knowing that if his brother was en route to the hospital, then Anjelica was too. He took a deep breath and proceeded to tell Roni about the shootout afterwards, leaving out the fact that Terrell left with Anjelica, of course.

"Oh my God. Who would be shooting at you?" she shrieked.

"Some dude was beefing with Terry about Darla or somethi—"

"Darla! I should have known her fat yellow ass would have something to do with this. Her hood rat, sleep-with-anyone-with-a-car, always-in-somebody's-face, no-hair-doing self need to just go somewhere and stay!"

"Calm down, Ron. The important thing is that no one was hurt and everyone's fine. Let me take a quick shower and then we can head back over to the hospital."

"Are you sure? I know you're tired after everything that happened last night."

"I want to go. I wanna be there for Kayla and her family." He kissed her quickly and headed upstairs to his room. Pulling out a pair of sweats and a T-shirt from his drawer, he walked into the bathroom. He couldn't help looking around and as he lay his clothes on the smooth countertop, he recalled the dream he'd just had of him and his old lover. Turning on the shower, he tried to push all thoughts of her out of his head, but they continued to flash in his mind like snapshots of a movie.

"Toby? You want me to make you some breakfast, sweetheart?" Roni called from downstairs.

"Naw, I'm good," he answered. *Man, get your head together*, he told himself. *You got a good woman downstairs that you need to be focusing on, and you're thinking about a damn memory of what could have been.* He stood in the shower and let his mind drift to thoughts of Kayla and her family, saying a quick prayer for them and Mr. John's recovery. He had just stepped out and was drying off when he heard the yelling.

"What the hell do you want?" Roni screamed.

"This ain't got nothing to do with you!"

"The hell it doesn't! You come knocking on my fiancé's door at eight in the morning demanding to see him and you telling me it doesn't have anything to do with me. You obviously don't even have as much sense as I thought you had."

"Look, I don't have to tell you shi—"

He heard the door slam and then someone began beating on it like a lunatic. The door opened again and this time he knew who Roni was talking to.

"Girl, I will beat your big ass into the middle of next week. You don't know who you're messing with."

"Toby!"

Toby quickly threw on his clothes and took off down the steps. His shirt clung to his still wet chest.

"What is going on?" he demanded. Roni was standing in the doorway about to bum rush Darla, who was standing outside the storm door, looking like a wild woman. Her clothes were rumpled and she kept folding and unfolding her arms as she demanded that Roni let her in. He knew from experience that Roni had no problem fighting, and he wondered if Darla remembered what happened the last time she popped up at his house and crossed Roni. That was the night Roni broke the windows of his truck and house because she thought he and Darla were hooking up. He wasn't about to go through all that again.

"I need to talk to you," Darla pleaded.

"I don't have nothing to say to you, Darla," he said calmly as he stepped in front of the door. Roni was right behind him, ready to pounce if necessary.

"Please, Toby. Just give me five minutes, that's all," she begged. Her face was swollen and he could tell she had been crying. He felt sorry for her, but was disgusted with her at the same time.

"Go away, Darla. There's nothing to talk to me about."

"I need to explain about last night. I need for you to understand what happened."

"What happened was that you almost got him and a whole lot of other people killed because of your ignorant ass!" Roni reached past him and tried to open the door.

"I didn't have anything to do with that! I swear. Toby, you gotta believe me. I would never have done anything as stupid as try to have somebody shoot at you or your trifling-ass brother. I need to talk to you, please."

"He already told you to get the hell away from here. What part of that don't you understand? Leave him alone!" Roni was using all her strength to get past him at this point and Toby had to actually struggle to restrain her.

"Darla, just go away. Now isn't the time or the place for this. Go," he said as he stepped back and reached to close the door.

"Toby, please wait," she pleaded. "That's it? After all the shit we been through? It's just that I told Terry—"

"Look, I didn't have anything to do with what you and my brother had going on. I got my own stuff to deal with and I'm not being in the middle of this. That stunt you and your friend pulled last night was crazy and uncalled for."

"Leave him alone. Leave Terry alone. Find somebody that wants you back for a change and quit being a doormat!" Roni yelled.

"Roni! Let me handle this," he turned and told her.

"Handle it then. I'm so sick of her," she huffed at him. It seemed that her attitude was now aimed at him and it took him by surprise.

"You're out of line," Toby told Roni.

"What? I'm out of line? You act like I should give a damn about her or her feelings, which I don't. Every time I turn my head she's over here crying on your shoulder about someone that's done her wrong. Maybe if her high yellow ass would stop screwing—"

"Just go inside," he cut her off.

She stared at him for a moment then rolled her eyes at Darla. "STD," she murmured as she walked away.

He made sure she was out of earshot then turned back to Darla, who was looking like she wanted to burn down his house with him and Roni in it. He went to say something, but she stopped him. "I thought I was your friend, if nothing else, but like your fiancée said, I'm nothing but a STD."

"I'm sorry, Darla, but right now the best thing you can do is let it go."

"Let what go? What are you saying?"

"I'm saying leave me and my brother alone." He closed the door, leaving her standing in the doorway, a defeated look on her face.

He stood there for a moment, staring at the back of the door, angry. Angry at himself for ever becoming involved with a girl whose self-esteem was so low that she would do anything to get anyone's approval. Angry for even bragging and joking that she was just an STD – something to do, nothing special. Angry at Terrell for taking advantage of her too, then getting her pregnant on top of that. Angry at Darla for allowing them to treat her like she was nothing. Angry at Roni for talking to her like that, making an already bad situation worse. He looked out the window and double checked to make sure that Darla had left. He saw her black Neon still sitting in front of his house behind Roni's silver Celica. Their eyes met briefly, then she left. His anger turned to relief as something told him that she finally understood and wouldn't be bothering them again.

Chapter 11

"Hey, baby. How's Mr. John?" Nicole greeted Terrell with a hug and a kiss as he walked through her front door. He was surprised she was still dressed for church because it was after 5:00 in the evening. He had remained at the hospital for the majority of the day, playing the waiting game with Kayla and her family. After making sure that there was no chance of any friction popping off between the sisters, he decided to leave for a while, promising to return later.

"Still in ICU. Everyone's pretty much still there. The doctor says the next few days are the most critical. I'm probably going back in a little while and take them some food. Did you cook?" He knew she did. Nicole cooked a full meal large enough for ten people every Sunday, although most days it was just the two of them.

"Yeah, I baked some chicken. You want me to fix you a plate?"

"Naw, I'll get it," he told her. "I wanna take a quick shower first, though. Is that cool?"

"Of course. You look exhausted. Why don't you lie down for a while before you go back to the hospital?"

He was tired, but he knew that if he lay down for a nap, he wouldn't wake up until the morning.

"Nickey, do you have any glossy paper?" A voice came from the room Nicole used for a home office.

Terrell cringed, knowing that it was her brother, Gary.

"Look at the top of the closet. It should be a pack up there," Nicole yelled to him.

"I looked and I don't see it."

"Never mind. I'll get it," she huffed and rushed down the hall.

Terrell shook his head in silence as he walked into the kitchen. Nicole had not only cooked baked chicken, but also cabbage, macaroni and cheese, rice and gravy, and cornbread. The growls coming from his stomach reminded him that he was hungry in addition to being tired. He grabbed a large plate and began piling it with food. Just as he sat down at the small kitchen table, Nicole entered with Gary right behind her. There was no denying that they were sister and brother. They were similar in looks, although she was older by two years, darker by two shades, and taller by three inches. Gary was barely five-five and she was easily five-eight.

Nicole had moved into the city to be near Gary after she finished nursing school. They never spoke of their father and their mother had passed away a few years earlier from cancer. Gary was protective, often overbearing of his older sister, and it wasn't a secret that he and Terrell didn't care for each other. He had served seven years in the penitentiary for drugs and acted like that fact alone made him hardcore. Terrell wasn't impressed with him, though, and didn't perpetrate like he was.

"Terrell," Gary said as he sat across the table from him. He was dressed in jeans and wife beater, which did nothing to complement his skinny frame.

"Gary." Terrell didn't look up from his plate.

Nicole offered Gary a plate, but he declined. "No thanks."

"I thought the reason you stopped by was to eat." She sucked her teeth at her brother.

"Changed my mind. I don't have much of an appetite now." He glared across the table. Terrell lifted his eyes and looked over at Nicole. He decided to let her respond, rather than giving Gary one of his own.

"Gary, don't start."

"Don't start what? You want me to sit here and act like everything is fine with this?" he snarled.

"Fine with what? You have a problem with me eating dinner at your sister's crib?" Terrell asked, placing his fork down and wiping his mouth. He had kept quiet long enough.

"Terrell, go ahead and eat," Nicole told him.

"No. What I have a problem with is you knocking my sister up!" Gary pulled out a piece of paper and threw it on the table. Nicole walked over and snatched it up.

"What? You're going through my stuff, Gary?" she shrieked.

"What is it?" Terrell asked, reaching for the paper.

"My ultrasound picture," Nicole answered. She shook her head at her brother in disbelief and began rubbing her temples. Terrell walked behind her and massaged her shoulders. He knew she was upset. The one thing she had been worried about for the past few weeks was how to break the news to Gary.

"I can't believe you, Nickey!"

"Calm down," she told him.

"You lied to me." Gary stood up.

"Gary . . . " Terrell's voice was calm. He knew this was going to be a difficult situation to diffuse.

"You shut up! I ain't talking to you!"

"Hold up, cuz." Terrell could feel his anger mounting although he was determined to maintain his composure.

"No, you hold up, and I ain't your cuz!" he spat.

Nicole shrugged Terrell's hands off her shoulders and took a step toward her brother. "Gary, you need to stop this right now."

"You lied. Straight up lied to me to my face. I thought we were better than that, Nickey. I asked you if you were sleeping with him, if you two were serious. You said no."

Terrell felt his body tighten as he looked from Nicole then to Gary, who was still talking.

"'No, Gary, I'm not serious about him. It's not even that deep.' That's what you said, remember? Well, let's see how deep it is, huh, Nickey? Is he gonna marry you?"

Nicole stood there, obviously stunned by her brother's outburst. Her lips were pursed together in anger and her chest rose and fell with each breath she took.

"Maybe I should ask him since you don't seem to know the answer. Well, *cuz*, are you gonna marry her?"

"Don't answer that." Nicole turned and touched Terrell's shoulder. Her eyes told him she was pleading, and he remained silent. "Gary, don't be ignorant."

"How is that ignorant? What's wrong, *cuz*? You can't answer?" He paused momentarily. "I guess not."

"He doesn't have to answer you! Don't answer him, Terry."

"I'm outta here," Terrell told her. "I'll call you later."

"Terrell, wait." She walked behind him as he exited the kitchen and headed out the door. He felt drunk, like everything was moving too fast and he couldn't keep up. His day had been filled with emotional chaos and lack of sleep.

"Let that nigga go, Nickey. You don't need him anyway!"

"Terrell, please stop. Don't listen to him, please," Nicole said as he continued out into the hallway of her apartment.

"Look, I ain't gonna disrespect you or your house by disrespecting your short-ass brother, so I'm leaving. I'll call you later," he told her.

"Wait a minute, Terrell, I don't want you to leave like this. Talk to me," she demanded as she followed him all the way to his car.

"I ain't in the mood for talking right now, Nicole. Now's just not a good time for me. It's been a long night and I just need to go home, take a shower and lay down before I go back the hospital. We'll talk later."

"I wanna talk now."

"You wanna talk now? Whatcha wanna talk about Nicole?"

"I know you're mad, Terrell. I'm sorry my brother is a jerk."

"You told him you weren't serious about me, Nicole? This whole thing has been a joke to you?" he asked. He had told himself that he was going to let it go, but since she wanted to talk all of a sudden, he decided to just put it out there to discuss.

"I said . . . I mean . . . " She looked down as she talked.

"Don't lie to me! What did you tell him?"

"I told him I didn't know what was up with us. And I don't, Terrell. That's the God's honest truth."

"What do you mean you don't know? What the hell is that supposed to mean? I love you, Nicole. I tell you that all the time." He rested against his car and put his hands in his pockets.

"And? You know how many times I've heard that? Look, I love you too." She sighed and reached for his hand. He stared at her and frowned. He could not believe she was saying this.

"I can't tell. It's not even *that deep*, according to what you told your brother. And I don't give a damn about anyone else or what they told you. I'm talking about how I feel about you. Damn, quiet as it's kept, I do wanna marry you."

Nicole closed her eyes then let out a small huff. "No you don't, Terrell. I know you love me. I never questioned that. But you're not ready to marry me. I don't think you're ready to marry anyone."

"How can you tell me what I'm ready for? You know what? Forget it, Nicole. I don't believe we're even standing here having this conversation."

"Terrell, how are you gonna marry me when you're not even fully committed to me?"

"What? I am committed to you. You're having my baby, Nicole. I want us to be a family. You don't want that?" He was totally confused by her response. From the moment she told him she was pregnant, he thought she wanted to get married. Now, it seemed that marriage was the furthest thing from her mind. He didn't want to question whether the baby was his.

"So, you think that because I'm carrying your child that automatically means I want to be your *wife*? Sorry, it doesn't work that way. I'll agree to be your wife when you show me you're ready to be my *husband*."

"What do you want from me, Nicole? I love you, I'm there for you, there's nothing in this world I won't do for you. I've told you that from the moment we got together. And now I find out that we aren't that serious." Terrell's head was messed up and he was ready to leave. He leaned his head back and closed his eyes. He felt Nicole's gentle touch on his cheek and he looked into her beautiful face.

"I love you, Terrell, and I have no doubt that you love me, too, in your own way. But you still go to the clubs every time the doors open, and let's not talk about your phone blowing up. You stay out all night and then get mad when I don't condone that behavior and tell you how immature you are. You even accuse me of trying to control you. Terrell, until you show me you love me, the thought of marrying me shouldn't even enter your mind. True, I am carrying your child, so maybe instead of focusing on marriage you should start with fatherhood."

"So what, you don't wanna have anything to do with me, Nicole?"

"Baby, no, that's not what I'm saying at all. I'm saying that when I get married, it's gonna be forever, and right now, you are definitely not at the forever stage." She smiled.

He looked at this woman who was saying the opposite of what he thought she would. She never ceased to amaze him. She was smart, talented and beautiful. He loved her and was going to marry her. He placed his hand on her stomach, which held their child. He knew that changing his ways was inevitable; he just assumed it was going to be after he was at least engaged. He now realized that he wanted to change. Spending the rest of his life with Nicole and making her happy was that important to him. *She may think I'm not in love with her. I can show her better than I can tell her.* He kissed her, again told her he loved her, and got into his car.

Terrell could see her waving in his rearview mirror, slowly disappearing as he drove off. He thought about everything she had told him as he drove home, realizing that she was more intelligent than he had even given her credit for. He began respecting her more and more as he reflected. There was no way he was letting her down. *Little does she know, the forever stage is right around the corner.*

Chapter 12

The sound of a baby crying on television caused Toby to stir in his sleep. He began feeling around in the bed searching for the remote to turn the volume down when he realized that the sounds weren't coming from the TV, but the other side of the room. Roni got up and walked over to the port-a-crib where her goddaughter, Day, was whining. She picked up the baby and placed her in the bed between them. It had been seven days since Mr. John's heart attack and Roni had kept Day for the weekend to relieve Geno and Kayla.

"Aw, baby Day, what's wrong? You hungry?" Roni cooed.

Toby smiled at the beautiful little girl's arms and legs flailing in the air. Roni told him she was going to get Day a bottle from the kitchen. He picked Day up and placed her on his chest, snuggling her close to him. She began to quiet down and her wails turned into a simple humming. He placed his thumbs into her tiny fingers.

"You're just spoiled, that's all, Miss Day. You're not slick." He picked up the remote and clicked on *SportsCenter*. He checked out the scores of the NBA playoffs, glad to see that Miami had won. It was only 6:00 in the morning and he wasn't used to getting up this early.

"You want anything while I'm down here?" Roni shouted.

"No, I'm good," he answered. The loudness of his voice startled Day, who raised her head in annoyance. "Sorry sweetie."

He rubbed his hands across her back in a circular motion and her eyes began to close. Just as he thought she was asleep, a loud noise came from her bottom and a scent traveled to his nose. *Oh, no she didn't.* He grimaced. *That's so disgusting.* As if she knew what he was thinking, she raised her head once again, looked him in the face, and smiled as she grunted this time. He raised her off his chest and placed her back in the center of the bed.

"You smell terrible, pretty girl," he told her. She continued to look at him, still passing gas and grunting. He grabbed a diaper, the wipes and some powder out of the diaper bag and placed them on the bed. He stood there looking at the items, realizing he had never changed a diaper in his life. From the smell of it, he wasn't ready now, either.

"Okay, Day. I got your breakfast," Roni announced as she returned to the bedroom.

"Breakfast is the last thing she needs, Ron. She's already full enough!"

"What are you talking about?" She leaned over and picked up the baby. "Whoo whee! Girl, you stink!"

"I told you she don't need nothing else to eat. Then again, she may be hungry because everything she ate is filling that diaper up. I was about to change her." He stretched and lay back down on the bed.

"You were about to do what? You don't know anything about changing a diaper and you know it." She laughed.

"That's what you think." He watched her carefully unfasten Day's pajamas and lift her legs out.

"Wait a minute. Get a towel and put her on, man!" He hopped off the bed, hurrying to the linen closet for a towel. He nearly tripped over the diaper bag in the process.

"Lord have mercy, Toby. It's only poop. She ain't bleeding to death!" Roni laughed. She snatched the towel from him and placed it under the baby's bottom. As she opened the diaper, the stench increased and he tried not to gag.

"That is so disgusting," he commented. He went and grabbed the air freshener from the bathroom and began spraying. "I'ma have to have this place fumigated."

He was contemplating lighting some candles as well when Roni told him, "Here, boy. Take this to the outside trash can."

He stared at the small white bundle she was holding out toward him. *She can't be serious.* He looked over at her and realized that indeed she was and he had no choice but to take it. He grumbled as he took the foul package out the back door. *Maybe I'm not ready for fatherhood after all, taking crappy diapers outside at six in the morning, bedroom stinking.* When he returned to the bedroom and saw his beautiful fiancée sitting on the bed, rocking Day and humming as she fed her, his thoughts changed. It was a beautiful sight to see them there. Roni looked so natural holding the bottle just right. He rarely saw her like this. So often she was dressed to the max, never a hair out of place, face made up perfectly, but here she sat, dressed in one of his old T-shirts and a pair of shorts, scarf tied on her head, and face void of makeup. She had never looked so beautiful to him. His heart leapt. He walked over and kissed both her and the baby as he sat beside them.

"What was that for?" she asked suspiciously.

Toby put his arm around her and whispered, "I want a baby."

"Yeah, right." She snickered.

"I'm serious, Ron. I want us to have a baby."

She lifted Day onto her shoulder and began patting her softly on the back. "Clearly you have lost your mind. You'd better stop spraying that air freshener because it's messing with your brain cells."

"No, it's not. I don't understand why my wanting us to have a baby is so crazy," he replied.

"I'm not having a baby, Toby. I'm still in grad school, and—"

"I don't mean right now, Roni. I'm talking about after we're married."

"I'm not having one then, either. I don't want to have a baby."

He was taken aback by her statement. He had just assumed that they would have a child someday. Roni was always babysitting or shopping for Day and he knew she loved it. He thought she was practicing for when she had her own baby, which he had also assumed would be some time soon after they were married. He didn't know how to react. Luckily, Day picked that very moment to throw up on Roni's shoulder, so he didn't have to.

Roni quickly passed him the baby as she grabbed the nearby towel and began cleaning up. "Can you put her to sleep while I take a shower and get dressed?"

"Sure." He sighed and watched in silence, still holding the baby, as Roni placed three outfits on the bed, deciding which one to wear. This was her usual morning ritual and he was used to it.

"Which one do you like, Toby?" she asked like always.

"All of 'em," he said, reaching on the nightstand for Day's pacifier.

"What's wrong, Toby? I know you're not tripping because I don't want a baby, are you?" she turned and asked, noticing his change in attitude.

"I just thought we would have children."

"Children?" She seemed appalled at the thought.

"Well, at least a child. I like kids, and I wanted at least one of my own." He rocked Day as he talked. Her big brown eyes were looking into his. She looked just like her mother and aunt. *Something about those Hopkins women,* he thought.

"I'm sorry, baby. I'm just not the maternal type. I have too many other things I want to do in life, and having a baby isn't one of them." She shrugged and walked into the bathroom.

Toby's gaze returned to Day, who was drifting off to sleep. He slowly laid her on the bed and pulled the blanket over her. He was tempted to walk into the bathroom and talk to Roni some more about having a child, but decided against it. It didn't seem like the time to discuss it anyway. He lay back next to the baby and flipped through the channels, closed his eyes and drifted off to sleep.

He woke to the feel of Roni's lips on his. His eyes fluttered open and she grinned at him. He had to admit, she looked damn good, dressed in a cobalt blue dress that clung to her curves. Her makeup matched perfectly and her hair was flawless. *Typical Roni.* She definitely didn't look like a sixth grade school teacher, that's for sure. *More like a supermodel.*

"Okay, sleepyhead, I'm gone to work. Kayla will be here to pick Day up around ten. You don't have to worry about dressing her. There are two bottles in the fridge and one by the bed. Are you sure you can handle this?"

"Yes, Ron. You act like I haven't watched her before."

"Well, after your panic attack this morning when she pooped, I was beginning to wonder, Mr. I-want-a-baby."

"Whatever," was his only comment.

"Oh, I forgot to tell you. I have a conference out of town next week. I'm pulling out Wednesday and will be back Sunday night."

"You're going by yourself?" he asked as he began drifting back to sleep.

"Yep. All by my lonesome." She looked at her watch and noticed the time. "I gotta get outta here. I love you. Call me if you or Day needs me."

"How's your dad?" Toby asked.

Kayla had arrived to pick up Day and was double-checking to make sure she hadn't left anything. She looked tired and he almost asked if she wanted him to watch Day a little while longer while she got some rest.

"Better. He's out of the coma and he's alert. If he continues to improve, they'll release him by the middle of next week."

"That's great. I'm glad to hear that," he told her.

"I really appreciate you and Roni doing this for me," Kayla said as she took Day from his arms. "You don't realize how much of a help it's been for me and Geno."

"It's not a problem. You know I love spending time with my beautiful goddaughter." He kissed Day's fingers.

"You'd better not let your brother hear you say that. He'll be ready to knock you out." Kayla laughed.

"Yeah, you know how his jealous ass is," Toby told her as he picked up the bag that held the port-a-crib and Day's diaper bag.

"It's about to get bigger too."

"Bigger? I doubt if that can happen."

"Believe me, it can. I got word that he was about to be promoted on the job. The announcement comes out today. Terrell Sims will be the new department supervisor," Kayla said matter-of-factly.

"Shut up! I didn't know. I can't believe he hasn't said anything to me. Supervisor?" he repeated to make sure he heard her correctly.

"Supervisor. Can you believe I'll be working for Terrell?" she asked as they headed out the door. As soon as she got to the driveway, she stopped. He looked to see what the problem was and he saw Craig standing next to her car. "What the hell are you doing here? What? You following me now, Craig?"

"I wanna see my daughter. I been calling you for two weeks now."

"And? In case you didn't know, my father had a massive heart attack. I haven't had time to deal with you or your mess." Kayla hit the alarm on her keychain and popped the trunk at the same time. She motioned for Toby to put the crib and bag in the back of the car as she fastened Day into her car seat.

"What's up, Toby?" he acknowledged, and Toby gave him a nod. "What mess? And I know all about your father being in the hospital. My mother called and offered to keep Day, but all of a sudden you don't want her to have nothing to do with the baby. But I bet you Geno's mom had her, didn't she? She can keep her whenever she wants."

"You know what, Craig? I don't have to explain anything to you about my child. It's none of your business. Now leave." She got behind the wheel and started the engine.

"What do you mean it's none of my business? Do you listen to yourself? That's my daughter you're talking about. I pay for her childcare and buy her clothes. I ain't one of these deadbeat niggas that ain't handling their business. I love my daughter. Even Toby can testify to that."

At the sound of his name, Toby slammed the trunk down. He had kept quiet because he didn't want to be involved. He knew that Craig did love Day. There was nothing he wouldn't do for her. He also knew that Craig had a wife who had recently moved in with Craig's parents along with their son, and that was the main reason Kayla didn't have anything to do with him or his family. Avis, Craig's wife, had harassed Kayla to the point to where not only did Kayla get the girl fired from her job for harassment, but had damn near taken a peace bond out on her after they had a fist fight. Why Craig was questioning Kayla's actions when he knew all of this baffled Toby.

"I don't need Toby to co-sign. His ass ain't no prayer book and his mouth ain't no Bible! No offense, Toby," she turned and said calmly. She returned her attention to Craig and her volume increased. "Again, what I do with my child is my business. You *and* your wife are full of games and I don't have time for that. You wanna play daddy? Go do it with your other child because this one doesn't need you." Kayla put the car in reverse, nearly hitting Craig and Toby as she barreled down the street.

"You know what, Toby? That girl is crazy," Craig turned and told him.

"I don't think she's crazy, Craig. She's just going through a lot right now," Toby replied. He could see the frustration in Craig's face and felt for the brother. Craig did try to be a good father in his own way. He made sure that Day was well taken care of, but Kayla was right; the brother played too many games. He had told so many lies that no one believed a word he said.

"I don't give a damn what she's going through. That doesn't have nothing to do wit' me seeing my daughter. She don't have no problem wit' me paying that daycare bill every month or buying clothes and toys, does she?" Craig asked. "Now, that's not fair."

Toby just shrugged. "I feel you, bro. Just keep taking care of your responsibilities and she'll come around, believe me. It's just a lot going on in her life right now."

"Oh, I'ma take care of some things. Believe that," he said. Toby didn't even want to know what he meant by it, so he didn't ask. "I'm outta here, Toby."

"A'ight, Craig." Toby watched him drive off then went back inside.

Looking at the issues that Craig and Kayla were having made him appreciate the fact that he didn't have kids yet. *And now it seems I may never have any*, he thought, remembering what his fiancée had told him earlier. He now

understood why she was adamant about him wearing a
condom whenever they were together. Even after he had
shown her his clean bill of health from his doctor, she still
insisted. There was another reason for the condoms. *She
doesn't want kids, ever.*

Chapter 13

"I'd like to propose a toast. To my little—"

"Younger," Terry corrected before Toby could go on.

"Younger brother Terry. He finally gets to be a *big dog* on the job." Toby raised his glass and his friends followed his lead. They were sitting in their favorite sports bar watching the basketball playoffs. The place was crowded and cheers were coming from the Lakers' and Pacers' fans throughout the bar as they enjoyed their teams.

Toby had called Terrell and they agreed that the beef they had in the parking lot was stupid. He invited his brother out for drinks to celebrate his new promotion. Jermaine agreed to tag along.

"So, what's up for the night, fellas?" Jermaine asked.

"It's your night, Terry. What are you trying to do?"

"I'm down for whatever," Terrell told his friend. "As long as you guys remember a brotha gotta be at work by nine in the morning."

"Man, please. You're trying to be home before Nicole gets home from work. Don't even try it," Toby joked.

Terrell looked at him and replied, "Don't even try it. The only reason you called me was because Roni is out of town."

"Ha! That's true. I been trying to get you to hang out since I moved back, and if you not working at the club, you're up under Roni." Jermaine nodded.

"Forget both of y'all. Don't hate because I'm 'bout to be happily married."

"We ain't hating because you're 'bout to be married. We're joking because your ass is sprung!" Terrell nudged Jermaine's arm. At that moment, his cell began ringing.

Noticing the time, he knew it was Nicole calling on her break, and he had to answer. He raised his eyebrow at Jermaine and Toby as he slipped it out of his pocket and answered.

"Hey, baby."

"Aw," the men groaned in unison as he walked away from the table.

"Looks like Toby ain't the only one sprung!" Jermaine yelled.

Terrell ignored them, knowing that they would probably joke him the remainder of the evening. Any other time, he would have let the voicemail pick up, but he had been gradually making a change and was determined to remain focused on making his relationship with Nicole work, especially when he realized that there was a possibility he could lose her.

"Hey. You enjoying hanging with your boys?" she asked him.

"Not as much as hanging with you."

"I'll bet." She laughed. "What time are you going home?"

"We're not hanging out late. You know I have to get to work early."

"Okay. Um, Terry, I have something to ask you."

"What is it?"

"I don't want you to get mad or upset. I just want to know."

His heart began pounding as he tried to think of what it could be. He knew he hadn't done anything in the past few weeks to cause suspicion, but there were so many other things she could have found out about.

"What's up?" he asked.

"Gary came by tonight to talk to me."

"And?" he asked. He tensed up, thinking about how much her brother irritated him. Since finding out about Nicole's pregnancy, Gary had become even more of a pain in the neck. He was always at her house, and when Terrell was there, he would purposely do things to irritate him, like talk about her old boyfriends or some guy he knew that wanted to holler at her. On more than one occasion, Terrell had been tempted to throw a punch, but he just ignored him.

"He's got a new girlfriend. He seems to like her a lot," she said. "He wants me to meet her."

"And?" Terrell asked, wondering what this had to do with him. He could care less whether Gary's short ass had a girlfriend.

"I told him we would go to dinner." She sighed.

"What? Nicole, come on, baby. Be real. You know your brother and I can't stand each other. It's no secret that he don't like me and I don't like him."

"Terrell, this is important to me. I know you and Gary don't see eye to eye at times, but you're both gonna have to get over it. I'm not going to be put in a position where I have to choose between both of you," she snapped.

"I'm not asking you to choose, Nicole. I just don't think us going to dinner is a good idea, sweetheart, that's all." He forced himself to remain calm as he stood in the small area near the pool tables, watching people play.

"Can you please just think about it, Terrell?"

"I'll think about it."

"I mean think about it with an open mind, Terrell. Gary is the uncle of your child, and might be your brother-in-law one day," she added.

He shuddered at the thought. If that was the case, that meant that he would have to get used to the idea of Gary being around, and he definitely wasn't ready for that.

"I said I'd think about it."

"Thank you. You know I love you for that, right? It may seem like—"

The phone went dead in the middle of Nicole's sentence. He looked at his phone and saw that his battery was gone. He looked up and saw Jermaine headed toward the restrooms. He waved toward him. "Jermaine! Yo, let me hold your phone."

Jermaine walked over to him. "What's wrong with your cell?"

"My battery went out in the middle of talking to Nicole."

"And that's why you're shouting my name out like that?"

"Shut up and give me the phone." He snatched the phone and redialed Nicole's desk number. "Weren't you headed to the restroom?"

"Sorry. I'll give you some privacy, lover boy." Jermaine laughed and walked away.

"Labor and delivery," Nicole answered.

"Hey, it's me. My battery went dead," he told her.

"I thought you hung up on me. Guess there's no need to leave the nasty message I was going to, huh?"

"Oh, so it's like that?" He laughed, glad that the mood of their conversation had changed. There was a beep and he looked at the phone. He blinked twice to make sure he was reading it correctly, "Yo, Jermaine got another call. I'll be home when you get off. Call me."

"Love you," he heard her say just as he hit the button.

"Yo," he said, answering the other line.

"Jermaine?"

"Naw, he's busy right now. Who's this?"

"None of your business, Terrell. What is he doing and why do you have his phone?"

"I'm saying. What's up, Anjelica? Long time no hear from. I see why I haven't now," he said. He thought that the reason Anjelica hadn't called him was because she was caught up with her family. Now he saw otherwise.

"I got your messages. Thanks a lot. I've been meaning to call you, but you know a lot has been going on," she told him. "I really haven't had time to talk."

"You got time to talk to Jermaine, though, huh?"

"Why Terrell, is that a hint of jealousy I detect in your voice? I do believe it is."

"Don't even try it. I'm saying, I thought we were cool."

"We are cool, Terrell. I can't thank you enough for being there for me and my family. I appreciate it, and you know that. Please don't trip about this."

As she talked, Terrell watched the door of the men's restroom open. Jermaine walked out. As he passed a group of females standing nearby, they all stopped and stared at him, one of them even making a comment about how fine he was. Jermaine just thanked her with a smile and kept walking.

"I ain't tripping. I was just saying that all of a sudden you find time to call Jermaine but not me."

"And how are Nicole and the baby?" she asked sarcastically.

"They're fine. Here comes Mr. Wonderful right now," he replied, passing Jermaine the phone. "You got a call, bro."

"Hello," Jermaine said. "Hey, sweetie. How's it going?"

Terrell shook his head and returned to the table to join his brother.

"What's wrong with you?" Toby frowned. "Where's Jermaine?"

"On the phone. And get this—you'll never believe who he's talking to," Terrell told him.

"Who?" Toby asked, suddenly curious.

"Anjelica."

"Get the hell outta here!"

"I'm dead serious."

"You gave him the number?"

"Hell no. She called him."

"On the cell?"

Terrell was beginning to get irritated. "Naw, at home. Yeah, on the cell. You know she ain't call him here at the bar!"

Jermaine returned to the table with a smile on his face. He ordered another round of drinks and sat down. "What's the score?"

"What's up with that?" Toby asked.

"What? Y'all don't want another round?" He looked at the two brothers, both looking back at him like he had stolen something.

"That's not what he's talking about," Terrell told him.

"What are y'all talking about, man?" Jermaine asked innocently.

"Man, don't play dumb. What's up with your girl hitting you up on the cell and you coming back to the table grinning like a kid on Christmas morning?"

Jermaine cut his eyes at Terrell. "Damn, just blow up my spot, why don't you?"

"Whatever," Terrell said and focused on the big screen television against the wall. The fine waitress brought their drinks, smiling and flirting with him. It took all he could not to flirt back and get her number, but he had to check out her thick behind as she walked away from the table.

"Anjelica is cool people," Jermaine told them. "I started calling to check on her pops then we just started talking on the phone. I like her. She's funny."

He wasn't saying anything Terrell didn't already know. "So, it's just a phone thing. That's cool. For a minute I thought you were gonna say you were trying to holler at her."

"I am. I got tickets for us to go check out Maxwell next month," Jermaine said, raising one eyebrow, his signature gesture.

"What?" Terrell asked before he could stop himself. He tried to play it off when both Toby and Jermaine looked at him. People at the table near theirs were staring as well.

"What's the problem?" Jermaine asked.

"Man, that girl is nothing but trouble. She causes trouble if nothing else," Toby said, taking a deep swallow of beer. "Tell him, Terry."

"She must not be that bad. Terry was hanging with her. That's how we met, remember? She was dropping you to get your car. Now, according to her, y'all weren't kicking it. Tell me now if it's anything different and I'll step off."

"Man, you know Terry wasn't kicking it with her like that. Were you?" Toby now turned and asked his little brother, wondering himself.

Terrell didn't know how to answer. Granted, he hadn't really kicked it with Anjelica, but they were friends. And they had slept together, even if it was only once. For some reason, the chance of her being with Jermaine bothered him, and he didn't want it to happen. For once, he had the upper hand in the competition and he didn't want to lose it. He thought for a minute then told them, "I'm just saying you need to think twice before you get caught up. She's cool and everything, but I ain't gonna lie; I hit it and I know someone else who did."

"Are you saying she's a ho? She doesn't come off like a ho, Terry. Is she out there like that, Toby?" he turned and asked.

Toby just shrugged, wondering why his brother was saying that about Anjelica. He didn't think she slept around the way Terry was making it seem.

"I ain't say she was a ho, Jermaine. I'm just telling you what *I* did with her. I didn't know you were into my *leftovers*," he said arrogantly. He hoped that would aggravate Jermaine to the point where he would leave Anjelica alone. "You always wanted fresh meat, remember?"

Jermaine picked up his half-empty bottle of beer and swallowed the remainder in one gulp, staring at Terry the entire time. When he was finished, he slowly told him, "Leftovers, huh? I don't think Anjelica would be called a leftover, Terry. I think you may have just been the *appetizer* before the main course. And I've had a few appetizers myself."

"What the hell are you talking about, Jermaine? Who?"

"That's not important, Terry. And don't front like you ain't had a few *appetizers* yourself. The difference is I ain't trying to put nobody's business out there like you are. I like the girl. She's good people, and as her friend, I don't think she would appreciate you trying to call her out like that. I want you and her to remain friends, so the fact that you did that will remain at this table unless you bring it up to her." Jermaine leaned back in his chair.

Terrell stood up and looked over at Toby, who hadn't said a word. "Man, I can't talk to him. You try and talk to him."

"I don't know the girl, Terry. You said yourself that I ain't know her for real. I only know what you and other people have told me."

"Fine. You can't say I ain't warn you." He was about to walk away when he heard someone calling his name.

"Terrell, what's up, man?"

He turned to see his friend, Theo, headed toward the table. "What's up, Theo?"

Theo worked for the same company as Terrell. He was also a manager, but he worked in the finance department rather than customer relations, where Terrell and Kayla worked.

"Nothing. Came here to check out the game." Theo spotted Toby sitting at the table. "DJ Terror, how you been, man? You set that date yet?"

Toby stood and the two men gave each other dap. Toby told him, "Naw, not yet. I'm waiting for you and Tia to set yours first."

"Man, the way she's talking about everything she wants for the wedding, it's gonna take about two years to save for it. At least two years." Theo laughed.

"Wait. You're getting married too?" Jermaine asked.

"Yeah, got engaged back in December," Theo told him.

Toby invited Theo to join them. "You remember," he told Jermaine. You met Theo and his fiancée at Jasper's the night of the proposal.

"Oh yeah. Tia, the fitness instructor." Jermaine nodded. "She came to the hospital the other week when we were there."

"Oh, you're the *friend* who was with Anjelica when her dad got sick?" Theo's eyes widened as he took a seat beside Jermaine. Terrell decided to sit back down and stay a little while longer.

"That's me, I guess." Jermaine smiled.

"So you own the security camera business, right?" Theo asked.

"Yeah, We Secure U."

"A friend of mine's brother just bought a crib and was looking for someone to install some equipment. You got a card?" Theo asked.

"Yeah, here you go." Jermaine reached into his pocket and passed Theo a business card. "Tell him to give me a call."

"Must be a pretty big crib if he needs security cameras," Terrell commented. He had remained quiet, still heated from the conversation earlier.

"Yeah, it is. It's over in Wheatland Heights." Theo nodded.

"Damn, Wheatland Heights. What does he do?" Toby whistled. Wheatland Heights was prime real estate property with homes starting in the half-million-dollar range.

"He's a pharmacist . . . I mean a real pharmacist in a drugstore, not a street pharmacist," he told them after he saw the way they were looking at him.

"Yeah, that brother's paid for real," Toby agreed.

"Your brother ain't doing so bad, either," Theo told him. "You know I was happy for you when they told me you got the promotion."

"You know I was surprised as hell when they told me. But it's cool," Terrell replied, once again fighting the urge to go after the waitress who kept asking him if there was anything else he'd like. He assured her he was fine, and she looked disappointed.

"I think she wanted you to ask for something else," Jermaine teased. "I can't believe I'm sitting here with three PWBs."

"What? You're crazy!" Terrell blurted across the table.

"Never that, son!" Toby added.

"I definitely don't fall into that category." Theo shook his head.

"There's nothing wrong with being pussy-whipped, my brothers. I mean, you should be glad. Some of us are still on that quest to find that special someone. More for me to choose from. Where did that waitress go again?"

The men continued joking as they watched the game. After watching the Lakers make it one step closer to the NBA championship, they said good-bye and got ready to head out, making sure they were all sober enough to drive. Terrell noticed Toby staring at an empty table in the back corner and tapped him on the shoulder.

"You a'ight?"

"Yeah, just got some stuff on my mind, I guess," his brother told him. "You going to Nicole's?"

"Naw, I think I'm just gonna head home," Terrell answered. "I don't feel like making that drive tonight, especially since the crib is only five minutes away."

"I feel you on that one." Toby sighed.

"You sure you're okay to drive?"

"Yeah, I'm cool. Let's go."

Terrell was concerned about his brother. Toby had seemed distant all night, as if he was deep in thought. He wondered if it had something to do with Roni, but he didn't ask. They were almost out of the bar when they noticed a group of women walking in. Terrell spotted a familiar face among them.

"Leaving so soon, fellas?"

"What's up, Meeko?" He walked over and gave her a hug. He was glad that even after all he had put her through, she was able to forgive him and they were friends. Meeko was a good person and he liked her. She told her friends she would join them in a moment and they walked away.

"Hey, Toby." She smiled. Terrell noticed her eyes brighten as she recognized Jermaine. "Well, well, well. I heard you were back in town. How are things going?"

"They're going good. What's up with you?" Jermaine stepped up and gave her a hug.

"Same old, same old. Working hard and still broke." She laughed, and Terrell noticed Jermaine's eyes lingering on her breasts a little longer than necessary.

"Aren't we all?"

"You guys aren't leaving, are you? Stay a little while and hang with us."

"Sounds good to me. You guys wanna hang out a little while longer?" Jermaine asked.

"I don't think so, Meeko. Thanks, though," Toby replied.

"Naw, I gotta be at work early," Theo said, checking out Meeko's friends. "Looks like I'd be in good company if I did hang around, though."

"Man, let's go," Terrell responded. He thought about Anjelica's claims that Theo was trying to hook up with one of her girls and wondered if there was any truth to what she was saying.

"You guys must be getting old or something. I remember a time when you would party all night, go get some breakfast, and the only reason you went home was to shower and change clothes, not even taking a nap." She smirked.

"Naw, they ain't old, Meeko. It's something else." Jermaine grinned. "But you go right ahead, fellas. Like I said earlier, more for me."

Terrell watched as Jermaine put his arm around Meeko and they joined her friends at the table. The women all greeted him with hugs and smiles and he turned around briefly to wink at Terrell. Terrell followed Theo and his brother out of the bar and into the parking lot.

"Man, back in the day I woulda been right in there with all them fine-ass women." Theo sighed.

"All of us would, man. All of us would. I'll check you guys later," Toby said and gave them each a pound with his fist.

As Terrell sat in his car, he looked through the window of the club. Jermaine was laughing with the waitress who had previously flirted with him. He tried to fight off the pangs of jealousy that were creeping in. He knew the waitress meant nothing to either of them. He also told himself that he was doing the right thing by leaving, especially since he already told Nicole he would not be out late, but there was something still bothering him. He couldn't put his finger on it. It was as if there was a building irritation deep within and Jermaine was the cause of it. *He was just messing with me.*

There's no way he was wit' anybody I was sleeping with. He looked up and saw Meeko hugging Jermaine once again. *No way. There's no way he would go there, and neither would she.* He knew he was tripping. *I've had a few appetizers myself.* Jermaine's voice echoed in his head.

Chapter 14

"Man, I appreciate you helping me out," Jermaine told Toby as he climbed into his truck. "This is a big job and it's kinda last minute."

"Yeah, yeah, yeah. You'd better be glad you're my boy," Toby replied, settling into the butter-soft leather. He was tired, even though it was 1:00 in the afternoon. He usually slept until 2:00 or 3:00 on Saturdays. Jermaine had called him at 11:00 this morning and asked him if he could help him out. He realized this meant a lot to his friend and agreed. "Where are we going, anyway?"

"To Wheatland Heights. Your boy came through. The guy called me late last night and asked if I could come out and give him an estimate this afternoon. He was upset and determined to have me get his house done as soon as possible. Told me money was not an object. You know I told him I'd be there first thing this morning. I just need you to help me measure stuff out, that's about it," Jermaine told him. "No manual labor required."

"Whatever. You still paying me regardless. Like you said, this is a big job."

"No doubt. You know I got you."

Toby felt his eyes getting heavy as they got on the Interstate. The weekend traffic was backed up, and he drifted to sleep, knowing it would be at least a thirty-minute drive out into the suburbs. When he woke, they were entering the sprawling neighborhood bearing the sign WELCOME TO WHEATLAND HEIGHTS, HOME OF PRESTIGE. He was amazed by the huge houses sitting on impeccable lawns which seemed to reach for miles. Some of them were surrounded by huge iron gates and circular driveways. *Some day, Roni and I will be living like this.* He smiled to himself as he admired the landscape.

"Man," he said as Jermaine turned into the driveway of the house at the far end of a cul-de-sac. There was a BMW, a Lexus, an Expedition and a Camry parked in front.

"Told you this was a big job. The guy said there's a lot of new construction in this area and people are looking for security system installation. This may be just the break I been praying for."

"Then you may be able to hire me part-time and I can get a piece of the action," Toby said as he got out of the truck.

Jermaine reached into the back and removed a briefcase and small tool bag. They made their way to the front of the house, careful not to step on the landscaped lawn, still damp from the sprinkler located in the center.

Jermaine rang the doorbell then began whistling lightly. Toby smiled slyly, remembering that his best friend always whistled when he was nervous.

"It's gonna be a'ight, son. This is what you've been praying for, remember? You got this." He nudged his shoulder.

"I know, but it doesn't make my nerves any easier." Jermaine laughed.

The door opened and a younger guy wearing glasses greeted them. He was dressed in a plaid shirt, khaki shorts and leather sandals. *He looks like a pharmacist*, Toby thought.

"Hello. Jermaine?" He looked at them hesitantly.

"How ya doing, Mr. Winston?" Jermaine extended his hand.

"Please, call me Stanley. Come on in. Glad you could find the place." He led them inside the massive marble-floored foyer. Sunlight was streaming into the connected living area through the skylights in the vaulted ceiling.

"This is my partner, Tobias Sims." Jermaine gestured toward Toby.

"Mr. Sims." The man shook his hand. He was a fair-skinned gentleman with a slight pot belly. Toby could tell he was quite jovial because he kept smiling at them the entire time he talked.

"Call me Toby. This is a beautiful home," Toby commented.

"Thanks. I'm still trying to furnish it. I've only been here about three months. Between work and teaching, I really haven't had time," Stanley told them.

"So you teach too?" Jermaine asked.

"Yes, I teach chemistry part-time at the university."

"Wow, you are busy," Toby told him.

Stanley gave them a tour of the home, telling them he needed the surveillance and security system installed immediately, and he wanted the top of the line, most extensive system on the market. "Cost is not an issue. I just need it done and done quick."

Toby looked at Jermaine and smiled. They had to be thinking the same thing.

"Stanley, can I ask you a question? I understand you wanting to protect your home, but you don't seem like the type of person that would need what you're asking for. That system is for politicians or even some rap stars."

"I know what you're thinking: What is up with this guy? And I feel comfortable enough to share this with you." The small man looked at them bashfully and said, "This may be hard to believe, but I really don't meet a lot of women."

"Really?" Jermaine looked at him like he was surprised by Stanley's revelation. It took all it could for Toby not to laugh.

"Yeah, believe it or not. A brother is paid, but he can get lonely. I think a lot of women are intimidated by my intelligence."

"I can see that happening," Toby agreed.

"Well, in my spare time, I began chatting online to various partners of the opposite sex. Just innocent conversations at first, but some of them actually began to develop into something more. Recently, I took a chance and invited a certain interest to my home to meet face to face."

"To meet for the first time?" Jermaine asked.

"Stan. You know you're always supposed to meet in a public place first. You're smarter than that, man." Toby shook his head.

"I know, I know. But what can I say, fellas? She had me wide open and there was a lapse in judgment, I guess. Call it temporary mental insanity. Needless to say, when she arrived, I noticed there was something strange about her."

"Was she ugly, Stan?"

"Naw, she was gorgeous. Beautiful, smart, funny. Everything she seemed to be online, but you know I'm in the medical field, and I pick up on some things. And when I realized what it was, I had to ask *him* to leave."

"What!"

"Naw, Stan. Tell me you're playing!"

"Seriously, guys, I couldn't believe it myself. Well, he didn't take it very well, and things around here have been crazy. It's to the point that I'm being stalked. I gotta get it done. When can you start?"

Jermaine looked at Toby, who gave him a nod. "I'll order the equipment tonight. We can start getting measurements right now."

"Fine with me." Toby shrugged. He should have known that he would be roped into helping Jermaine with the installation. He really didn't mind because he could use the extra loot.

"Thanks. I really appreciate it. Come on back to my office and I'll get you a check," Stanley gushed.

They followed him down the hallway leading toward the back of the home, where they entered a large office. They could hear music and laughter coming from outside, along with water splashing.

"You got a pool?" Toby asked, walking to the window and looking out.

"Yeah, my rowdy brother is here visiting for the weekend. He and his girl must be back there," Stanley answered, reaching into the large mahogany desk and taking out a checkbook. He sat down and began writing.

Toby saw a man dive into the swimming pool. He came up beside a sexy, bikini-clad woman, sitting poolside, tanning. Her back was toward the house. The guy soon swam nearby and came up from under the water, splashing some on her. She screamed and jumped up, running over to the nearby table and grabbing a towel. She wiped her face then began threatening the culprit. Toby's heart began pounding as he watched from inside. The Isley Brothers singing "Summer Breeze" faded from the surround-sound speakers.

"I told you I didn't wanna get my hair wet! You play too much!" she screamed.

"Aw, I ain't thinking about your hair," the guy said, walking over and putting his arms around her.

"Get off me! You're getting me wet!"

"I'm sorry, baby. Do you forgive me?" he asked playfully. The woman turned around and faced him, looking at him tenderly, then kissed him softly on the lips. Toby blinked, wanting it to be a bad dream he was caught in.

"Toby! Man, did you hear anything I just said?"

Jermaine was speaking to him, but Toby couldn't move. He continued to watch as the couple returned to the pool and sat on the side. The guy was muscular, the same light complexion as Stanley, dressed in a pair of black trunks.

"What's your brother's name?" Toby finally spoke.

"Sean. You know him?" Stanley asked, looking up.

"Naw, I was just wondering," Toby said solemnly. He finally turned and walked away from the window. Jermaine was staring at him.

"What's going on, T?"

"Nothing," Toby answered. He was still flabbergasted by what he had just witnessed. He was about to sit down but then walked back over and looked out the window again. Anger began to creep within him as he continued to watch the couple. Her legs were wrapped around his body and they were grinning at each other.

He was so caught up that he didn't realize Jermaine was standing next to him, observing as well. "What the—? You gonna go handle this?"

"Handle what?" Stanley asked.

"The measurements," Toby quickly answered. "Naw, we can get them later. You know we got that other thing to take care of and it's getting late."

"Right, right. So, we'll get started Monday. Is that cool, Stan?" Jermaine asked, picking up his briefcase.

"Sure, Monday's fine. I appreciate you guys coming out here, especially on a Saturday. But like I said, things have gotten crazy, and it's imperative that I get it taken care of," Stanley said as he walked them out.

"We'll see you Monday morning. Will your brother be here?" Toby asked, looking over at Jermaine.

"No. He's flying out at six o'clock tomorrow."

"All right then, it was nice meeting you," Jermaine said.

"Nice meeting you. I look forward to doing business with both of you."

Neither man said anything as they got inside the truck. Jermaine drove in silence for a good fifteen minutes before asking, "You a'ight?"

"Yeah, I'm good."

"You sure? Because we can go back and handle it i
you want."

"Naw, I'm good. It's cool," he answered. His head was
throbbing, but the pain was nothing compared to the hurt he
felt in his heart. He continued to sit in silence and stare ou
of the window. It seemed to take forever for them to get to his
condo.

"You want me to come in for a while, man?"

"I need some time alone to think. Thanks for offering,"
he said when they pulled in front of his townhouse.

The phone was ringing as he walked inside.

"Hello."

"Hey, baby. What are you doing?"

"Just walking in the door," he said, going into the
kitchen. He opened the refrigerator door, not knowing what
he was looking for. He scanned the shelves, suddenly
realizing that he was hungry.

"I thought you'd still be 'sleep."

"Nope, I did some running around with Jermaine. I'm
just getting back." He tried to think of how he would handle
this situation without losing his cool. "How's the conference?"

"It's going good. Do you miss me?"

"Of course I do. What time are you coming back?" His
voice cracked and he cleared his throat, hoping she didn't
catch it.

"Probably around three. Can you meet me at the car
rental place?"

"Sure. Which one?" he asked. He located a frozen
pizza and popped it in the microwave.

"The one by the mall. What time are you going to
work?"

"I'll be leaving here around eight-thirty, I guess. Same
time."

"Then I'll call you around eight. I have another seminar about to begin, baby. I'll talk to you later. I love you."

"Love you too," he said then hung up the phone. He stared at the floor, still thinking about what he had seen earlier. He felt the anger that had subsided beginning to return. The sound of the microwave beeping brought him back to reality.

He took his food out and placed it on the kitchen table, grabbed a beer out of the fridge and sat down to eat. As he closed his eyes and lowered his head to pray, the image of the guy and girl at the pool interrupted him. He shook his head in an effort to extinguish the mental image. *God, help me. I don't even know how to handle this*, he prayed then picked up a slice. He tried to eat, but the appetite he had just moments earlier was gone. He wrapped the food up and put it back in the fridge then poured the untouched beer down the sink. He decided that he was more tired than anything and went to the bedroom. He took off his shoes and climbed into the huge bed and fell into a deep slumber.

Chapter 15

"That's not player." Terrell frowned at Nicole. She was holding a yellow-and-white sleeper with a matching hat. They were in the mall and had been shopping all afternoon. He had been ready to go for a while.

"I'm not worried about it being player, Terrell. I'm worried about it fitting the baby." She sighed and rolled her eyes at him.

"I want it to fit *and* be player. I can't have my son around here sporting yellow footie pajamas."

"Who said you were having a son? That hasn't been determined yet, remember?" she asked, putting the outfit back. He laughed as he looked at her belly, which was beginning to poke under her shirt.

"I wouldn't even want my daughter wearing that." He laughed, taking her by the hand and leading her out of the store. "Come on, let's go. I'm hungry."

"We just ate a little while ago. And I thought I was the pregnant one," she teased. They left the mall and headed to the car, both carrying large shopping bags. Terrell popped open the trunk and placed the bags inside.

"Better job, more money. Must be nice."

Terrell looked up and saw Geno and Kayla walking toward his car. Geno was pushing Day in the stroller. Nicole got out of the car when she saw them.

"Aw, don't you all look like the perfect family? How's your dad?" He hugged Kayla and greeted Geno with a pound. Day was chewing on a toy and he began teasing her with it.

"Released this morning. He's home, thank God. We just left there and decided to walk the mall this afternoon. We're not buying up everything like you all, though," Kayla told them.

"Girl, please. You know I'm not buying anything, unlike your buddy here." Nicole laughed.

"Don't even try it. If y'all think all those bags in there belong to me, then you're—"

"Exactly right." Nicole finished the sentence for him. They laughed because there was no doubt in anyone's mind that the majority of the bags belonged to Terrell. "I'm not even complaining, though. I'm just gonna let him get his shop on now because in a few months the only thing he'll be shopping for is diapers and formula."

"I know that's right." Geno nodded. "Where are you all headed to now?"

"To eat, of course," Nicole told them.

"Y'all wanna roll?" Terrell asked.

Kayla looked at Geno, who nodded. "Yeah. Where y'all trying to go?"

They decided on a restaurant and agreed to meet there in an hour. Terrell and Nicole arrived first and gave their name at the door. The hostess advised them that there would be a twenty minute wait, which they expected. Kayla, Geno and the baby soon arrived and they sat on the benches outside, enjoying the evening air. Terrell told them all about his new job and his new supervisor, CJ.

"I can't stand her," Kayla told him. "She talks to me like I'm dumb. She talks to any female that isn't a manager like she's dumb, matter of fact."

"Aw, she's not that bad. I don't have any problems with her, myself," he told her. That was true. People, mostly women, complained about CJ being arrogant, nasty and short-tempered. Terrell had never seen that side of her, and he had come in contact with her on several occasions. She was always pleasant and cordial toward him. He had chalked their comments and complaints up to being jealous of CJ's position as one of the highest-ranking managers in the company. That, plus she was the finest woman in the office.

She was tall, dark and exquisite. She wore her hair long and dressed the executive part. When she entered a room, she commanded attention and always got it. He was beginning to admire her the more he got to know her, and she had actually suggested that they go to lunch one day soon.

"I bet you don't. I mean, you are a man. She doesn't have a problem with men. Now, let that have been me that got the position, then it would be an entirely different story." Kayla smirked.

"Oh, so it's like that, Kayla? He didn't tell me it was like that," Nicole uttered.

"Mm-hmm." Kayla nodded in a gesture of sisterhood.

"Both of y'all need to quit." Terrell shook his head at them. "It's not like that. You know Kayla's gonna *exaggerate* everything."

"Oh, so now I'm *exaggerating*?" Kayla gasped dramatically.

"See, DQ in full effect," he responded and they all laughed.

Their name was announced over the loudspeaker, so they proceeded inside to be seated. Terrell was holding the door open when he felt his phone vibrating in his pocket. He lingered behind and took it out. Recognizing the number, he told Nicole he would return momentarily. He went out and stood in front of the restaurant, redialing the number that had just appeared on his caller ID.

"Hey, Terrell, I got your message. What's up?"

"Nothing. I was just calling to check on you. What's going on with you? Kayla told me you dad was released today."

"Yeah, he's home and doing good. When did you talk to her?"

"We're actually at dinner right now. You should come too," he told her.

"Yeah, right. Family crisis is over, she's back to hating me, so no thanks. Anyway, I have plans already," Anjelica told him.

"What plans?"

"None of your business." She laughed into the phone. "You are a funny dude, you know that?"

"Naw, I ain't funny. I know you don't have plans with Jermaine, do you?"

"What difference does it make? Did I ask who you were out with? No, because it's none of my business."

"It's not even like that. I'm telling you that he's no good for you and I'm telling you because you're my friend." He began pacing up and down the sidewalk.

"No, you're telling me that because you don't want to even think about the possibility of your boy sleeping with me. That's what it is."

He could hear the agitation in her voice and met it with his own. "The fact that we slept together has nothing to do with it. I'm telling you so you won't get hurt. I know Jermaine; he's my boy, and I know how he is. I saw that nigga the other night at the bar hollering at another friend of ours. What does that tell you, Anjelica?"

"It tells me that maybe you need to check yourself, putting someone that's supposed to be *your boy* on blast like that, telling me all of his business. Now, I don't know what's going on with you these days, but you need to chill. I have to go. Like I said, I got plans." She hung up in his ear.

He stood speechless for a minute, trying to figure out what had just happened. Not only had he pissed Anjelica off, but he had put Jermaine out there like he was trying to play her, which he hadn't intended to do.

"So, how long you been fucking her?"

The hairs on Terrell's neck stood up as he realized someone was standing right behind him. He put his phone back in his pocket, trying to think of something to say. He slowly inhaled as he turned around.

"Damn," was all he could say.

"Answer me. How long have you been sleeping with her?"

"It's not like that."

"Not like what? Oh, don't tell me. That was another Anjelica you were talking to on the phone, right?"

"Hold up for a minute. Please just let me—'

"Let you what? Explain? What is there to explain? There's no need. You know what? This kind of explains a lot of things. I thought it was kinda funny that you and she arrived at the hospital together, but I thought that had something to do with her maybe hooking up with Jermaine. But it was you she was with, and Jermaine was covering for you two. Damn, I can't believe this." Tears began streaming down her face and Terrell realized how hurt she was. He hadn't meant for her to find out this way.

"Kayla, wait." He reached for her arm but she snatched away from him.

"Don't touch me!"

People entering and exiting the restaurant stopped to look at them. He took a step back, not wanting to appear like he was hurting her.

"Kayla, I need for you to listen to me. It's not like that, for real."

"You were my friend—my best friend, at that. And this entire time you been screwing my sister! Now I know why you defended her every time I said something. I guess you all sit back and have a good ol' laugh about me, huh?"

"Kayla, chill. Listen."

"No, you listen. I never want to see or talk to you again! Leave me alone, and I mean that." Kayla wiped her eyes with the palm of her hand and took a deep breath. She scowled at Terrell as she walked past him and re-entered the restaurant, snatching the door.

Terrell waited a few moments before going in. When he arrived at the table, Geno was putting Day back into the stroller.

"What? You guys leaving?" he asked, avoiding looking at Kayla.

"Yeah, Kay has a migraine and she forgot her medicine. She went to the car to get it, but it wasn't there," Geno told him. "Guess we'll have to take a rain check."

"Yeah, we'll have to do that." He watched Kayla grab her purse and the diaper bag. She paused and looked at Nicole. His heart began pounding, wondering what she was about to say.

She looked over at Terrell then said, "Nicole, give me a call later."

"Sure thing, girl. I know how those migraines can be. Take care of yourself." Nicole stood and gave her a hug and watched them as they left.

"You still wanna eat?"

"Yeah, I'm still hungry," she assured him. "I wonder what happened to Kayla, though. She seemed fine when they first got here. She went to the car, and then when she came back to the table, she was like, 'Let's go!'"

"I don't know." Terrell seemed to be engrossed in the menu.

"Well, she's been under a lot of stress these past few weeks, so she's probably just tired."

"Yeah, probably."

Nicole's phone rang and she took it off the side of her purse. "It's Gary. He's probably with Arianna."

"Who? Who the hell is Arianna?"

"Gary's girlfriend. She's a nurse too. Can you believe that?" she said and began chatting into the phone to her brother.

"No, I find that hard to believe," Terrell muttered. Gary was probably lying to Nicole. His girlfriend being a nurse would require her having some level of intelligence, which obviously she didn't have if she was with his dumb ass. He had more important things to deal with than Gary and his fake-nurse girlfriend. He had to smooth things over with Kayla, Anjelica, and possibly even Jermaine if Anjelica told him what he had said. *I can't believe I've messed up all the way around. Tonight just ain't my night.*

"They're right around the corner. I told them they could join us. Is that cool?"

"Whatever," he said, not really paying attention to what she was saying. He told her he'd be right back, got up and walked over to the bar, ordering a Tanqueray and orange juice. He contemplated calling Toby, but thought about the warning Toby gave him when he found out Terrell was messing with Anjelica. He paid for his drink and returned to the table.

"They're on their way," Nicole told him when he sat down. "Please be nice—well, at least be civil."

"What are you talking about?"

"To Gary and his girlfriend," she replied.

"What about them?"

"I just told you they were eating with us. Matter of fact, here they come now."

Terrell turned around to see Gary walking toward them, decked out in a two-piece linen suit with matching gator shoes. *This guy really thinks he's a pimp,* Terrell thought as Gary threw up a peace sign and waved. Then, Terrell felt as if he was in a Quentin Tarrantino movie and things began moving in slow motion. Gary turned and reached back for someone, and his date appeared by his side. She was beautiful; an attractive blond who reminded him of one of the girls from the TV show *Friends*. He had seen her once before, and never in a million years had he thought he would ever see her again—definitely not with Gary, of all people.

"What's up, peeps?" Gary smiled at them.

"Hey there, you!" Nicole gave her brother a big hug. She faced the girl and said, "You must be Arianna. It's nice to finally meet you."

"Nice to meet you too," the woman replied.

Terrell wanted to run before she saw him. He wondered if she would recognize him. If she did, would she remember from where?

"Gary has told me so much about you. This is my boyfriend, Terrell." Nicole took Terrell by the hand and pulled him to her side.

"How are you?" He extended his hand toward her nervously.

She took it into hers and their eyes met. He saw her eyebrows rise, and a look of surprise crossed her face. He knew that she remembered him. She blinked then took a step back. "Nice to meet you."

"Uh, sweetheart, I need to go to the restroom. I'll be right back," Terrell said to Nicole. "Please excuse me."

Terrell walked into the bathroom and stood over the sink. He turned the water on and let it run while he closed his eyes and tried to calm down. There was no way his life could be turning out this way. Stuff like this didn't happen to him. Shit was beginning to crumble left and right. *Tonight ain't my night. It just ain't my night.*

Chapter 16

Toby turned into the parking lot of the car rental company. He spotted Roni getting out of a gold Camry, waving at him. He pulled behind her and got out. She ran over and threw her arms around his neck. He inhaled her sweet scent as he kissed her.

"I missed you, baby," she whispered into his ear.

"I missed you too." He cupped her face in his hands and looked at her intensely. She kissed him fully on the mouth and he held her tight. After a few moments, they pulled away.

"I'm going inside and take care of the paperwork. It should only take a few moments," she told him.

A young guy wearing a uniform came out and began checking the car. Toby had loaded Roni's things into his truck and was about to get in when the guy yelled for him.

"Yeah?" Toby walked over, thinking maybe Roni had scratched the car or something.

"Found this under the seat. You know this guy?" he asked, handing the small piece of plastic to Toby.

He looked at the driver's license and smiled at it, thanking the guy. "Yeah, that's her brother. I'll give it to him. He'll be glad you found this."

"No problem. Have a good day," the guy said.

He drove to the front door and waited for Roni to come out. She finally did, and he walked around to open the door for her to get in.

"Thank you, sweetie," she said and gave him another kiss.

"You going to my crib or yours?" he asked.

"Mine. I need to unpack and get ready for the week."

"But what about spending time with me? I thought we'd go to dinner or something this evening. I want to have you in my bed tonight."

"I know you do, but I'm tired, sweetie. It's been a long trip. I'll make it up to you." She reached over and began playing with the back of his neck.

"Promise?" He looked over at her.

"I promise. Besides, soon you're gonna have to start kicking me out of your bed because I'll be over there so much."

He asked her to fill him in on her trip and the seminars she attended. She told him about the speakers that attended and the different topics covered, talking all the way to her house. He took her things inside as she checked her mail.

"You want me to go grab you something to eat?" he offered, pulling her into his arms. "Or is there something you'd like for me to eat before I leave?"

"Hmm, that's an offer I'll definitely be taking you up on later," she said as she kissed him. He walked her over to the sofa, both of them falling down onto it. She groaned as his hands crept along her thighs and worked their way up. She was wearing a short jean skirt and tank top. He went to reach under, knowing that she was wearing a thong, but she grabbed his hand.

"What's wrong?" he asked.

"I'm just tired, that's all, babe. I'm sorry."

"I understand," he told her, easing up. He stood and reached to help her up. He took a deep breath and said, "I guess I'ma leave. You go ahead and get some rest. I'll call you later."

"Okay."

He opened the door then snapped his fingers. "Man, I almost forgot. The guy found this under the seat of the rental car."

He reached into his pocket and handed her the license. She took it and looked at it. He waited for her reaction.

"Oh wow, this is a guy that was at the conference with us. I gave him a ride to his hotel one afternoon." She laughed nervously. "I know he must be looking for it. He's not gonna be able to get on the plane without his ID."

"Good thing you found it, huh? Maybe you should call him. You got his number?" He folded his arms.

"I sure don't."

"He had to catch a plane? Where's he from?"

"I don't even remember. Philly, I think. Yeah, Philly."

"It's right on the license. What's his name? Dean?"

"Sean," she corrected.

"That's right, Sean. And you're sure you don't have his number?"

"No, I just gave him a ride that one night." Roni looked at him innocently. He almost believed her.

"Roni, you're not lying to me, are you? You met this guy at the seminar and you gave him a ride back to your hotel?"

"His hotel! And what's with the third degree, Toby? I told you what happened. It's no big deal. I'll drop the license in the mail to him tomorrow when I leave school. Damn, why are you tripping all of a sudden?"

"Why am I tripping? Did I tell you where Jermaine and I went Saturday?"

"You told me you ran some errands or something." She walked past him. He grabbed her by the arm and looked her in the face. "What is wrong with you?"

"Jermaine got a huge contract Saturday for a house in Wheatland Heights." He watched her face become clouded with confusion and held onto her arm as he spoke. "That's right, Wheatland Heights. It's a nice neighborhood. As I was driving through, I was thinking, man, Roni and I will have a house like one of these someday. Have you ever been there?"

"No," she said quietly.

"Don't lie to me. Please don't lie to me, Veronica." He looked at her, eyes wide with shock. He still had a grip on her arm and was determined not to let go. She stared back at him, saying nothing. "Tell me who Sean is."

"I told you," she whispered.

"I saw you, Roni! I was there at Stanley's house when you were frolicking in the backyard by the pool! 'Don't wet my hair!' Remember? Isley Brothers blasting from the surround-sound. You were having a ball. You and Sean."

"Toby, please."

"Please what? Oh, now you wanna talk? Well, I don't wanna hear it. You been with this nigga since last week, Roni? You spent the weekend with him. I wonder how many other seminars you've been to with Sean, huh? Correction—no, I don't wanna know how many other ones. Seminar, my ass!" he yelled. She flinched and he released her arm. He walked out, and she chased behind him.

"Toby, I need to talk to you. Don't leave like this, baby. Please."

He got into his truck and drove off. He was tempted to look back but didn't. He couldn't believe that she had tried to play him. He had pondered all weekend about how he would approach the subject with her. He knew she would deny it initially; that was why he gave her the opportunity to come clean. But she didn't, and that disappointed him. He was more hurt by the fact that she tried to lie about the situation than he was about catching her with another man.

He drove around aimlessly for an hour, eventually winding up at Jasper's. There were a few cars in the parking lot, although it was only 6:00. He didn't understand why he was torturing himself by thinking about the last time he was here, the night he proposed. His emotions were sending him into a combined state of confusion and devastation. For most of his adult life, Jasper's was the comfort zone he could go to whenever his life was filled with turmoil.

He could hear soft jazz playing as he walked in and headed straight for the bar.

"Tobias, man, what a nice surprise," Uncle Jay called from behind the bar.

"Hey, Uncle Jay. What's going on?"

"Nothing much. What'll it be? The usual?"

"I don't even know, Uncle Jay," Toby said, looking at the bottles of liquor on the glass shelves behind the bar. "I may need something a little stronger today."

"What? It can't be that bad." The older man looked at Toby with his face full of concern. Monica, one of the regular waitresses, walked up and put in a drink order. She made small talk with Toby while Uncle Jay prepared the beverages.

"Uncle Jay, why are you tending the bar?"

"We're short-staffed tonight. Well, actually, we're short-staffed every Sunday since business picked up. Word got out about the kitchen being open at five. I guess that's a good thing, huh? So, I fill in back here."

"It's gonna be really busy tonight because we're short-staffed in the kitchen too," the waitress said, picking up the tray of drinks. "Nice seeing you again, Toby."

"Uncle Jay, why didn't you tell me you needed help? I'll work the bar for you tonight," Toby stood up and told him.

"You don't have to do that, Tobias. You came in here to drink yourself. Seems to me like you already got enough on your mind." Uncle Jay leaned on the bar. "Now, tell me what the problem is."

"I don't have a problem, Uncle Jay. Go ahead and work the kitchen. I got this out here," he told him. When his uncle hesitated, he assured him, "I want to do it, Uncle Jay."

"Well, once the evening crowd is served then I can come back out here. I appreciate this, Tobias. I really do." Uncle Jay removed his apron and Toby made his way to the back of the bar. "You sure you know what you're doing?"

"I learned from the best, Uncle Jay. You taught me well." Toby smiled. His uncle set out for the kitchen, leaving him to familiarize himself with his new surroundings as bartender.

People began coming in the door, and soon Toby was hard at work. The wait staff was patient and friendly as he racked his brain in an effort to remember how to mix drinks and cocktails. Monica teased him, but she helped out a lot. *Uncle Jay is right; this place is the spot on Sundays.*

Toby was in the middle of making a round of Harvey Wallbangers for a rowdy bunch when someone yelled, "Can a brother get some service?"

"Coming right up," he called and carefully handed the loaded tray of drinks to the server. He looked up to see his brother sitting with his back to the bar, checking out the scene. "What the hell are you doing here?"

"What are you doing behind the bar?"

"Helping Uncle Jay out."

"I feel you. This place is really jumping, huh? I heard them talking about it at work."

"Yeah, I think it has a lot to do with Liquid," he said, pointing to the band that was setting up. "What are you drinking?"

"Ginger ale."

"You came all the way to Jasper's for a ginger ale?"

"That and the atmosphere, of course." He gestured toward a table full of females, laughing and talking. One woman waved for Terrell to come over, but he shook his head and waved back, surprising Toby. *Maybe he is changing his ways*, he thought.

The two men made small talk as Toby continued to work the bar. He noticed Terrell seemed distant, but he was too preoccupied with his own drama to even ask what was wrong.

"Get this," the waitress said as she walked up to the counter. She had to yell in order to be heard over the band. "This chick ordered something called a Slow Screwball or something. I told her you wouldn't know what it was."

"A what?"

"Maybe it was a Screwball with Sloe gin." She tilted her head to the side.

"Go make sure what she wants," Toby told her and began filling other orders. Soon she popped back at the bar, smiling at him. "Did you find out what she wanted?"

"Yeah. A slow, comfy screw."

He leaned closer to make sure he understood what she was saying. "What did you say?"

"A Slow Comfortable Screw." The voice came over Monica's shoulder, causing Toby to damn near drop the bottle of Courvoisier he was holding. His eyes met hers and they stared at each other for what seemed like a lifetime. Her hair was cut short, yet it did nothing but enhance her deep-set, keen eyes and broad cheekbones. Her face was exquisite, and he thought that even if she had shaved her head bald, it would only make her more beautiful than she already was.

"Yeah, that's it." Monica smiled. "A Slow Comfortable Screw."

"Damn, Isis, you look good as hell." Terrell stood up and walked over to her. She gave him a hug, but her eyes never left Toby's.

"You're not looking so bad yourself, Terrell. Hi, Toby."

"What's up, Isis?"

"You wanna just sit here at the bar instead of your table?" Monica asked. "I already put your food order in to the kitchen."

"Sure, that's fine," Isis told her. "If these two gentlemen don't mind me joining them."

"Heck naw. Besides, Toby's the bartender anyway. He doesn't count." Terrell grinned as Isis took a seat next to him. "Where the hell you been? I mean, you showed up at the proposal and graced us with a song, and the next thing I knew, you were ghost and we ain't seen you since. What's up with that?"

"I was only in town for one night. It was a beautiful proposal. I have to admit I was impressed." She looked over at Toby. "You two looked very happy together."

Toby thanked her and began mixing her drink. He concentrated on mixing the exact amounts of Sloe gin, Southern Comfort, vodka and Galliano, but instead of orange juice, he used pineapple, topping it off with two cherries, the way he knew she liked it. It had to be perfect.

"So, you're visiting again?" Terrell asked.

"Yeah, for a minute. You know how I do," she answered.

"Meeko was pissed that you came to town and didn't holler at her. I thought she was your girl."

"She is. I called her and explained what happened."

"We saw her at the club a few weeks ago. When was that, Toby?"

"About a month ago," Toby said, placing the drink in front of her.

"Why thank you, Isaac—I mean Toby." She winked.

"Oh, you got jokes, huh?" He grinned.

Her smile met his and she picked up the glass. "Should we toast?"

"I think we should." Terrell held his glass up as well.

"Toby, you're not joining us?" Isis asked.

He grabbed a glass and filled it with soda, lifting it to theirs. "To old friends."

"To old friends," they repeated. He watched Isis take a long swallow of her drink.

"Perfect," she told him.

The bar got busy and Toby got back to work. He eavesdropped as Terrell began filling Isis in on the latest gossip and caught her up on the people they knew. She tossed her head back in laughter; it sounded like music to Toby's ears.

"Your food should be out in just a few minutes," Monica said as she walked up to the bar with another order of drinks for Toby to fill.

"Thanks," Isis replied. She looked up and caught Toby staring at her again. He smiled, knowing he was straight busted.

"Uh, hello. Can my customers get their drink on, please?" Monica snapped her fingers at Toby. He snapped back to reality and had Monica repeat the order.

"Hey, check it out. Why don't I take over for a little while, Toby? You and Isis can talk," Terrell suggested. Toby didn't know how to respond. He looked over at his brother, who was already headed behind the bar.

"What are you doing?" he whispered as Terrell pulled on a white apron emblazoned with the Jasper's logo.

"Helping out." Terrell raised his eyebrows as he answered. "There's no point in you staring at each other all night and her sitting at the bar acting like I'm doing standup. Go sit down and talk. Well, never mind. It's too late. She's already gone."

Toby turned to see that the space where Isis had been sitting was now empty. He looked around the club, but she was nowhere to be found. There was no way to hide the disappointment he felt. *Stop tripping. You didn't have no business sweating her like that anyway. Her leaving is a good thing. You are engaged, remember?*

"Yeah, you're right," he told himself aloud.

"Right about what?" Terrell asked.

"Nothing." He stood in silence, still scanning the crowd, hoping to find her. The faces of people laughing and enjoying themselves were too much for him. It had been a hell of a day and he decided it was time for him to leave. "I gotta go talk to Uncle Jay. I'll be right back."

Terry nodded and began talking with some female patrons who were now sitting at the bar. Toby set off to find his uncle. He was about to enter the kitchen when the door swung open. Monica walked out carrying a tray of food. He held it open for her.

"Thanks. Tell your friend I'll bring her food to her as soon as I take care of this other table."

"Don't bother. She dipped."

"What?"

"She left. I'm leaving too. Terry's gonna work the bar. Where's Uncle Jay?"

"Back there." She nodded, looking at him strangely. "I can't believe she left."

"Believe it. She's known for pulling disappearing stunts like that. Not the first time, won't be the last," he replied.

He found Uncle Jay piling plates with his famous fried catfish and potato salad. "Uncle Jay, I'm leaving."

"So soon? I thought you were gonna help me close up," his uncle said jokingly. "Thanks for pitching in tonight, Toby. I guess I can get outta this hot kitchen now. Especially since the cook finally showed up."

"Terry took over the bar, so you can relax for a little while, Uncle Jay."

"Terry? When did he get here?"

"About an hour ago. He's got everything under control out there. You know him."

"Yeah, he's probably out there giving out drinks in exchange for telephone numbers." Uncle Jay laughed. "I sure appreciate you boys. Can you believe how busy this place has gotten? That band packs a house, I tell you."

"Yeah, Uncle Jay." Toby sighed.

"Something wrong, Tobias? What's on your mind?" Uncle Jay continued piling plates as he talked, peering at Toby over his wire-rimmed glasses.

Toby inhaled deeply, not knowing where to start. He didn't want to put his and Roni's business out there, but he needed to talk to someone. Uncle Jay had always been the father they never had.

"Toby, you are such a liar!"

Toby frowned at Monica as she walked past him, reaching for the trays of food.

"What are talking about, ghetto girl?"

"That girl is sitting right in the back, waiting on you."

"Where?"

"What girl?"

Toby and Uncle Jay spoke at the same time.

"Some girl he and Terry were talking to," Monica answered. "She's at the table in the far left corner."

"Is that her food?" Toby asked.

"Yep."

"Show me where she is." He turned to Uncle Jay. "Can I get a plate?"

"Humph. I thought you were leaving," Uncle Jay said suspiciously. "Who's out there?"

"Isis."

"The singing girl?" Uncle Jay's eyes lit up and Toby couldn't help smiling. "I ain't even gonna ask."

"Please don't," he replied. His uncle fixed him a plate and placed it on the tray next to the plate for Isis. "Thanks, Uncle Jay."

He followed Monica out of the kitchen. She pointed to a secluded table located in the far corner of the restaurant. He thanked her and made his way through the crowd, balancing the tray. The saxophone player was playing a killer rendition of "For the Love of You" by the Isley Brothers. Isis was bobbing to the beat of the music and her eyes were closed. She was zoning, and he was tempted not to disturb her.

She looked up and saw him standing there. "So, you're the waiter too?"

"Don't hate because I'm multi-talented," he replied, putting her plate in front of her.

"I was beginning to wonder if you had decided not to join me. I know you're an engaged man, Toby. I ain't trying to start no stuff."

"You're good," he said, taking the seat next to hers. "So, what's been up with you? You just dip and no one has seen or heard from you in damn near two years."

"I did a little bit of traveling. Stayed with some family out west for a bit, and now I guess I've made my way back here."

"You could've called and let someone know you were okay. I mean, I thought we were cool. Hell, I thought we were better than cool."

"You're right, Toby, and I'm sorry. But my head was all messed up, and I just needed to get away from everything and everybody. We were more than cool, and we always will be. You know that." She reached across the table and covered his hand with hers.

Toby looked at Isis and shook his head. "I guess it's just good to know that you're okay. And yeah, we'll always be cool."

She gave him a relieved smile and asked, "Anyway, where is your fiancée?"

Roni was the last thing Toby wanted to talk about right now, especially after the conversation he had with her earlier. He could feel his previous anger growing and pushed it down further. His only response to Isis's question was to shake his head as he began picking at his food. He still could not believe he caught Roni cheating.

"Toby, what's wrong? I know I've been gone for a minute, but I'm still me. If you wanna talk, I can listen." Isis picked a piece of fish off her plate and bit into it. "Mmm, good."

He raised his eyes from the plate and looked up at her. "I just found out some things that are making me question my decision to get married right now."

"Big things or little things?"

"Both."

"Things about her, things about you, or things about marriage?"

He thought about that question long and hard. There was the fact that Roni didn't want children, how she questioned his decisions and challenged him constantly, and now the fact that he had just caught her cheating. These were just a few of the things that were causing him to be doubtful that they were ready for marriage.

"Okay, no answer. Well, let me ask you this: Have you talked to her about it?"

"Not yet."

"Then maybe that's where you should start."

"Simple as that, huh?"

"Yep, simple as that. No point in speculating without communicating. Talking is the most important part of the relationship. How long have you two been together?"

"A year in July."

"A year?" She looked surprised.

"What?"

"Nothing. I just thought you had been with her longer." She shrugged.

"Nope, only a year."

"She's a pretty special girl."

"What makes you say that?" he asked, knowing that they had never met.

"She got you to turn in your player's card and commit to her. Only an exceptional woman can do that. She got you to marry her," she said matter-of-factly.

"I turned my card in the day I met you, but you didn't want me, so I had to get it back. And I haven't married her—*yet.*"

"You will. You love her. I could see it in your eyes the way you looked at her. Now, when you think about the way you felt the night you proposed, any doubts you may be having about getting married should vanish. Think about the love you felt at that moment." She looked at him so intensely that he could feel the words as they escaped her lips. She had a way of reading him like no other woman could.

Before he could react, Uncle Jay appeared at the table. "You two need anything?"

"No thanks, Uncle Jay. You remember Isis, don't you?" Toby asked.

"How could I ever forget someone so beautiful—and talented, at that?" Uncle Jay smiled. "How are you? Is the food okay?"

"Yes, everything is fine," she told him. People began to applause as the band announced they were taking a five-minute break. Toby could tell his uncle was up to something. He watched, curiously, wondering what it was.

"Isis, since the band is here tonight and you did such a wonderful job the last time," Uncle Jay began, "do you think you can sing another song for us?"

"Huh? I . . .uh . . .I really didn't plan on singing, Mr..."

"Sims," Toby told her.

"Uncle Jay," he corrected.

"You didn't plan on singing that night either, did you? But you got up there." Toby winked.

"That was a gift." She gave him an evil look, which was obviously a fake one.

"Go on up there and sing, girl. Unless you're scared," Toby challenged.

"She ain't scared. I know you ain't scared, are you?" Uncle Jay asked.

"No, Uncle Jay, I'm not sacred, and Toby knows it," Isis told them. She shook her head at Toby and Uncle Jay. "I'll be right back."

Toby's eyes followed her as she stood and walked toward the door leading backstage. The silk dress she wore fit the contours of her body just right, and he forced himself not to think about what was underneath.

"I like her," Uncle Jay said as he sat in the chair Isis had just vacated.

"Forget it, Uncle Jay. She's too young for you," Toby joked.

"Believe me, your uncle ain't as old as you think he is. I still got a lot of hang time in me."

"All right, Uncle Jay," Toby told him as he began eating his food.

"I'm serious, Tobias. You can ask—"

"I believe you!" Toby quickly interrupted before his uncle began calling names. He had no desire to know who his uncle was having relations with.

A few moments later, the band came back on the stage, followed by Isis. The saxophone player placed a stool in the middle of the stage in front of the microphone. "Ladies and gentlemen, Liquid is pleased to present the vocal style of Miss Isis Adams."

There was a thunder of applause and a hush fell over the crowd as she took her place. She didn't say anything as she sat on the stool. The band began playing a few chords and she began singing "Feel the Fire" by Peabo Bryson. Her eyes remained closed, as if she was afraid to open them. She was in her own world, and her voice exuded power.

As he watched her sing, Toby recalled the first time he saw her and how this woman had turned his world upside down. Feelings he thought were long gone and buried began to rise, and he knew that he had to leave now for fear he would act upon them. He whispered good-bye to Uncle Jay as he stood up and headed for the exit. Toby looked back once more, locking his eyes to hers. He gave her a small nod of his head and he knew she understood why he couldn't stay.

Chapter 17

"I need to talk to you. I'm at Jasper's, working the bar," Terrell said into his cell phone after he heard the voicemail pick up. "Meet me up here."

Chills ran down his spine as Isis's voice floated through the club. The girl had a voice that would make Patti LaBelle do a double take. He looked over at his brother, who seemed to be in awe as he watched her perform. There had always been a connection between Toby and Isis, yet nothing ever jumped off between them, and he always wondered why they never hooked up. Too late for that now, because Roni had staked her claim and he had no doubt in his mind that his brother was in love.

"They must really be desperate for help."

Terrell turned around to see Meeko standing near the bar. "No, they needed a skilled brother like myself for a change."

"Skilled brother like *me*," Meeko corrected. She pointed to Isis and asked, "How long has she been on stage?"

"She just got up there. Tearing it up, as usual."

"I see," she replied. They stood watching Isis pour her heart and soul into the song. "Damn, that girl can sing."

"No doubt about that. Did she know you were coming?" he asked as he looked her up and down. She was still the baddest redbone he had ever met.

"Yeah, I told her I'd meet her up here and check out the band. She didn't mention you'd be here, though," she said, sitting on an empty stool. He made an apple martini and placed in front of her. "Thanks."

"So, where your man at?" He couldn't resist asking.

She cut her eyes at him. "What are you talking about, Terry?"

"Your man. Where's he at?"

"I'm gonna ignore that question. Especially coming from you."

"Why's that?"

"Don't you have a woman?"

"Yeah, I got a woman. That's not the issue. The question I asked you was where's *your* man at?" He grinned.

"I don't have a man. Unlike your lockdown ass, I'm a free agent."

Terrell scowled at her as she killed herself laughing. He decided not to give her a rebuttal. Isis was completing her song and people were on their feet clapping. He saw Toby ease out the door without even saying good-bye. *Roni must've called and told him to come home,* he thought. Good thing, too, because the heat between him and Isis was obvious enough for Stevie Wonder to see.

"Was that Toby?"

"Yep," he replied, leaning past her to take an order from Monica.

"What's wrong with him? He didn't even speak. Did Isis see him?"

"They were sitting together before he left," Monica volunteered. Terry shot her an angry look and she shrugged. "Oh, sorry."

"They were sitting together?" Meeko asked. "Uh, I know this is none of my business, but where's his fiancée?"

"You're right; it's none of your business," Terrell warned, passing the tray of drinks to Monica.

"Whatever," Meeko told him, finishing off her martini and requesting another. "So, you seen Jermaine?"

"Haven't talked to him." He refilled her drink. "Were you expecting him?"

"Not really, but I did mention that Isis and I were gonna come check out the band this evening," she commented.

"And you think that because you told him were coming through he would automatically be here?" he asked, wondering just how often they had been talking. "Sorry to disappoint you, but looks like your date's a no show."

"He's not my date," she said, sucking her teeth. She waved at Isis, who was coming through the stage door. People were on her like bees to honey. *Probably paying her compliments. That girl is a true talent.*

"I'm saying, you trying to kick it with him now?"

"No, and why are you acting like a jerk, Terry? What's going on with you?"

Terrell knew he was being a total asshole, but he had a lot on his mind already, and the fact that Meeko was asking about Jermaine of all people didn't help his mood. He was about to apologize when he saw Jermaine enter the club. "There's your boy now."

Meeko shifted around then turned back to Terrell. "Guess my date showed up, huh?"

He watched her walk over to Jermaine and hug him. Isis soon joined them and pointed over to Terrell. Jermaine was all smiles as he sauntered over to the bar, a beautiful woman on each arm.

"What's up, Terry? What are you doing behind the bar?" he asked. "I thought you were a big exec now."

"Aw, man, you never know where you'll find me when it comes to Jasper's. This is home. You know that." Terrell reached out and gave him a pound. "What you drinking? Long Island?"

"Naw, I'm taking it easy tonight. I got an new job to start on in the morning."

"Really? Where?" Meeko asked, sitting a bit too close for Terrell's liking.

"Over in Wheatland Heights." Jermaine beamed.

"Must be a pretty big job," Isis commented. Terrell followed her eyes to the table where she and Toby had been sitting, and he saw the sadness in her eyes.

"Isis, girl, you should really think about hitting a studio and laying down some tracks. That was beautiful," he told her.

"Thank you, Terry. I appreciate that, but I don't think so." Isis sighed. "Singing is just a hobby."

"I can't believe I missed you singing," Jermaine told her.

"She blew the roof off, too, Jermaine." Meeko nodded. "Didn't she, Terry? Toby was here but he left."

"How long ago did he leave? I need to talk to him," Jermaine quickly asked, looking at Terrell.

"I'm surprised you didn't see him in the parking lot before you walked in. He just left right before you got here," Terrell told him. He wondered why Jermaine looked worried all of a sudden, especially since Toby had been so distant earlier. Something was going on, and he wanted to know what it was. "What's up?"

"Uh, nothing," Jermaine said, glancing at Isis then back to Terrell. "He's supposed to be helping me out tomorrow and I need to get with him about the logistics of what we need to take care of, that's all."

Terrell didn't believe him for some reason. Maybe it was the bullshit way Jermaine answered or the obviously bogus excuse he quickly came up with. Helping Uncle Jay out at the club was one thing, but moonlighting for Jermaine was something else. He gave Jermaine a look to let him know he wasn't buying it and to come clean. Jermaine just stared back at him like he didn't know what was going on.

"Let's get a table, Jermaine," Meeko said after they talked with Terrell for a while longer.

"Cool. It's an empty one over there," Jermaine told her, taking her by the arm. "I'll holler at you later."

"You coming, Isis?" Meeko asked her girlfriend, who wasn't moving.

"I think I'm gonna get out of here soon. You guys go ahead and enjoy yourselves," she told them.

"They look cozy, huh?" Terrell asked Isis after they had gone.

"Yeah, maybe Jermaine will be the next one popping the question," Isis replied.

"I knew something was up with them," Terrell hissed.

"What is your problem, Terry?" Isis asked, realizing he was serious. "You can't possibly think that something is going on between the two of them. You know Meeko is probably trying to get him to give her the hookup on a security system or something."

"Or she's trying to hook up with him."

"So what if she is? You didn't want her, so why can't someone else have her?"

"Because he's supposed to be one of my best friends and she's my ex. That ain't even cool."

"If you say so, but believe me, there's nothing going on there. I'm leaving." She leaned over and kissed him on the cheek as she said good-bye. When she was gone, he couldn't help looking over at Meeko and Jermaine sitting at their table, laughing. Suddenly, he heard his name being called from across the club. He looked up to see his manager, CJ, walking toward the bar.

"Hey there, CJ, what's going on?"

She smiled. Terrell couldn't help noticing how nice she looked in the red sundress she was wearing.

"When they told me you were over here at the bar, I thought they meant you were having a drink. I had no idea that you were the bartender. Do we not pay you enough at your day job?"

"No, that's why I have to tend bar on the weekends. You think you can talk to someone and handle getting me a raise?"

"Depends on how good my drink is," she said seductively, leaning on the bar in a manner that left no question about whether she was wearing a bra.

"So, that's the determining factor?"

"That's the determining factor. You can show me just how good your job performance is." She nodded.

"Well, I hate to brag, but my performance has always exceeded expectations. What's your pleasure?"

"Um, let's see. How about a Long Island Iced Tea?"

"That's it?" he asked. "I'm about to be paid."

"We'll see," she said. She continued flirting with him as he made her drink and he wondered if she was serious.

"Here you go. I think you'll find it's well beyond your liking."

"We'll see," she said, taking a sip. "Brother, you're about to get a raise."

"Told you. I'm a man of many talents."

"So I see. You'll have to display more of them to me one day. It was nice seeing you, Mr. Sims." She paid him and waved good-bye.

"No, what she should've said was you're a man of much bull."

Terrell didn't even see Anjelica until she spoke. He had actually forgotten that he had called and left the message for her to come up there. Now he was wishing that he hadn't, especially when he remembered that Jermaine and Meeko were having drinks at a table a few feet away. He wasn't sure what type of relationship Jermaine and Anjelica had, but he was pretty certain that his boy wouldn't feel comfortable being seen at a table with another female.

"What's up, girl? Took you long enough to get here."

"I just knew you were lying about being the bartender. I would think such a job is beneath you, Terrell. I hope you notice that I didn't bring a purse, so my drinks will have to be on the house," Anjelica remarked, looking good in jeans and a crop top. Her long hair was in a mess of curls, surrounding her pretty face.

"No job is beneath me when it comes to Jasper's. If Uncle Jay needs me to clean the toilets, I would," he told her.

"Well, it's nice to see you can be loyal to something."

"What's that supposed to mean? You know what? Never mind. What do you want to drink? And you only get one on the house, so if you want more than that, I suggest you use the ATM located in the lobby."

She ordered a Tequila Sunrise and sat down. "So, talk."

He decided to talk as long as possible in order to distract her from looking around the club and seeing Jermaine. He told her about having dinner with Nicole and Gary and his girlfriend, whom he happened to be familiar with. Instead of being concerned, Anjelica found the entire situation funny. She nearly choked on her drink when he told her.

"What the hell is funny about that?"

"I mean, the fact that your future brother-in-law's girlfriend is the nurse from the abortion clinic you took your booty call to. If that ain't hilarious, I don't know what is."

"First of all, she was the receptionist, which is another thing. I think she told Gary and Nicole that she was a nurse, not a receptionist."

"Then there you have it. She was probably just as uncomfortable as you were. You know her dirt and she knows yours. Did she say anything?"

"Nope, not a word. We acted like we didn't even know each other. She didn't mention it to me and I didn't mention it to her. We had dinner, that's it."

"Then what makes you even think that she remembers you?"

"I can tell she remembered me. I'm not that forgettable, and it wasn't that long ago that we were there. She remembers. I don't know what I'm gonna do." He sighed. He was glad he had finally told someone about the situation he found himself in. He wanted to talk to his brother about it, but Toby seemed to have a lot on his mind, so Terry didn't bother him with it.

"I say be like the Army—don't ask, don't tell. If she doesn't bring it up, then you don't bring it up."

"I guess that's one way of looking at it, but there's something else that happened Saturday night."

"Damn, something else happened? You had a rough weekend, huh? Is this as funny as the other thing? If so, let me put my drink down before you tell me." Anjelica smiled.

"No, this one isn't that comical," Terrell told her, his voice full of tension. He had also been thinking of how to tell her about the other situation he found himself in.

"What is it?" she asked, noticing his grim face.

"Kayla . . . "

"Mr. Sims, I'm about to leave. I just wanted to say good-bye and thank you for a wonderful drink. We will talk about those other talents really soon," CJ called over the bar as she headed for the exit. He turned toward her and noticed Meeko and Jermaine standing right behind her. He prayed that Anjelica wouldn't turn around and see them, but CJ's yelling was hard to ignore. Anjelica swiveled around on the stool and got a full view of the couple. The look on her face confirmed just what he suspected; she was obviously not pleased with seeing them together.

"Okay, CJ, we'll do that. Drive safely," Terrell called to her and turned his back to Anjelica. He pretended to be busy washing glasses and putting away bottles of liquor, waiting for her to speak before he did. When she didn't, he turned back to see why she was so quiet. He was flabbergasted to find her chair empty. She was talking with Meeko and Jermaine. He stood, waiting for the catfight to break out between the two women, but it didn't. Neither one looked angry or even uncomfortable as they stood and talked. Soon she returned to her seat and Meeko and Jermaine walked out the door.

"You really are funny," Anjelica snapped. "I can't believe you did this."

"What are you talking about? I didn't do anything."

"I guess you called me up here to catch Jermaine with another woman, huh? Was that your little master plan? You thought I would clown and get all ghetto and show my behind like some crazy, jealous person? You must have me confused with . . . what's Craig's ghetto wife from New York's name?"

"Avis," he replied, thinking Craig really did have his hands full with both his deranged wife and Kayla as his daughter's mother.

"Yeah, Avis. Sorry, that's not how I roll. I may be a bitch sometimes, Terrell, but I do have class. Jermaine's not my man. I told you before, I am a free agent."

Before Terrell had a chance to respond, Jermaine strutted up to the bar and put his arms around her. "What's up, sweetheart? You want another drink?"

"No, I'm good. I thought you were gone."

"Do you think I would have left without spending some time with you?" Jermaine asked. "Terry, have Monica send another round to the table, man. Okay?"

"No problem," Terrell told him.

Something about the way Jermaine ordered the drinks let Terrell know that his friend was a bit pissed, and he wondered if Jermaine also thought he had set this entire thing up. He wasn't about to hang around to find out.

Chapter 18

Toby had been tossing and turning in his bed for thirty minutes, trying to fall asleep. He had turned the ringers off all the phones in his house and ignored the beep of the answering machine, letting him know that he had messages waiting. His cell phone remained in the glove compartment of his truck, where he had placed it before he even went into Jasper's.

He knew he had to have been dreaming when he felt someone climb into his bed. The warm body snuggled closer to him; he felt its nakedness and the familiar scent of Victoria's Secret Pink filled the air, letting him know that indeed Roni was there beside him.

"Baby?" she whispered in his ear.

"What do you want?" Toby groaned, refusing to roll over. He'd avoided her calls all evening and thought she would get the hint that he needed some time to deal with this situation. Considering the mood he was in right now, it definitely was *not* the time.

"I am so sorry, Toby. You have got to know that," she told him, her voice trembling.

"I don't wanna deal with this right now, Ron. I think you should just leave. Seriously, I need some time."

"I love you, Toby. We need to talk about this. Please, baby." He felt her drape her arms across him and his back remained to her as she rubbed across his chest. "Toby, please talk to me."

"Who the fuck is he, Roni?" he heard his mouth say. He had told himself to remain quiet, not to say anything, but that was one question he wanted to know the answer to.

"He's not you, Toby. That's all that needs to be said. Who he is isn't important. You are the most important person in my life, and I don't wanna lose you. I need for you to understand how sorry I am. It was a mistake and it will never happen again. I love you, that's all. Tell me you forgive me, Toby. Please." She caressed him as she talked, wrapping her legs around his.

Her soft feet ran up and down his calves. He could feel her breasts pressing on his back as she continued to whisper, pleading for his forgiveness. His mind told his body not to respond, but he felt himself getting hard, his physical wants ignoring his mental commands. She had aroused him and he was ready. He turned over to face her, and wasn't surprised to see the tears running down her cheeks. Her eyes were swollen and he could tell she had been crying for a while. She blinked as if she was surprised that he had turned over so soon. He didn't say a word as he pulled her mouth to his, kissing her fiercely, positioning his body on top of hers. He reached between her legs, touching the wetness that welcomed his fingers. Her response was to meet his touch while stroking his stiffness, making sure he was as eager as she was.

He entered her with such intensity that he felt her body tense in surprise. His eyes remained open because he wanted to watch her facial expressions as he made love to her. Her eyes were shut tight and he wondered if it was from the roughness of their lovemaking or because she was thinking of her other lover, the one she was with just hours before, the one that she had her legs wrapped around just yesterday in the swimming pool. *Did she make the same face as she is now when she was fucking him? Did she call his name out and beg him not to stop as she's calling out to me?* He could feel her muscles contracting as he drove in and out, and hear the sounds of his body meeting hers as she screamed in ecstasy. Flashes of red and blue collided with he darkness as he shut his eyes tightly. His passion was mounting and he could no longer hold back. Faster and faster, harder and harder, until he couldn't take it anymore. Once again, her muscles tightened against his and he felt her nails scrape across his back as he came deep inside of her. It was a much needed release. The tension he had been holding in for the last two days seemed to subside.

"Baby, are you all right?" she finally asked him.

Toby remained silent as he eased off her and sat on the side of his bed, reaching on the nightstand to turn on the lamp. He walked into the bathroom and washed himself. He realized that this was the first time they had ever made love without a condom, and couldn't help but wonder if she had done so in an effort to prove her sudden loyalty to him. He stared at his reflection in the mirror and became angry at the tears that he saw in his eyes. *Get yourself together, T,* he told himself, taking a deep breath.

"Toby, please talk to me," she said once again as he came out of the bathroom. He didn't even look over at her. Instead, he walked over to the dresser where he noticed her purse. He opened it, taking out her keys. He went through the ring, searching until he found the one he wanted. She sat up in the middle of the bed, not bothering to cover her nakedness. "What are you doing?"

Silently, he removed the key and climbed back into bed. He turned the lamp off again then lay back down with his back to her.

"Toby, please say something. Don't you dare lay there and ignore me like I'm nothing!"

"Lock the door when you leave," he told her.

"When I what? Oh, so you want me to leave? You just gonna sleep with me and then kick me out? Is that how you wanna end this, Toby? You know what? Fine then, I'll leave. But if I walk out that door . . . "

"Lock it behind you," he repeated. He had told himsel
that he wasn't going to argue, fuss or fight with Roni. The
less he said, the easier it would be. He remained quiet as she
continued to rant and rave about him being unreasonable
about the situation. Finally, he listened as she gathered her
things, took the keys off the dresser and descended the
steps.

The door slammed behind her and he waited. With
Roni, there was no telling if something was gonna come
through the window or his car alarm would start blaring,
letting him know that she had taken her frustration out on
something he possessed rather than on him. She had done it
before, and he prayed that she wouldn't do it again. But
there was no sound of breaking glass or piercing alarms.
Just the sound of her car as she drove away. Then, and only
then, did Toby drift into a deep slumber.

"You sure you're up to this, man?"

"I told you I was. Now, will you quit asking me dumb
questions? I told you, I'm cool," Toby replied. Jermaine had
been asking him if he was okay for the past fifteen minutes.
He had to admit, he had even surprised himself when he got
out of bed and called his best friend to ask if he still needed
help this morning. He didn't know whether it was because he
didn't feel like moping around the house all day and was
looking for something to take his mind off Roni or that he
wanted to return to the place where he actually caught his
fiancée cheating on him. There was no doubt in is mind that
once they got to Stanley's house he would have to relive the
images he witnessed the last time they were there. And
somehow, he wondered if in the back of his mind he really
hoped to run into Stanley's brother and talk to him. Either
way, he had called, Jermaine picked him up, and they were
well on their way.

"I know you're cool. I know you got a lot on your mind, that's all. Did you talk to her about what happened?"

"Yeah, she tried to deny it until I told her I saw her," he told him.

"No, I know she ain't try the 'It wasn't me' line. Please don't tell me that. I don't think I can take it."

"No, but only because she realized she was busted. I couldn't believe it myself, especially when I gave her the opportunity to be honest with me. I think that's what hurt me the most, the fact that she just straight up lied to me about him. Come on, J, Roni was just as big a player as I was before we hooked up. I know that. It was one of the things that attracted me to her . . . Well, that plus she's fine as hell." He tried to laugh, but it came out like a pitiful sigh. "But when I told her it was all about her, I left everyone else alone. I just assumed she did the same thing. All she had to do was be honest wit' me when I asked her about him. I would've been pissed, but I would've respected the fact that she was honest."

"I feel you on that one. Let me ask you something. You said you left everyone else alone, but I hear you was up in Jasper's last night with Isis. How do you explain that one?"

Toby explained how he wound up working the bar and Isis happened to come to the club. He assured his friend that he left long before she did and he went home and went to bed. Jermaine was stunned when he told him of how he and Roni made love and then he took his key from her. "I told her to lock the door behind her when she left."

"And then what did she do?" Jermaine asked, focusing on both Toby and the morning traffic.

"She was pissed, but she left."

"And then what did she do?" Jermaine repeated the question as if Toby didn't hear him correctly the first time.

"I told you. She left. She locked the door and left."

"She keyed your truck?"

"Nope."

"She ain't slash your tires?"

"No, none of that. Nothing thrown, no broken glass, no property damage. I'm telling you, she locked the door and left."

"She's planning something big, then. Either she's gonna burn all your shit while you ain't home or she's plotting to kill your ass," Jermaine told him assuredly. Toby looked over at him like he was as crazy as what he just said. "I'm telling you, she's planning the big payback. You screwed her, didn't say anything to her, took your key off her key ring and then told her to lock the door when she left? She's gonna hire someone to kill you, for real." They turned into Wheatland Heights and onto Stanley's street.

"Are you listening to yourself? You sound so retarded."

"Are you listening to yourself? This is Veronica Black we're talking about. Has Roni ever taken anything that calm before? Don't worry. I got this new system we can install in your place later."

"Shut up, Jermaine. I already got a security system that works fine. You're blowing this way out of proportion. Roni couldn't overreact because she was wrong. Not only was she wrong, but she was caught. You can't act crazy if you're the one who's busted. Her tearing stuff up like she normally does, that would've just added fuel to an already lit fire," Toby replied, opening his door and getting out.

"And I'm telling you, you better pray your joint ain't a bed of ashes by the time we make it back this afternoon." Jermaine laughed, passing Toby a large tool bag out of the back of the truck.

Chapter 19

"Is this one of your accounts?" Terrell walked up to Kayla's desk and asked. He knew it was; he was just using it as an excuse to talk to her. He had put off calling her, trying to give her some time to cool off. This was the first time they had ever had a falling out of sorts and he felt bad, mostly because it was his fault.

"Does it have my name on it?" She didn't even look up from her computer.

"Yes, but I don't understand the notes on it. Can you explain them to me?"

Kayla rolled her eyes as she took the file from his hand. She frowned, trying to figure out what he was talking about. After turning a few pages, she told him, "You were the last person to notate this account. I notated it three months ago. I don't understand the notes either."

"Can I see you in my office?"

"I'm busy," Kayla snapped, turning back around to her computer.

"Kayla, come on. Stop tripping. Come to my office so we can talk."

"I told you I'm busy. Call Anjelica. I'm sure she would have no problem talking to you. You need her number? Oh, my bad. You already know it."

"Fine then, Kayla. Be stubborn. You aren't even giving me a chance to explain myself," he hissed, making sure he spoke low enough that no one could hear them over the small cubicles.

"There's nothing to explain. You're a grown-ass man, Terrell. I ain't your woman or one of your hoes. You don't owe me an explanation for nothing you do," she told him.

He turned around to see CJ standing nearby. She waved at him and asked, "Is everything all right, Mr. Sims?"

"Yeah, CJ. I'm just going over something with Ms Hopkins here."

"Well, don't forget we have that meeting coming up soon. I'll be stopping by your office later." She gave him a knowing look.

"I'll bet she will," Kayla said sarcastically.

"What's that supposed to mean, Kay?"

"That she'll be coming to your office later, Terrell—I mean Mr. Sims." She continued, "You know I can't stand her. I advise you to deter her from coming over here because if she does, there's nothing you can do to stop me from cussing her out. Today is not the day, and I am not in the mood."

"She ain't coming over here. Just come into my office so we can talk. I need for you to understand what went down," he told her.

"Is there a problem? Can I help with something?"

Terrell felt the hand on his shoulder and turned around. CJ was looking over him at Kayla's computer. Her hand made its way to the center of his back as she moved closer. He tried to move a little in case someone happened to notice her obvious gesture of affection.

"No, we're fine, CJ. I was just going over some notes with Kayla in regards to an account. Everything's under control," he assured her. Kayla continued typing, not even acknowledging CJ's presence, which was probably a good thing.

"Really? Ms. Hopkins, do we need to retrain you in notating accounts?" CJ asked.

Kayla's fingers stopped immediately. She stood up and turned toward them. Terrell began praying that she wouldn't start talking without thinking, which she had been known to do on more than one occasion. The look she gave CJ said everything without anything coming out of her mouth as her eyes traveled from the top of CJ's head to her feet then back up again. Other employees nearby sat frozen, waiting for whatever was going to happen next.

"I believe it was a mistake that Mr. Sims made on the account that needs to be corrected. I'm sure you'll have no problem retraining him, since he's the one having difficulties. Excuse me. It's my break," she said with a smile.

Snickering could be heard from the onlookers and CJ turned around, giving them a threatening look. They quickly went back to work and Terrell excused himself as well. When he returned to his office, Kayla was there waiting.

"Look, Kay—" he started, but she cut him off.

"I didn't come in here to talk. I came for you to listen. Nicole is a nice woman with a lot going for herself, despite the fact that she is with you. We all make mistakes. That being said, you need to get your shit together. I know Nicole well enough to know that she's not stupid enough to be waiting in the wings for you. But even still, she loves your unfaithful, noncommittal ass for some strange reason, and I don't want her to be hurt or look stupid." The words came out of her mouth so fast that he doubted she had even taken time to breathe.

"What are you talking about, Kayla? I'm telling you that your sister and I were together one time and that's it. We're just cool. It's not even like that."

"I'm talking about you being with everybody, Terrell. Anjelica, Darla, CJ . . . "

"CJ! You really are out of your mind, Kayla. I'm telling you I'm not like that anymore. I've changed. I know I gotta get my shit together if I want things to work with Nicole, and I am. Part of the reason I know that is because your sister Anjelica pointed out a lot of stuff to me and I know I was wrong."

"Oh, so now you're taking advice from a whore? Well, I am so glad that she is being so helpful to you and has given you such great advice when it comes to your love life," she said, standing up. "I can see that I've done nothing here but waste your time."

She opened the door to his office. Terrell quickly ran over and pushed the door closed. "Kayla, wait a minute. Anjelica didn't say anything to me that you haven't said in the past. The reason I pointed that out was to show you that she's not this monstrosity that you make her out to be. I know you believe she's this evil sex fiend of a woman who tries to sleep with any man she comes in contact with, but you're wrong."

"I don't have to listen to this. I've known my sister all of my life and you've known her what, two hours? Please, spare me."

"Spare you what, the truth? Why should I? You come in here all condescending like you're holier than thou, without even giving me the chance to talk. I'll be the first to admit that I've done some trifling stuff over the past few months, but I've changed. I love Nicole and I'm not gonna do anything to jeopardize what we have. She's invested a lot into me and our relationship, and I respect that.

"Believe me, Kayla, even that night with Anjelica was a one time thing. It was the last time I even did anything that stupid. But your sister is a good person, just like you are. Maybe that's why she and I became cool, because you are somewhat alike. You never talked to her to give you the chance to see that side of her," Terrell told her.

He released his arm from the door and walked behind his desk, sitting in soft leather chair. The initial tension that had embraced him when he first entered his office was subsiding. Kayla stared at him then opened the door. She turned and left without saying a word. He didn't expect her to, because he knew she needed time to absorb everything they had just shared with each other. That was how their relationship was. He was her backbone and she was his conscience. They were each other's strengths when the other was weak. She was his best friend and he loved her. But Anjelica had become his friend, too, and it hurt him to see the two beautiful, intelligent sisters hating one another.

Kayla's silence was good enough for him because he knew he had caused her to think. He would call her later and they would talk some more and by the end of the week, they would be having lunch together like old times. *Maybe she can help me figure out this Arianna dilemma that's been haunting me*, he thought as he sorted through the pile of work that he was supposed to have completed by the end of the day.

He was in the middle of working on a report when he heard a knock at the door. He looked at the clock and saw that it was after 5:00. *Kayla must be stopping by before she leaves.* He was surprised when it wasn't Kayla but CJ who walked in and took a seat on the edge of his desk. Her skirt began rising on her thick thighs, and he saw that a garter belt was holding up her black silk stockings.

"Are you busy?" She smiled, not even pulling the skirt down. He could've sworn that she maneuvered her body so that it rose up even more.

"Finishing up this report for the meeting tomorrow. You on your way out?"

"Yep, I'm all finished. I just stopped by to see if I could interest you in a bite to eat." She leaned over his desk and picked up a picture of him, Jermaine and Toby from his desk. It was one of his favorite pictures of the three of them, taken one summer after he had graduated from high school. They were posed on a set of rocks on the beach and looked like they had it going on, dressed in denim overalls, Cross Colors shirts and black Doc Martens. She giggled as she looked at it.

"Okay, what's with the sunglasses? You all look like body doubles for Jodeci."

"Boyz 2 Men," he corrected. "And back then, you couldn't tell us that we weren't."

"Don't tell me you all were a group."

"Triple Threat. We won the talent shows every year. Shoot, you're laughing, but we were the bomb. We had backup dancers and everything."

"Is that a curl, Terrell? Did you have a curl?" she shrieked.

He snatched the picture out of her hands. "No, I didn't have a curl. Those are dreads."

"Let me see. That is a curl! I can't believe you had a curl." CJ reached for the frame, but he held it out of her reach and she wound up nearly falling off the desk. He reached out and she landed in his arms. They both ended up across the desk. He found himself staring at her cleavage then back into her dark eyes. CJ licked her lips at him and at that moment, the door opened.

"I brought you a picture of Day—oh, shit. Sorry."

Terrell quickly stood up, knowing what this must've looked like to Kayla when she walked in.

"Have you ever hear of knocking?" CJ barked as she readjusted her clothes.

Kayla looked at Terrell and shook her head at him. He tried to catch her before she got out of his office, but she was out the door before he knew it. Rushing into the hallway, he called out to her. "Kayla, Kayla!"

He made it to the end of the corridor just as the elevator chimed. He pressed the button in an effort to stop the doors from closing, but saw that Kayla was pressing just as hard on the inside to make them close. He looked over at the door leading to the steps and was tempted to beat her to the parking lot, but he knew that it wouldn't matter. There was no way she would believe anything he said at this point. He sulked back to his office.

"So, where shall we dine?"

"Huh?"

"Hello, dinner? Where do you want to eat? We were deciding when we were so rudely interrupted." CJ stood up and strolled over to him. She began playing with the knot of his tie. "Let's see if we can't straighten this a little. Now, that's better."

"Uh, thanks," he said, quickly moving from within her reach. He took his seat behind his desk and leaned back, groaning as he exhaled. His life was falling apart at the seams and there was nothing he could do about it.

"Maybe a massage would help. You seem a little stressed," CJ suggested. "I give a pretty mean one. Want me to demonstrate?"

"That's okay. I don't think that would be a good idea. I don't think our going to dinner would be a good idea either," Terrell told her.

"So, what do you think is a good idea, Mr. Sims?" she asked suggestively.

"I think my going home would be a good idea, Ms. Ware. That's a good idea."

"Does our sudden eagerness to run off have anything to do with that hussy rudely interrupting us? She's nothing but trouble anyway. She thinks she knows everything."

Terrell ignored her comments regarding Kayla and grabbed his jacket off the back of his chair. "No, that doesn't have anything to do with it at all. I just think that picking up some Mexican food and going home to rub my pregnant fiancée's feet is the best idea for me right now. I'll see you tomorrow, CJ." He left her sitting stunned in his office, closing the door behind him.

Chapter 20

Toby pushed the button on his answering machine. He kept his hand on the delete button, knowing that most of the messages weren't worth saving anyway. Just as he thought, they were mostly sales calls, but a few were requests for him to deejay at weddings or parties. He even had an offer from a woman who wanted him at her family reunion.

"Money is no object. Just let me know how much," she said into the machine. This one was definitely worth keeping. He skipped to the next message.

"Toby, it's me. I know you said that you needed time to deal with this, but I need you to at least call me and tell me you're dealing with it. I love you so much and I—" He hit delete at the sound of Roni's voice. She probably thought he would have called by now, but he hadn't, although he was tempted. It was especially hard late at night when he rolled over to pull her warm body close to his and it wasn't there beside him.

The day had been long, but enjoyable. Working with Jermaine had provided just the diversion he needed. Not only did he learn a lot about the business, but his friend kept him amused, all the while putting a few extra bucks in his pocket. Out of all the jobs they had done that week, working at Stanley's had been the most strenuous. Not because of the manual labor, but because of the mental capacity it took for Toby to do it. The entire time they were working, he continually had flashbacks of Roni in Sean's arms by the pool. He paused to look at pictures Stanley had throughout the house of family members, especially the ones containing Sean.

"I see you checking out the horrible family photos," Stanley commented.

"Yeah," Toby answered, embarrassed that he had been caught looking.

"My brother keeps telling me to take them down, but I won't. These pictures of us are my prized possessions. Besides, I may need them one day to blackmail him." Stan laughed.

"I swear I think I know him from somewhere," Toby lied. "Does he live here in town?"

"No, he moved to Atlanta after he finished school. He comes to town every now and then to visit and spend time with his on again/off again girlfriend."

"Oh yeah, the girl he was with the other day. So, she lives here and he comes to see her. Must be serious."

"With those two, you never can tell. Like I said, it's an on again/off again thing that's been going on for years. Well, I'm outta here. You guys are doing an awesome job and I really appreciate it."

"Thanks, Stan. You stay cool, man." Toby pounded his fist on Stan's and went back to work, still thinking about Sean, Roni and the insight that Stan had given him. It took some effort, but they completed the job and Jermaine told him he had mad respect for him.

It had been a while since he had worked out at the gym, but he was full of energy and it seemed like a good idea. Grabbing his duffle bag out of the closet, he changed into some sweats and set out to get his workout on. He noticed that the regular crowd was there in full effect as he walked to the locker room. Vinny, the manager, greeted him with a smile.

"Hey, Toby. Where you been? We missed you." The short, young guy gave him a handshake.

"What's up, Vinny? I know it's been a minute, huh?"

"Well, I know you got engaged and I figured that had something to do with it. Where is your beautiful wife-to-be, anyway?"

It was the first time anyone had asked him about Roni, and Toby felt a twinge of discomfort. He thought about telling Vinny that they had broken up, but technically that wasn't true because Roni still had his ring. He didn't ask for it back and she didn't offer to give it. They really hadn't said that the wedding was off; he just took his key back.

"She's not here. I'm rolling solo today, Vin," Toby told him.

"Well, tell her I said hello." Vinny smiled. "Good to see you, Toby."

Toby began stretching, trying to decide whether to start with free weights or the exercise machines. The machines were almost all taken by other fitness gurus, so he opted for the free weights. He lifted, bench pressed, pushed and pulled for an hour, until his black We Secure U T-shirt was soaked and clinging to his body.

He was tired, but somehow convinced himself that thirty minutes on the elliptical machine was the perfect finish for his workout. By now, people had gotten off from work and the gym was packed. Somehow, he located and empty machine and rushed over to it before someone else snagged it. He was so busy trying to find some Janet Jackson on his mp3 player that he didn't notice the woman smiling at him on the machine next to his.

"So, how long are you gonna ignore me, Toby?" she asked. He looked up and saw that it was Isis. Her arms and legs were moving rhythmically like she was cross-country skiing. She made the machine look like a breeze, which he knew it wasn't.

"What's going on, Ms. Adams? I see how you stay looking fine; you work at it."

"And I thought those rippling muscles you have came from spinning and mixing records. I see I was wrong."

"Since when did you start coming here? I've never seen you here before," he said, getting on and setting the timer.

"Hmph. I've been here every day almost since I joined a month ago. What does that tell you? I think someone has been slacking on their workouts." She grinned.

"Well, I have to admit it's been a minute since I've been in here. So, you joined the gym. Does that mean you'll be here for a while?" he asked, trying to convince himself that the only reason he asked was to make general conversation. But he knew he really wanted to know the answer. He didn't even bother putting his headphones on.

"For a while. How are things going with you?"

"All right, I guess. You going back to your old job?"

"No way. You know I hated it when I was working there. I'm not cut out for that kind of work. I was on my feet all day, every day, dealing with dumb customers that think they have ten dollars in their accounts so they can talk to me any kind of way. I don't think so. Besides, nothing good ever came to me at that job." She huffed as she talked, her arms and legs moving faster and faster.

"That's not true," he said, smiling at her. "What about me? I came to you there."

She shook her head, blushing, which surprised him.

He remembered the first time he saw her. He had just gotten his first check from the club, and he went into the bank. He wasn't really paying attention. He was busy two-waying this girl he had been trying to get with for a week, and she had finally agreed to go out with him. He moved up in line and walked to the window with no one standing in front of it.

"Excuse me, but I'm closed."

"Huh? Oh, my bad. I didn't even see the sign." He smiled.

"Well, it's right there in front. See." She pointed at the small sign that indeed read CLOSED, SEE NEXT AVAILABLE TELLER.

He looked around and saw that all of the other tellers had customers and by now, the line was longer than when he first walked through the door. There was no way he was going to stand in it again. "I'm saying, you can't just help me out? I just need to cash this check right quick. It won't even take that long. Come on. Please?"

"Sorry. I'm closed," she said icily. She looked down at his check. "Besides, you have to have an account here to cash a check from another institution. Do you even have an account?"

"No, but I'm saying, can't you just open one up for me real quick?" he asked.

"Like I said, I'm closed. See the manager." She said abruptly then turned and walked away. He was livid. He was about to call her out about her nasty attitude when he noticed the sign on a nearby door directing him to new accounts. He figured he would go ahead and open the new account since he was there. There was a small white man in the glass office, and Toby softly knocked on the door.

"Can I help you?" the man asked, looking up from the newspaper he was reading.

"Yes, sir. Are you the person I see about opening a new account?"

"Yes, I am. Come on in and we can take care of you." He welcomed Toby and told him to have a seat. Fifteen minutes later, Toby was the newest member of their financial institution, complete with checking and savings accounts and the Christmas club. "Welcome, Mr. Sims. If you step right over here, Ms. Adams will be happy to take care of your accounts for you."

Toby looked at the window where the sign still sat. "I think she's still closed."

"Closed? She shouldn't be. I can get her for you and she can get you squared away." He pushed a few buttons and walked through a large wooden door, coming out on the other side of the teller windows. "Here she is. Miss Adams, this is Mr. Sims, our newest customer. I'm putting him in your hands, and I've assured him that you'll take good care of him. Nice meeting you, Mr. Sims." He nodded to Toby.

"It's a pleasure doing business with you, sir," Toby told him. He smiled at Ms. Adams, who did not seem so pleased to see him. "I guess you're open now, Ms. Adams?"

"How can I help you?" she asked, her face and voice void of any emotion.

"I need to make a deposit into my checking and savings accounts, but I want to get two hundred back in cash." Toby signed the back of his check and passed it to her. His two-way began beeping, and he reached into his pocket and took it out. He quickly scanned the message and began typing a response. His date was acting like she was going to cancel on him, and he was pissed.

"I need a deposit slip and a photo ID." She sighed.

He looked at her like she was crazy. "I just opened my account. The branch manager just introduced me to you. You know who I am."

"Can I see a photo ID, please? *And* a deposit slip."

Toby reached into his back pocket and pulled out his new checkbook along with his wallet. He snatched out a deposit slip and flashed his driver's license in front of her. She peered closely at it and thanked him. He watched her as she quickly took care of his transaction, meticulously counting his money. Her nails were neatly groomed, and he could tell they were real, not those acrylic things women usually wore. His gaze drifted to her face. Her eyes were frowned with intensity, yet she was gently biting her bottom lip as she flipped through the bills. She paused and looked up at him.

"Damn, you're beautiful." The words slipped out of his mouth before he could stop them. She went back to counting and he smiled. *She's funny. A straight, first class—*

She interrupted him before he could complete the thought. "Here you are. Twenty, forty, sixty, eighty, one. Twenty, forty, sixty, eighty, two. Here's your receipt. Have a nice day," she said. He tried to search her face for any signs of kindness, but there were none.

"You too, Ms. Adams. See you next week," he made sure to tell her. He looked at her once more before turning to leave. Indeed, she was gorgeous, and for some reason, her stank attitude made her even more attractive to him.

For weeks, Toby continued coming in to the bank, refusing to go to anyone's window but hers. On the days he would walk in and see that she was working the drive-through, he would go back and get into his truck. He knew he irritated her, and it became a game to him.

Then one night, she strolled into Dominic's with her girlfriend. Terry, who happened to be in the booth with him, pointed the two women out as they sat at a table near the back of the club.

"Man, look at the two hotties over there. They are fine," Terrell announced. Toby looked over at them and shook his head.

"That's shorty from the bank, the mean one I pick with. She thinks she's all that."

"Which one? The redbone one or the other one in the skirt? She looks mixed. Is she mixed?" Terrell was stretching his neck to get a better view. "They both look good."

"The other one. And I don't know if she's mixed or not. I think she is," Toby told him. He often wondered that about her. She had thick, wavy hair and keen eyes along with her satin toffee skin, which led him to believe that she was not one hundred percent African American. Her looks were what he considered a combination of Janet Jackson and Amiel

Lareaux, with a touch of Kimora Lee. He said her name aloud to no one. "Ms. Adams."

"If it's the other one, then she is all that. And since you got dibs on her, I'm about to go holler at the redbone. I'll tell her you said hello," Terrell said as he headed down the steps.

"I ain't got dibs on nobody. I told you I just mess with her because she always has an attitude. And you'd better hope and pray that she doesn't cuss you out when you tell her you know me." Toby laughed. The crowd was kind of thin since it was a rainy Thursday in March, but he tried his best to entertain them. It took some coaxing, but soon a few people were actually on the dance floor, including Terry and the female who was with Ms. Adams. Noticing his prey standing at the bar alone, he popped in a slow mix CD and took it upon himself to join her.

"Slow Comfortable Screw, please," she told the bartender.

"Why, Ms. Adams, I would be honored, but don't you think we should go on a few dates first?" he asked her, grinning.

"Oh God. What are you doing here?" She rolled her eyes at him and asked, "Am I giving off a vibe attracting wannabe smooth operators or something?"

"Don't even try it. You know I work here. I've invited you several times and you read my paychecks every week when I bring them to the bank. It's okay to admit that you came to check me out."

She turned away from him, reaching for the drink the bartender handed to her. She was dressed somewhat conservatively in a simple black shirt and a denim skirt. It was fairly long, almost to her ankles, but there was a sexy split that reached all the way to her thigh, revealing just enough to make a man want to see more.

"Believe me, checking you out is the last thing I want to do. The only reason I'm here is because Meeko dragged me. She told me she heard this was the spot. And by the look of the crowd, obviously it's not. There's no one even here."

"Come on. It's cold and raining outside. Most people are at home hugged up in front of the fireplace with their boo, getting their groove on. Those people that have a boo, that is. The only people that come to the clubs on a night like this are those who are *looking* for a boo to get their groove on with."

"Well, that definitely isn't me," she told him.

Another woman who had been giving him the eye all night walked up and spoke to him. She introduced herself as Darla and offered to buy him a drink. He kindly declined, telling her he'd take a rain check, but to come by the booth and he would hook her up with a CD.

"See. On the prowl," he said. "What'd I tell you?"

"She's desperate."

"Now that's cold." He laughed. He leaned closer and asked her, "Why you always gotta look so mean?"

"How do you know how I always look?" she asked then swiveled back around to the bar. Damn, she looked good.

"I'm saying, though, it makes it difficult for a man to approach you. That evil look could easily intimidate a brother, discourage him from coming over here and talking to you."

"Good," she replied with attitude. "I don't wanna be bothered with a man without balls anyway."

Before he could respond, she grabbed her drink off the bar and walked away. Toby was right on her heels as she returned to her table.

"This is much nicer. Now we can have some privacy." He laughed, startling her as he sat down. "So, what's been going on?"

"Don't you have some records to spin or some shout-outs to make over the mike or something?"

"You know, this stuck-up attitude is getting real old, Ms. Adams. Here I am trying to be the nice guy that I am, and you still got this hardcore, queen bee, I-am-me-and-I-don't-need-you attitude, which, by the way, isn't cute."

"You can just leave me alone. I didn't ask for you to come over here, so you can go right back to being DJ Terror, hooking up with these *boo prowlers* out here buying you drinks and blowing up your two-way. And you're right; I don't need you!"

A big grin spread across his face and suddenly Toby was laughing. He couldn't believe that from the first day he walked into the bank, she had been playing him. It became so funny to him that he was crying. He saw that the corners of her mouth were actually starting to curl up, and although he could tell she was fighting it, soon she was laughing with him.

"Can someone tell me the joke?" a deep voice asked. They both looked up to see a man standing over them. He was average height and build, dressed in grey slacks and a conservative shirt. Toby wondered why he was interrupting them.

"Oh my goodness, Jeff! What are you doing here? When did you get in town? I thought you were gonna be gone another month. How'd you know I was here?" she asked all in one breath.

"I called Meeko's house after you weren't home, and her sister told me you all were coming here. I wanted to surprise you, which I see I did," he said, motioning toward Toby.

"Oh, Mr. Sims, this is Jeff, uh, my—"

"Fiancé." Jeff finished her sentence for her and reached out for Toby's hand. "How you doing Mr. . . . Sims, was it?"

"Toby, man, and I'm good." Toby stood up.

"Mr.—uh, Toby is one of my customers at the bank," she explained.

"Oh. Well, it's nice to meet you. Isis usually complains about her customers, so you must be one of the few she likes. I'm gonna grab a drink. You guys want anything?"

Isis. Her name is Isis. It's perfect for her.

"I'm fine," she told him quickly.

"Naw, I'm good," Toby said. "I gotta get back up in the booth anyway."

"I'll be right back," Jeff said and walked off, leaving Isis and Toby alone again.

"Why didn't you tell me you had a man?"

She shrugged and replied, "I didn't think it was any of your business."

"You're right; it's not. Well, you have fun and enjoy the rest of your evening," Toby told her, turning to leave.

"Toby, wait!" she said unexpectedly. He did an about face and she rose to her feet, her eyes meeting his. The chemistry between them was so strong that the hairs stood up on the back of his neck. Without warning, he reached out and touched her cheek. She closed her eyes then they quickly fluttered open and she took a step back, away from his reach. "I'm sorry."

"No need to apologize." He smiled at her. "I'll see you later."

For the rest of the night, he fought urges to look over in her direction, knowing she would be staring back at him. He let his music speak for both of them as he chose the last song of the evening. He began packing up as couples took advantage of their final opportunity to dance, including Isis and Jeff. It was the first time they had gotten on the dance floor. As the music played, his eyes drifted to them and he locked eyes with her.

Erykah Badu put his feelings into words as she sang about seeing him next lifetime. He wound up taking Darla up on her rain check that night.

Strangely enough, Toby and Isis continued the cat and mouse game when he came to the bank. He continued to go only to her teller window, and she continued to give him the cold shoulder. But now, there was a look in her eyes that told him that there was more to it than she was letting on.

After Meeko and Terrell started dating, he often asked about her. Meeko volunteered information on Jeffery, Isis's fiancé, telling him that they hadn't been together that long and that he was a merchant seaman, often out of town for months at a time.

"And when he is in town, he's such a cornball that she wishes he was gone. I don't know why she's marrying him," Meeko told him. "But that's my girl, and if she's happy, then I'm happy."

One evening while leaving the 7-Eleven, he noticed a woman parked to the side, struggling to change a flat tire. He pulled his truck over and hopped out, offering to help, then smiled when he recognized Isis.

"No, I got it," she said, not even looking up. He waited for a few minutes then watched as she threw the tire iron down in a fit of frustration.

"Let me help you out, Ms. Adams," he told her. She sucked her teeth when she saw that he had been standing there looking at her struggle.

"I should've known it was you. I don't think I have the right tire iron. I can't get my rim off."

He picked the iron off the ground and walked over to her Honda Accord. He placed the end on the edge of what she was calling a rim and popped it off, revealing what really were the lug nuts of the tire, "You don't have *rims*, boo. You have hubcaps."

Isis tossed her head back in a fit of laughter. "No wonder."

"Women. I swear . . . " He sighed and quickly changed the tire for her.

"Thanks, Mr. Sims. How much do I owe you?"

"Let's start with you calling me Toby. Then let me take you out to dinner tonight." He already knew from Meeko that Jeff was gone, and he had been waiting for the perfect opportunity to ask her out.

She began biting on her bottom lip, instantly turning him on without even knowing it. "I don't think that's a good idea. Besides, I already have plans for tonight."

"Come on, Isis. It's just dinner, nothing else. I wanna take you out, get to know you, and I know you want the same thing. Tonight is Tuesday, and I don't have to work."

"I told you I have plans."

"What plans? Who has plans on a Tuesday?"

"I do! Meeko and I are going to karaoke," she answered.

"Karaoke? You've gotta be kidding." From the look on her face, he knew she wasn't. "Fine, then Terry and I will go with you. Tell me where and what time."

"You and Terry are going with us to karaoke? I don't think so. You two don't know how to act and I am not gonna be embarrassed."

"I promise we won't embarrass you," he assured her.

She stared at him for a few moments then told him to meet her at Floyd's, a small bar downtown, at 7:30. He agreed. After pleading with his brother, who wasn't too keen on the idea of going to karaoke, they arrived to find the two women already seated inside.

Toby knew that after a few drinks, most people actually believed they could dance in the club, but this gave him the opportunity to see firsthand that alcohol had the same effect on their belief that they could sing too.

Surprisingly, they had a blast, laughing at most people and applauding others.

"What are you gonna sing tonight, Ice?" Meeko asked.

Isis gave her a look of horror. "Nothing! I'm not singing."

"That's right. I heard you can blow, Isis. What's up with that? You not gonna demonstrate your skills for us?" Terry asked.

"I didn't know you sang," Toby leaned and whispered into her ear. As he got closer, he could smell the scent of jasmine. He looked at her full lips and wondered what her mouth tasted like.

"I don't," she told him.

"She does so. Ask the emcee. She sings every week." Meeko nodded.

"Come on, sing for me," he told her. She cut her eyes at Meeko then said she'd be right back.

A few moments later, the emcee appeared on stage.

"Okay, we have a real treat for you, ladies and gentlemen. One of our regulars, Ms. Isis Adams."

The room fell silent and Isis stepped forward. She gave a perfect rendition of "Inseparable," and Toby knew at that moment that it would always be their song.

They began spending more time together, just talking and going on "unofficial dates," as he called them. There was no denying their attraction to each other, but he was enjoying living the single life and his newfound status of being the area's hottest deejay. There was also the small problem of her engagement, which caused him not to think about becoming involved with her, no matter how much he wanted to.

He often questioned her uncertainty about Jeff, but she said that it was time for her to be married. Toby became content with their friendship. There were times when the urge to pull her close and savor the feel of her soft lips on his was almost too much for him. He knew that she was just as much aware of how much he wanted her, but they never acted upon any of their desires, physical or emotional. Toby wondered if it was just as hard for her as it was for him.

Now here they were, nearly three years and several lifetimes later, talking and working out in the gym like no time had passed between them.

"So, what is it that you do now?" he asked.

"I work at a day spa called Tasteful Tranquilities. I'm a masseuse," she said proudly.

"Tasteful Tranquilities? Sounds like a cemetery. So, can a brother get more than a massage?"

"Shut up. It's a day spa, not a brothel. See, that's how men think."

"I'm saying. I figured I would ask, just in case."

"Just in case what?"

"Just in case I could get a hand job—I mean a manicure." He laughed.

She stopped the machine and got off, wiping her face with a towel. "You are so trifling. Good-bye."

"Wait a minute, Isis," he said, getting off the machine and walking beside her. "I was just playing. There you go being all sensitive and stuff. Hey, I'm about to leave. How about we go get a smoothie or something from the juice bar?"

"A smoothie?" She frowned.

"Hell, I don't know. Isn't that what people go get after they work out?"

"How about we just go outside and talk, Toby?" she said. "I'll meet you out front. Just give me enough time to jump in the shower and change."

He agreed and was waiting for her when she walked out of the locker room twenty minutes later.

"I thought we were gonna meet out front."

"I was talking to Vinny and decided to catch you in here instead. You ready?"

They each grabbed a bottle of water and walked outside the gym. Sure enough, there were small tables outside the juice bar in the same shopping center, and they took a seat there.

"You sure you don't want a smoothie?"

"I'm sure." She laughed. "This water is fine. So, tell me what's going on? Did you and your wife-to-be talk the other night?"

"Uh, I saw her, but we didn't talk," he admitted.

"Say no more. I don't even wanna know what you all did. Things will work out for you." Isis took the cap off her water and took a long swallow. Toby could see that her hair was still wet from the shower, her curls glistening from the dampness.

"I don't think so. She has some major issues that I'm not up to dealing with right about now."

"Toby, this is what marriage is all about, working through those issues. It's not a walk in the park."

"I don't expect it to be a walk in the park, but there are some things I expect from the woman I marry, and right now, Roni isn't willing to do those things." He was trying to go about this conversation without giving Isis details, but she wasn't making it easy for him. It wasn't that she was trying to get in his business intentionally; Isis would never do that. After all they had been through, he considered her a friend.

"I know you don't expect her to quit her job, cook, clean and stay home to take care of you. Please don't tell me that's what this is about."

"No, not at all. But I do expect her to be faithful!" There, he said it. He had admitted that his fiancée was cheating on him. And now that the words had come from his mouth, the numbness he had been feeling for the past few days instantly turned into pain. He needed to be alone to deal with it. He stood and told her, "I'll talk to you later."

"Wait a minute!" Isis jumped up. "I mean damn, I'm sorry, Toby. I just . . . I thought you guys were having problems over dumb stuff like wedding colors. I definitely wouldn't have pushed the issue if I would've known it was like that."

"It's all good. You were just trying to help and I appreciate that." Toby was grateful for her sincerity. He pulled her to him and hugged her tight. "Thanks. I'm out of here."

He was crossing the street into the parking lot when he heard her calling his name. He turned to see her jogging toward him, carrying his gym bag. "You might wanna take your funky clothes with you, Mr. Sims."

"Thank you, Ms. Adams. But I know if I left them with you, they would be in good hands."

"Yeah, right into the trash can over there." She grinned. "Just kidding. Here you go. And Toby, know that I'm here for you if you need me. Don't forget; Man's rejection is God's protection."

"Thanks."

"Everything happens for a reason."

"I know."

"If He brings you to it, He'll bring you through it."

"Yep."

"Weeping may endure for a night, but joy cometh in the morning."

"That's right."

"If you love someone, set them free."

"How many more of these do you have, Isis?"

"After all the heartache I've been through, I can quote 'em all, Toby." She sighed. "You sure you're gonna be okay? Because I have some more if you need them."

"No, you've given me enough for today."

"All right, then. Bye, Toby. Take care." They embraced once again and he opened the door of his truck, tossing the gym bag in the back seat. "Ice!"

"Yeah?"

"Same time tomorrow?" he said sheepishly.

"Wash those funky clothes before you put them on. I'll meet you on the treadmill."

Chapter 21

Nicole looked like she had swallowed a beach ball
other than that, you could hardly tell that she was si
months pregnant. Terrell couldn't believe that it was June
already. It had been a struggle, but for the past three
months, he had been the loving, faithful boyfriend that he
knew Nicole wanted and deserved. He no longer hung out in
the clubs or had females blowing up his cell phone. Outside
of the occasional conversation he had with Anjelica, there
weren't even any females that he talked with on a socia
level. And now it seemed that she was so caught up in
Jermaine, even that didn't happen all that often.

And then there was CJ. He had been avoiding her as
often as possible since that evening in his office when she
asked him to dinner and he declined. That was also the las
time he had talked to Kayla. She let him know in no
uncertain terms that she didn't have anything to say to him
outside of business, and he respected that. Their sudden
distance did draw some attention from people, though
including Nicole.

"Babe, why don't we invite Kayla and Geno over
tomorrow and cook out on the grill?" Nicole asked, climbing
beside him on the couch. This was one of the rare weekends
she had obliged him to stay at his place rather than him at
hers, and he was enjoying it.

"I thought we were gonna go pick the crib and stuff up
this weekend. I was gonna finish the nursery," he told her
She leaned back in his lap and he wrapped his arms around
her belly.

"You've been saying that every weekend since Easter
and it hasn't happened yet." She laughed. "Seriously, Kayla

hasn't hung out over here in a while and she really hasn't called. Is something going on between you?"

Terrell knew this conversation was coming, and he had thought long and hard about what he was going to tell Nicole when she brought up the subject. He was prepared to answer. "She thinks I have something to do with her sister hooking up with Jermaine. She's mad."

"Why would she be mad about that? And how did you hook her sister and Jermaine up? I thought Anjelica was bad news."

"I didn't have anything to do with that. That's the thing. Jermaine met Anjelica at the club one night."

"If they met at the club, I'm surprised you didn't have anything to do with it. Heck, I'm surprised you didn't try to hook up with her." Nicole laughed.

"Girl, please. I keep trying to tell you that I went to the club to hang out with Toby, that's all. I didn't go there to meet women. For what? I have the best woman in the world right here." He kissed her on the side of her neck and she giggled.

"Please, Terrell, save it. You are full of it. And I still don't understand how Kayla could be mad about something as simple as that. I'm going to call her and see what the real deal is. It probably has something to do with the job and that CJ woman."

"What?" Terrell sat up, nearly knocking Nicole off the sofa. "Oh sorry, boo. What are you talking about? What does this have to do with CJ?"

"She said that she couldn't stand CJ from the jump. Then you get the promotion as CJ's right hand man, then you don't have any time for Kayla anymore. I'm sure she feels frustrated, especially when you're her best friend."

"That's crazy. I have time for her."

"I just told you to invite them to a barbecue and you gave another excuse. That's okay. I'm going to invite her to my baby shower. I still love Kayla and have time for her."

"I had no doubt in my mind that she would be coming to your shower. And I still love Kayla too."

The phone rang, ending their debate over who loved Kayla more. Nicole reached over and grabbed the cordless. "Hello. Who's calling? One moment please."

"Who is it?" he asked, wondering if letting her answer his phone was a bad idea.

"Somebody named Meeko." She shrugged.

Terrell took the phone out of her hand. "Yeah," he said nonchalantly.

"Terry, It's me. I didn't think a female would be answering your phone. My bad," Meeko told him.

"It's all good. What's up?" He couldn't imagine what Meeko wanted with him, especially on a Friday night.

"I need to ask you a question, Terrell, and I need for you to be very honest with me," she told him.

"Okay, I'm listening."

"Did you know Jermaine got engaged?"

"Huh?" Terrell asked, confused by what she was saying and who she was saying it about.

"Jermaine. He got engaged."

He didn't know how to answer. There was no way that Jermaine could be engaged. Who would he even be engaged to?

"Wait a minute, Meeko. First of all, where is all of this coming from? How do you figure Jermaine's engaged?"

"Who is that?" Nicole asked. "And why is she calling you asking about Jermaine?"

"Shhhhh!" Terrell told her, covering the mouthpiece with his hand. He knew that if Meeko heard Nicole getting loud, she would get louder.

"You remember my cousin Leslie? Well, she works at Weinstein's," Meeko told him.

"How the hell did she get a job at Weinstein's?" Terrell asked, remembering Meeko's crazy cousin who got locked up for beating her husband in the head with a tire iron when she caught him in bed with another woman. "Does she get a discount?"

"Yeah, you know if you go in there she'll hook you up, Terry. But that's not what we're talking about right now. Wait a minute. Don't tell me you're about to get married too," she shrieked into the phone.

"Calm down, Meeko. Who told you Jermaine was engaged?" Terrell demanded.

"Oh, well Leslie said Jermaine and this girl came in the other tonight and they were trying on rings. He was asking her which one she liked. Well, when she got to work today, she saw a receipt for two thousand-something dollars with his name on it."

"Get the hell outta here! Yo, I'ma call you back," Terrell told her.

"Are you saying you didn't know anything about this, Terrell?" Meeko asked.

"I'm telling you I don't, but I'm about to find out," he answered. Nicole maneuvered herself off the sofa and he sat up. "I'll call you back later."

"Okay," he heard Meeko say before she hung up.

"What was that all about?" Nicole asked.

Terrell didn't answer. He was too busy dialing Jermaine's cell number.

"Thank you for calling We Secure U security installations service. Unfortunately, we are unable to take your call right now—"

Terrell hung up without leaving a message. He dialed Jermaine's home number and there was no answer there, either. *He's probably at Dominic's with Toby. I'll go up there and see what Meeko is talking about.*

"I'll be back," he told Nicole.

"Where are you going, Terrell? I know you're not going to the club, are you?"

"I'll only be gone an hour at the most, baby. I promise. I just need to talk to Jermaine and see what's going on, that's all," he assured her as he put his Timbs on. "It's not even that late."

"I don't care how late it is, Terrell. I'm saying, what difference does it make if Jermaine got engaged? What's wrong with that?" She stood at his bedroom door.

"It's who he may be engaged to that's the problem. He's barely even known this girl more than a month. I just need to go holler at him right quick. Go ahead and get in the bed. By the time you finish watching *Law and Order* I'll be right there beside you."

"Whatever," she said and disappeared in the room. He heard her fussing, but he left anyway. Just as he made it to the bottom of the steps, he heard the phone ringing. Thinking it could be Meeko or even someone worse, he ran back upstairs to answer it himself. He quickly unlocked the door and dove for the phone.

"Hello," he panted.

"Damn, T. What, you running a marathon or something?" Jermaine laughed. "Imagine that, your big behind running."

"Forget you, Negro. Yo, where you at?"

"At the crib, chilling."

"I need to talk to you. I'm 'bout to roll over there."

"Naw, son, don't do that. I got company."

"Who? Your fiancée that I heard you got now?" Terrell blurted out.

"What? You're tripping. I ain't saying she's all that."

"Oh, I ain't all that now? You weren't saying that a few minutes ago." Terrell recognized Anjelica's voice in the background. "Who are you talking to anyway?" he heard her ask.

"Terry. He was about to come over here, but I told him that was a bad idea."

"Your coming over here is definitely out of the question, Terrell," she yelled to him. "I'm going to see what I can find in this empty fridge to eat."

"For real, Terry. What's up? Something wrong?"

"Naw, I just heard that wedding bells were in your near future and I wanted to make sure you hadn't done anything dumb like asking her to marry you without telling us. That would be like thinking with your little head instead of the big one. Know what I mean?" Terrell chuckled.

"Maybe yours is small, but that ain't my business. But who told you some stuff like that?"

"I just heard you made a major jewelry purchase for her, man, and I was just checking, that's all," Terrell said, very much relieved.

"And if I did, why would I have to tell you? You think that because you hit that three or four months ago that you still got dibs on it? Be for real, man. I told you I'm feeling this girl. You said yourself that she's good people. But what she and I do within our relationship is between us. I don't care who she's been with in the past; I care about her being with me now. Believe that."

"I hear you," he replied.

"So you can call Meeko and tell her that ain't nobody engaged, because I know that's who told you about the whole thing. Her girl probably couldn't wait for us to leave out the damn jewelry store before she called and told her that I was in there looking at rings with some girl."

"Okay, you got me."

"Look what I found. Some Popsicles," Anjelica sang in the background. "Wanna lick?"

"Gotta go. Bye!" Jermaine told him. Terry thought he heard a click in the background before the sound of the dial tone filled his ear.

He got up and looked toward the bedroom door where Nicole was, but only heard the television. *She's probably already asleep.* He went into the living room and sat down, flipping through the channels. He tried to be content just being there, but temptation got the best of him. *I'll just run by the club for a minute.* He prayed Nicole didn't hear the door closing behind him as he sneaked out of the house.

The line to get into Dominic's was wrapped around the building. Terrell parked his car and walked past the anxious patrons, straight to the front door. He was greeted by the security guard, who let him in without even doing a search. He was making his way through the crowd to the deejay booth to see Toby when he heard his name being called. He turned to find Roni heading toward him.

"What's up, Ron?" He met her halfway. He hadn't really seen her in a while, and Toby told him they were taking a break. She still had the ring on her finger, though, and she still looked fine as hell.

"Nothing much. What's going on with you? How's Nicole?"

"She's good." He nodded.

"Getting big? You know if it's a boy or girl yet?"

"No, not yet. We're supposed to find out next week. But I ain't betting no money on it. Remember Kayla was supposedly having a boy when big-headed Day came popping out." He laughed. They walked over to the VIP section and the bouncer lifted the rope, allowing both of them access.

"So, who you here wit'?" he asked, thinking maybe Kayla or Yvonne was with her. Roni rarely frequented the club by herself.

"Rolling solo tonight, believe it or not."

"Wow. Where's your crew?" He held the chair out for her to sit down. He caught her looking over at the booth where Toby was mixing a slamming old school combination of Doug E Fresh and Dana Dane that had everyone who wasn't on the dance floor nodding their heads.

"They all have lives, I guess. Tia has Theo, Kay has Geno, Von has Darrell. I am the remaining member of the Lonely Hearts Club," she told him.

"Aw, come on. You're not lonely, Roni. You got Toby."

"No, I don't. I messed up, Terrell. And no matter what, I can't fix it. He won't talk to me. I've tried and tried for the past three months, but he still won't talk to me." Roni sighed.

She looked so sad and Terrell felt bad for her. Toby didn't give him the details of what went down, but he knew it had to be pretty big for his brother to act the way he had been acting lately. Toby always pulled himself into a shell when things got to him, shutting everyone out, and lately, he had been keeping to himself. Terrell couldn't remember the last time his brother had hung out and had fun. It was killing him not to ask what happened, but he didn't.

"I know, Roni. Just give him some more time. I'm sure he'll come around," he told her, though he knew that his brother could shut people out for months at a time. If it had been three months, Roni must've hurt him pretty badly. "Look at it this way; you still got the ring, right? That must mean something. Believe me, if he wasn't gonna come around, he would have asked for the ring back."

Roni looked down at the ring, which was on her right hand, and began twisting it. She looked up at Terrell and smiled. "I hope you're right, Terrell."

"He loves you. He just takes his time dealing with things. Uncle Jay calls him a thinker. He thinks things through before reacting to them." He bobbed his head to "Ownlee Eue" by Kwame. He glanced over to the dance floor wanting to be out there in the middle doing the Whop with everyone else.

"But how long does it take to think about things?" she asked.

"Did he ever tell you about the time I got a ticket and gave the cops his social security number?"

"You what?" She laughed.

"I told the policeman I was Tobias Sims and I got a ticket."

"Now that's just wrong, Terry."

"No, the wrong part was that I never paid the ticket and his license got suspended. I never told him about it."

"So, how did he find out?"

"He got pulled over on a traffic violation."

"No."

"And he was driving with a suspended license, so they arrested him and towed his truck," Terrell admitted.

"I betcha he whooped your ass when he got out!"

"Naw, but he was pissed, I'll tell you that much. He didn't speak to me for a year, not even when he came to my college graduation. Just gave me a hug and a card and then he left."

"So, when did he start speaking to you?"

"A year later. We had just gotten back on good terms right before that night when we all came to Dominic's for the first time. You remember that?"

"And Kayla and Janice were about to fight." Roni laughed. "Man that night was crazy. We had such a good time. I miss those days."

"Me too," he agreed. He thought about that night and all that happened after. "How is Kayla?"

"She's good. I guess she's a lot like your brother. They just need time to deal with things. I heard about what you and Anjelica did."

Terrell looked at her. "It's not what you think. It just happened. We did it and it was nothing, really."

"But why her, Terrell? Of all people."

"Kayla and Anjelica are alike in more ways than just looks. They are both loving, intelligent women with magnetic personalities. And they are both headstrong about making people believe what they want them to."

"So, are you saying that Anjelica is misunderstood because of Kayla?"

"Could be." He shrugged. "But let her know I asked about her and give Day a big kiss for me. I'm gonna go holler at Toby and then go home to curl up beside my baby."

"That is so sweet, Terrell. I'll deliver your message. Take care." Roni stood up and gave him a big hug.

He walked over to the booth and joined his brother, who was flipping through albums. He had the headphones wrapped around his neck and beads of sweat appeared on his forehead.

"What's up, Tobe? You a'ight?" he asked and gave him a grip.

"Yeah, man. This place is jumping tonight, huh?"

"You putting it down, man. That's for sure. You are in rare form tonight, kid. Does that have something to do with your girl being here?" He gestured over to Roni, who was still sitting in the VIP section, rocking to the music.

Toby looked over at her and shook his head at Terrell. "Nope, not at all." He pushed Terrell aside and put the headphones back over his ears.

"So, are you even gonna talk to her?" He tapped Toby on the shoulder. His brother paused long enough to look at him then went back to spinning music. Terrell took this as his cue to leave. "I'll check you out later."

Toby nodded. "I'll hit you up over the weekend, Terry."

"Cool," he replied. He waved at Roni, who was now holding a drink. He hoped that everything would be cool between them, because she was a good woman and he knew how much his brother loved her.

Terrell stopped at 7-Eleven on the way home and picked up a Slurpee for Nicole. He figured he was saving himself a trip because she was sure to send him out at 3:00 in the morning because she was craving one. He wasn't mad, though. He liked doing things for her and his unborn child, and he was looking forward to them being a family in the near future. In a few months, he would be a father, a dad, a pop. He didn't have a relationship with his father. He died when Terrell was only two years old and Toby was three. Now, he would have the chance to do all the things with his child that he and his dad never had the opportunity to experience, and he was excited.

Being extra quiet as he unlocked his door, he walked into his pitch black bedroom. He leaned across the bed, reached out for his sleeping girlfriend and whispered, "Baby, I brought you a Slurpee. Cherry, of course."

There was no answer and to his surprise, no sleeping Nicole. He checked the bathroom to see if she was there, but she wasn't. She wasn't anywhere in the apartment. He walked out to the parking lot to see if her car was there, but it was gone. He hadn't noticed it before when he first got home. He rushed back inside and dialed her home number, but she didn't answer. She didn't answer her cell number either. He called the hospital to make sure that she wasn't admitted, and was relieved when they told him she wasn't. He waited another thirty minutes before jumping in his car and searching for her. He drove around trying to think of places she could be, but eventually wound up back at home.

Something was wrong and he knew it. Nicole would never just leave without calling his cell and telling him something or at least leaving a note saying good-bye. He checked the caller ID to make sure that she hadn't called. The last call had come in at 11:34, while he was still at the club. The number belonged to an A. Moore, but he didn't recognize it. Not caring that it was after 1:00 in the morning, he called the number.

"Hi, this is Arianna. I'm sorry I can't take your call, but leave me a message and I'll call you back. If this is an emergency, feel free to call 911. Peace."

Arianna. What does she want and why is she calling my house? He leaned back on the couch and rubbed his tired eyes. He sat up quickly when he answered his own question. *She must've talked to Nicole.* He tried to convince himself that maybe Gary used Arianna's phone or something and he was panicking for no reason.

He tried calling Nicole once again and still got no answer. Hours later, he didn't even realize that he had fallen asleep until he woke up to the sun shining through his window. After still not being able to reach Nicole at home or on her cell, he called Arianna's number again.

"Hello," she answered. There was still a hint of sleep in her voice.

"Arianna, its Terrell. Have you talked to Nicole?"

"Huh?"

"Did you call here and talk to Nicole last night?" he questioned, trying not to sound frustrated.

"What time is it, Terrell?" she asked.

"Eight thirty," he answered, looking at the time on the cable box. He knew it was too early to be calling someone on a Saturday morning, but at that moment, it didn't matter. "I see on the caller ID that you called here last night. What did you want? How did you even get my number?"

"Nicole called here from that number and I called her back. Is that okay?" She whined. "Now, I need to call you back, Terrell. It's too early in the morning for this."

"I don't give a damn how early it is. I need to find my girl. When I left here last night, she was asleep. I come home an hour later and she's gone. She's not at home, not answering her cell, and you're the last number on the caller ID. Now, I need to know number one, was Nicole here when you called? Number two, if she was, did you talk to her? Three, do you know where the hell she is?"

"Look, Terrell, I don't have to deal with your attitude. I really don't have to deal with you, period. But out of the kindness of my heart, I will tell you that I talked to Nicole last night and you don't need to worry. She's fine."

"What the hell do you mean you don't have to deal with me? You call my house and talk to my girl and then she ups and leaves without saying anything to me? What did she say? Where is she?"

"I don't know where she is."

"You're lying. You know she's okay, but you don't know where she is? That's bullshit and you know it! What did you talk about? What did you say to her?"

"None of your business. I tried being nice and telling you that she's fine, but it didn't work, so now I'm hanging up. And don't call back," she said.

"I will come over there and—" The sound of the dial tone in his ear stopped Terrell from finishing his threat. He redialed the number, but the voicemail picked up immediately. There was no point in calling back because she had obviously turned her phone off. He had no idea where she lived. Deciding he couldn't just sit there, he grabbed his keys and hurried to his car.

Terrell hoped that by the time he made the fifteen-minute drive to Nicole's place, her car would be parked in front and she would be home. To his disappointment, neither of those things happened. He became desperate and went to the only other place he thought she could possibly be. He prayed all the way there, asking God to help him. *Lord, I need you to be there with me and help me remain calm as I do this. I know I haven't been the best brother on the earth, but I love her. Make her see that.*

He turned down the street and pulled in front of the house. His stomach was a bundle of nerves as he got out of the car and knocked on the door. He didn't know what he was going to say to her or what to anticipate.

"What the hell do you want?" Gary growled when he opened the door.

Terrell took a deep breath before answering. "I don't want no trouble, Gary. I just wanna talk to Nicole."

"And?"

"Don't play games with me. I just wanna talk to her."

"Nigga, ain't nobody playing. Obviously you did something wrong to think that she's over here! Where the hell is my sister? What did you do to her?" Gary stepped out the door toward Terrell.

Taking a step back in case Gary tried to swing on him, he replied, "When I came home last night she was gone. The last person she talked to was Arianna, so I figured she was over here, that's all. Now, is she here?"

"No, she ain't. Wait right here while I go call my girl and find out what the hell is going on." Gary turned and went back inside his house. Terrell looked around, peeking inside the storm door. He noticed that even though it was small, it was nice. There wasn't a lot of furniture, just a small grey sofa with a matching chair, a coffee table and a television. Everything was in its place. He didn't know why, but he expected Gary's place to be on the junky side.

A few moments later, Gary came back outside. "Well, looks like my sister finally came to her senses. Seems like your little secret has been found out and she's got firsthand knowledge that you are the loser I told her you were."

"Gary, you've got to believe that I never did anything to hurt Nicole. I swear. I love her. That was one of the reasons I did it!"

"You are crazy! You did something as trifling as that out of love? What the hell was that supposed to prove? How is that love? That's selfishness. And you never thought Nicole would find out about it, but she did and she's hurt. I don't blame her."

"I don't blame her either. And I'm sorry she had to find out about it the way that she did. I didn't want Arianna to be the one to tell her. I should have. And yes, I did it out of love—love for Nicole. There was no way that I could have a baby with that girl. I thought that I was doing the right thing by taking her to get rid of it. Especially since Nicole was carrying our child."

"What the hell are you talking about? Arianna ain't tell Nicole nothing. Nicole overheard you talking to your boy on the phone before you went to the club, and y'all was talking about some girl you boned three months ago. If that shit wasn't foul enough, now you standing here talking about some girl you took the clinic for a vacuum job? Nigga, you is foul!" Gary hollered.

Nicole must've been listening on the other end, Terrell thought. His heart began pounding in his chest as he realized what was about to happen. With a swiftness, Gary's right arm came out of nowhere and caught him in the face. In an attempt at self-defense, Terrell blocked his next shot and recovered with one of his own to Gary's abdomen. His opponent doubled over in pain but was determined not to be defeated. He raised himself up and charged at Terrell, knocking both of them to the ground. They rolled across the front of the lawn, ending up near the edge of the driveway. Neither of them noticed the green Toyota pulling up as they fought.

"Oh my God! What are you doing?"

"Stop it! Stop it!"

The two men continued to wrestle on the ground, ignoring the screams. Terrell had pinned Gary when he felt someone tackle him from behind. He fell to the side, landing next to Gary. He looked up just as Arianna pounced on him. It was then that he recognized Nicole's screams.

"Please, please, all of you! Stop it right now!" she cried as tears rolled down her face.

Terrell rolled over, pushing Arianna off of him and rushed over to her side. "Nicole, baby. It's okay."

He tried to grab her, but she pushed him away. "What are you doing here? What is your problem?"

"I came here to find you. When I came home last night, I was worried to death." His face was drenched with sweat and the taste of blood was in his mouth. He wiped it with the palm of his hand, checking to see if he was actually bleeding.

"Ari, are you okay?" Nicole walked over to the woman who was still sitting on the ground. Gary rolled over and crawled beside her as well, scowling at Terrell.

"I'm fine," she replied, checking her arms and legs for war wounds.

"I'm sorry," Terrell told them.

"You need to leave." Nicole shot him a look of hatred, which made him feel worse than he already did.

"I will, but I need to talk to you first," Terrell told her. She stood up and walked over to him, her round belly leading the way.

"There's nothing I have to say to you, especially right now. You know my brother is on probation, and you come over here and fight him in front of his house? Just leave right now, Terrell."

He reached for her once again, thinking that maybe if he could just touch her face and look into her eyes she would feel how much he loved and needed her. She stepped back from him and shook her head.

Gary jumped up and stood in front of his sister. "You'd better do what she says before I whoop your ass again!"

"You ain't whoop my ass the first time. Your girlfriend saved you," Terrell hissed. Gary charged at him again, but this time Terrell was ready for his attack. He stood firm and pushed him to the ground in one quick movement.

"What are you doing?" Nicole screamed at him. "Leave!"

A look of horror came over her face and she grabbed her stomach. Arianna rushed over, putting her arms around her. "Nicole!"

"Aaaaaaaaauuuuugh!" Nicole grimaced. Terrell caught her right before she collapsed.

"Call 911!" Arianna shouted to Gary. Before he even made it off the ground, Terrell had already lifted Nicole and was headed to his car. He hit the alarm and Arianna opened the door for him.

"Wha . . . shouldn't we . . . where . . . " Gary started mumbling.

"Shut the hell up and get in the car!" Terrell told him. He glanced over at Nicole, whose face was filled with pain, and told her, "Hold on, baby. I'm right here."

As he sped off to the hospital, he wasn't the only one praying this time.

Chapter 22

"So, did you talk to her?" Isis asked as they got to the stationary bikes in the center of the gym.

"Yeah, I did," Toby answered.

"Good. That's a start." She straddled the bike and set the timer. "Thirty minutes?"

"Forty-five," he told her, "and we didn't really talk that long."

"But you talked to her. That's all that matters. I mean, let you tell it, you were never talking to her again. That means you're healing."

"No, that means she cornered me at my truck as I was leaving the club." He began pedaling.

He and Isis had been working out every weekday for a while now, and he looked forward to the two hours he spent with her each day. It was therapeutic for him, and it was easy for him to open up to her. "But you're right; for some reason, I talked to her."

"Because you're no longer bitter toward her. I told you time heals all wounds." She smiled at him. He couldn't help laughing. Her 'Isisms,' as he called them, had become a part of their daily workout. Each day she had a quote, scripture or line from a movie that somehow suited whatever situation they were discussing.

"Okay, Ice, okay."

"What did you all talk about?"

"Like I said, nothing really. She asked me about Fourth of July and if I was having my annual backyard bash and I told her no." He shrugged.

"Why not? I heard that's become like a must attend event around here. People have already started looking for outfits," she told him. "What's wrong?"

"I'm just not in the partying mood, I guess. And I've only had two, so it can't be that big of an event."

"I heard the one last year didn't end until two days later."

"That's not true; it lasted two days," he corrected her.

"Well, what are you gonna do to celebrate the Fourth? It's next month, you know. And what are the masses gonna do without a DJ Terror backyard bash to celebrate?"

"That's not my problem," he said, panting. The bike was on uphill mode, and he adjusted his pace. "Like I told Roni, I'm not hosting it this year. She suggested we go away for the weekend."

"That's a nice idea. It would give you two the chance to spend some quality time together. You should go." Isis pedaled with ease. Toby looked over at her bike to see what setting she was on. He did a double take when he saw that she was also on uphill.

"I don't think so. I'm taking things nice and slow. I have to admit she looked good. I was glad to see that," he said.

"You guys will work things out. You just need time. I've been telling you that. I haven't been wrong yet, have I?"

"No, you haven't," he answered, "but I don't think we'll be getting back together. I don't trust her. Even after I got home last night, I was wondering if she went to see him after she left the club."

"I thought you said he lived out of town." She looked over at him.

"He does, but you know what I mean. I always wonder how many other times she lied about where she was and who she was with. It's gotten a lot better, because I was tripping after I first found out," he told her. "But you already know that."

Isis just laughed and continued pedaling. He knew she understood what he was talking about. Toby had been on an emotional roller coaster. Some days his mood was dark and depressing, and others he was full of rage. The only people in his life that he found it necessary to talk to were Isis and Jermaine, who he now worked with regularly.

Both of them seemed to understand what he was going through in their own way. Jermaine was always reminding him that he had his back with whatever he needed him to do, including using his business contacts to seek Sean out and beat him down. Isis was there for him every day to encourage him, and he found himself confiding in her more and more. That also added to the attraction he had for her. But when he mentioned it, she told him that what they both needed in their lives was a true friend, and that's what they would remain to each other, nothing more. He agreed and never brought it up again.

"Is she still wearing your ring?"

"Huh?" he asked, slowing his pace.

"You heard me. Is she still wearing your ring?"

"Yeah," he said slowly. It was a hearty laugh that escaped her this time, and he looked over at her like she was crazy. "What?"

"You'll get back together."

"Why?"

"She's still wearing the ring. Let me ask you this: have you ever asked for it back?"

"No. I wouldn't ever do that. I bought that for her. She can keep it. I know most guys would've took it off her finger the day they walked up on her and another dude, but it was a gift, and that would just be petty. You know what I mean?"

"No, but I can tell you what I think. I think that you're hurt and mad, but you're still in love with her. And she's still in love with you, because she is still faithfully wearing that ring and reaching out for you. It's only been three months. I say that by the end of July, you all will be back on the road to romance."

"Why are you pushing this, Isis? I mean, you push this harder than Roni does. Is she putting you up to this?" He reached for his towel lying across the front of the bike and wiped his face.

"I'm trying to stop you from making the mistake of throwing away happiness, that's all. You deserve to be happy."

"What about you?" He frowned.

Her legs worked faster and faster on the pedals. Her sports bra was wet with perspiration, drops of it running down her back into the basketball shorts she was wearing. He could see the muscles in her calves as he admired her smooth, shapely legs. He knew she was ignoring him because she refused to look at him.

"Don't ignore me. What about you, Isis?"

Her legs stopped and the bike slowed down. She hopped off the seat and snatched her towel off the back of the bike. Toby knew he had struck a nerve with her, but he was tired of being the only one sharing his issues and Isis keeping all of hers inside. He stopped his bike and stood up as well. He touched her arm, forcing her to look at him.

"What about me?" she asked, placing the towel around her neck.

"Don't you deserve to be happy? What about your true love?" He stared at her. He could see the rising of her chest as she inhaled and wondered if it was from the workout or anger at his question. "What about you?"

"I lost my chance at happiness that night, remember? I don't deserve true love," she answered. He was speechless as she turned and walked away from him, leaving him standing alone.

A chill went down his spine as he thought about the night she was speaking of. It was a night that played in his head a million times, like a dream etched into his memory. For him, it was one of the greatest moments of his life, but he knew that for her, it only reminded her of the worst moment of hers.

That night, both couples decided to hang out together, Meeko and Terry along with Isis and Toby. They went to check out Rickey Smiley at the comedy club then went down to the waterfront to have dinner. They had a ball, and were finishing up dessert when Terry suggested they walk along the pier.

They all looked at Isis, who knew she was outnumbered. She shrugged her shoulders and sighed. "I don't care."

The tab was paid and the two couples exited through the back door of the restaurant, leading directly to the pier. It was a nice fall night, with just a hint of a breeze. Terry and Meeko walked ahead of them, hand in hand. Toby strolled beside Isis, close enough to notice the small chill bumps that were beginning to form on her arms and shoulders.

"You cold?" he asked, taking off his blazer and wrapping it around her.

"Not really." She smiled and thanked him. "It actually feels nice."

"Then what's up with the goose bumps?"

"I don't know."

"Don't worry. I have that effect on women sometimes." He smiled.

"Don't flatter yourself." Isis rolled her eyes at him.

He couldn't resist stepping behind her and putting his arms around her waist. She squealed and tried to get away from his grasp.

"What are you doing?" she shrieked, turning toward him.

He looked down into her big brown eyes and got lost in them for a moment. She looked so funny standing with her hands on her hips and her head cocked to one side, waiting for his answer.

"What? I was trying to keep you warm, that's all. I'm not trying to attack you. You got people looking at us about to call 911." He gestured toward an older couple who was staring at them, cell phone in hand.

"Oh, sorry. I'm fine." Isis waved at them. They nodded and turned away.

"See, that's how innocent black men get locked up," Toby told her, sitting on a nearby bench.

She paused, looking ahead and asked, "Where did Meeko and Terry sneak off to?"

"Do you really want me to answer that question?"

"I guess it was kind of dumb of me to ask." She took a seat beside him. Her pager began beeping and she looked at it.

"You need to use my cell phone?"

"No, I know who it is. It can wait." She sighed, placing it back in her purse.

He noticed her sudden somberness in attitude and asked her what was wrong. She shook her head and looked out into the darkness. He could hear the sounds of the waves breaking against the nearby shore and embraced the silence between Isis and himself. After a few quiet moments, he finally spoke.

"So, what's the deal between us, Isis? I mean really."

"What are you talking about, Toby? There is no deal. Has it totally slipped your mind that I'm engaged to be married in a few months?"

"I know that's what you and everyone else keeps telling me, but I've never seen you wearing your ring, and you really don't act like you're excited about your upcoming nuptials. I'm beginning to wonder if you're even in love."

From the way she reacted, he knew he struck a nerve. "First of all, you don't know me, so how would you know how I act? I don't have to explain to you why I don't wear my ring and I . . . I . . . " She stopped mid-sentence.

Toby rubbed her back as he noticed the tears falling from her eyes. "It's okay, Isis. It's going to be all right. You can talk to me."

"I don't know what's wrong with me. Jeff is a good man, he has a good job, and he cares enough to wanna marry me. He doesn't hang out at the club; I don't have to worry about him beating on me. Why shouldn't I marry him? He's a good man."

"But you're not in love with him. What about love, Isis?"

"What about it? My father loved my mother, but when he found out she was pregnant, he left her high and dry because she was black and he was Japanese, and the reality of bringing her and a half-black child home was enough to make him forget all about her," she said in one breath. "So what makes me so much better than her? Jeff is a good man. We've been together for five years. When my mother died and I had nothing or no one, he was there. I had no family. My mother's people acted like I was a throwaway doll, and my father's family didn't even know that I existed. But Jeff was there for me. The fact that I'm biracial never mattered to him."

"You're crazy. I can't believe that someone as beautiful and intelligent as you has such low self-esteem that you think you have to marry the first man that asks you. You're making a mistake, Isis." He turned to face her. "The world is full of good men that don't give a damn if you're polka dotted. I'm a good man, Isis. At least you can say that you're in love with me. I understand that he was there for you, but you're with him out of obligation, not love. I love you."

He watched her shoulders slump in frustration, and he held her in his arms as she wept. There was no denying that she was caught between a rock and a hard place, and he wasn't making it any easier for her, but he was tired of denying his feelings—feelings that he had never held for anyone else. He was just as much in love with her as she was with him. He knew that.

"What do you want from me, Toby? You want me to just tell him that it's over? After all we've been through and all that he's done, you want me to just throw all of that away? That's not even fair to him."

"I know. But it's not fair to you to marry a man you know you don't love. Is that how you want to spend the rest of your life?"

Isis looked into his face then kissed him tenderly on the mouth. It was what he had been waiting for the entire night. Her lips felt so soft and warm on his, and her taste was all that he imagined it would be.

She finally pulled away from him and said, "I can't risk throwing away a sure thing for a *what if*, Toby."

"Hey, you guys ready to roll?" Terrell called from the darkness. Soon, he and Meeko strolled into the light, walking hand in hand, looking very much like the happy couple they were.

"Yeah." Isis stood. They walked back to Terrell's car in silence, which continued until they pulled in front of Toby's condominium.

"I'll check you guys later," Toby said, climbing out of the back seat. He had made it to the front door when he heard someone behind him. He quickly spun around, ready to swing on the prowler he thought was there. Instead of a robber, he found Isis holding the suit jacket he had loaned her. "Oh, thanks. You could've left it with Terry and I would've gotten it later."

"No, I wanted to talk to you anyway, Toby. I don't like the way things ended between us. Terry and Meeko said they'd wait for me."

"Yeah, we can talk. Come on in." He opened the door and led her inside.

Isis blew out a long whistle as she looked around his den. "Oh my God. How many of these do you have?"

She was speaking of the walls of CDs he had in the room. There were hundreds of them that he had collected over the years. He smiled. "I don't know. I think I stopped counting at four hundred thirty-three. Anything in particular you wanna hear?"

"No. Besides, I should really be going." She sighed.

"You don't have to leave. I can take you home. I don't mind."

"No. I should be going, really."

"Have a seat," he said and picked up the phone. "Yo, Terry. Y'all go ahead and roll. Isis is gonna chill for a while and I'll take her home. What? Meeko, don't go there. What? Okay, okay, hold on."

He passed the phone to Isis. "Yeah. Yeah. Uh-huh. I know. It's cool. I will. Girl, please. I don't think so. Definitely not. Okay, I'll call you when I get in. Bye."

"Did you convince your girl that you were safe?" he asked, taking the phone from her.

"Don't get mad because your reputation precedes you, Toby. She just wanted to make sure that you hadn't put nothing in my drink to make me stay." She sat back on the soft cushions of his sofa.

"Would you like something to drink?" he asked.

"No, I'm good. I thought you were gonna play me some music."

"I got you. Let's see . . . " He tried to think of what she would like. He walked over and kneeled toward the bottom case, finding what he was looking for. He placed the CD in the stereo and hit play. She tossed her head back in laughter when UTFO began singing. They talked and laughed about old times, and she even relaxed enough to dance a little bit.

"Hold up, hold up. I got something for you."

"Is it Klyymaxx? You know those were my girls." She nodded and then sang, "Don't you know the men all pause when I walk into the room?"

"No, it's not Klyymaxx. You probably only liked them because they had the Japanese-looking chick!"

"You are such a bum!" Isis reached out and punched him in the arm. "You know they could throw down."

"Check it out. What about this one?" he asked her.

Music played through the speakers and she closed her eyes, rocking. She started singing, and then he was right behind her. His arms came around her body and they started dancing, his front to her back. He sang into her ear and she leaned her head against his shoulder. She smelled so inviting, as if she had just stepped out of the shower. The feel of having her in his arms made him smile. There was no doubt this was indeed love.

The song faded and another one of his favorites, "Fairy Tale Lover" came on. This time, as he sang, she turned to face him. He brushed her thick, long hair from her shoulders and noticed a small mark on her collarbone. He rubbed his fingers across it.

"A mole," she told him.

"No, a beauty mark," he corrected her, then leaned down and licked it. He could feel her tense up in his arms, so he stopped.

They continued to dance, Toby holding her close in his arms. They made their way to the sofa, where she sat down and he kneeled before her.

"Toby, this is crazy," she whispered and shook her head at him. Her face was illuminated by the glow of the light coming from the small lamp in the corner of the room.

"The only thing crazy is the way I feel about you," he told her. "Now, just chill and relax."

As if on cue, "Let's Chill" by Guy began to play, and they began laughing. Unable to control his desire to have her mouth on his again, he kissed her with a passion. He felt her hands reaching under his shirt, and helped her by pulling it over his head. He began unbuttoning the dress she was wearing, slowly revealing the black lace bra she wore underneath.

"This is crazy. This isn't supposed to be happening. I'm engaged," she told him.

He looked deep into her eyes and told her, "But you're in love with me. You can't marry him."

"If I do this, something bad is going to happen. I know it is," she said, removing his belt and licking his earlobe.

"No, it won't. I promise. I am just as much a good man as he is. And you know that. Let me show you," he told her, pulling her onto the floor with him.

By the time Isis was naked, Toby was performing a full pelvic examination with his tongue. She called out his name over and over, making him want to fulfill her every desire. He raised himself over her and felt her fingers around his swollen hardness.

"No way! There's no way you're putting that big thing in me." She tried to sit up.

"Don't even try it. It's not even that big." He couldn't help grinning at her.

"Maybe if you plan on being a porn star."

"Just relax and let me take care of everything, Isis."

She leaned up once again and asked him about protection. He reached over into his pants pocket and pulled out a condom.

"Do you do this very often? Because you certainly are prepared." She giggled.

He could feel her legs shaking under him and he kissed her again, telling her to relax, everything would be okay. He began to slowly make love to her, wanting it to last forever. He wanted her to feel how much he wanted her and wanted to be with her. And as he felt her legs around him and looked into her face, she called out to him, letting him know that she felt the same way. It was as if they were meant for each other, and after it was over, they lay on the floor, holding each other tight. She lay against his chest, and he kissed the top of her head.

Their perfect moment was interrupted by a knock at the door.

"Who the hell—?" he asked, reaching for his pants. Isis scrambled for her clothes, and he showed her to the bathroom. He rushed back to the door, peeping to see who it was. Meeko stood shivering on his doorstep.

"What's wrong? Where's Terrell?" he asked when he opened the door.

"Where's Isis? I need to talk to her," she blurted out. "I've been paging her, but she hasn't called me back. Where is she?"

"She's in the bathroom. She'll be out in a minute. Where's my brother? Did something happen?"

"He's at home. He doesn't even know I'm here. I came right over here to get Isis."

"I'm here, Meeko. What's wrong?" Isis came out of the bathroom looking like the last hour with Toby had never even happened.

"We've gotta go. You gotta get home!" Meeko began pulling at her arm.

"Meeko, you're scaring me. I'm not going anywhere until you tell me what the hell is going on," Isis insisted.

Toby stood waiting for Meeko to answer her friend.

"Isis, there's been an accident. Jeff and some guys were on the road headed back when an eighteen wheeler came into their lane."

"Jeff isn't supposed to come home until next month." Isis shook her head as if she didn't want to believe what Meeko was saying.

"His mom said he wanted to surprise you, so he told you it was next month," Meeko explained, tears streaming. Toby could see in her face that this was not going to be good news, and that she had even more to tell.

"Well, where were they? I have to get to him. Where's Jeff?"

"Isis, he died about an hour ago on the operating table. I'm so sorry," Meeko whispered.

Isis stood in shock. Toby reached out for her, but she snatched away.

She looked at him and told him, "I told you something bad was going to happen. I killed him. This is all my fault!"

Isis left his house that night with Meeko, and it was the last time Toby had seen her until the night he proposed to Roni. He knew that she blamed herself for Jeff's death, and Meeko told them that she left to deal with her grief. Toby dealt with his own grief for several months, then he found himself back in the swing of things, being the player he was before Isis Adams had even entered his life.

Chapter 23

"How is she?" Terrell asked as Dr. Fisher came out into the waiting room. They had been waiting over an hour for someone to come and tell them something.

"Is she gonna be a'ight?" Gary brushed past Terrell and asked.

"And who might you be?" Dr. Fisher questioned.

"This is Nicole's brother, Gary, and his girlfriend, Arianna." Terrell introduced them out of respect for Dr. Fisher.

"Yes, Nicole has told me about you. Well, we were able to stop the contractions, so that's a good thing. But we are going to monitor her for the next day or so. After that, if all goes well, she'll be released, but she is to remain on bed rest for the remainder of her pregnancy. That means the only reason she is to get out of bed is to go to the bathroom, nothing more."

"I understand, Dr. Fisher. Can we see her?" Terrell asked.

"Right now, she's resting. Give her a little while. Her blood pressure was extremely high, and our goal is to keep her as peaceful as possible. Stress is what caused her to go into premature labor, and we don't want that happening again," the doctor warned.

"You don't have to worry about *nobody* stressing her out, Doc. I'ma see to that." Gary glared at Terrell.

"You don't have to see to nothing. I can take care of Nicole."

"You ain't taking care of shit! My sister don't wanna have nothing to do with your trifling ass! You'd better stay—"

"Gentlemen, gentlemen, gentlemen! This is a hospital. Now is not the time or place for this. I just told you how sensitive this situation is." Dr Fisher's voice boomed.

Terrell was immediately embarrassed. Usually he was the voice of reason in a time like this, and here he was being one of the causes.

"I apologize, Dr. Fisher," he quickly told him.

"You can come back when you've calmed down, but for now, you both need to leave." Dr. Fisher turned and left them.

Arianna, who had been quiet this entire time, finally spoke. "You two are so stupid! I am so embarrassed. Both of you are acting like children. Now, listen. This is how this is gonna go down. I'm staying here until Nicole wakes up. Terrell, you need to take Gary to get my car from his house. When you get back, if Nicole wants to see you, then fine. If not, then you'll have to deal with it."

Gary began to smile at him surreptitiously. "Don't worry. She won't wanna see you."

"Shut up, Gary, because you aren't gonna make matters worse by telling Nicole anything either. Neither am I. What goes on in that clinic is nobody's business but the people involved, and that doesn't include you, me, or Nicole. So get over that too, Gary, and I mean it. If I find out Nicole knows anything and Terrell didn't tell it, you're gonna regret it."

Terrell was amazed at the spunk and attitude that was coming out of this white girl. She always seemed so timid to him, but he now knew that was merely his perception of her. He should have figured out that she had to have some sort of backbone to deal with Gary's simple behind, though. He now had a newfound respect for her, and he could see that she was demanding all of this because she had Nicole's best interests at heart.

The two men agreed and somehow made it back to Gary's house without killing each other. As his future brother-in-law got out, Terrell looked at his face, still swollen from their early morning rumble. He could see that he was worried.

"Gary."

"What?" Gary turned around and frowned.

"Nicole and the baby are gonna be fine. I know they are."

"Yeah," was all that he mumbled, looking down.

"You also have to believe me when I say that I love your sister. I swear I ain't gonna do nothing to hurt her."

Gary looked at him and replied, "Terrell, you'd damn well better show me better than you tell me."

Terrell nodded and pulled off. He went home, took a quick shower and raced back to the hospital. He stopped at the gift shop and picked up some flowers, a card and a big teddy bear wearing a yellow ribbon. Gary was in the waiting room when he got there.

"Any word yet?" Terrell asked him, setting all the gifts in the middle of the table.

"Ari is back there with her now. She should be out here in a minute," he replied.

Terrell took a seat and picked up a magazine from the table. There was a cute little girl on the cover, smiling with only two teeth at the bottom of her mouth. She was the cutest thing, and he wondered if he had a daughter, what she would look like. He sat back and closed his eyes.

"What's up? How is she?" he heard Gary ask. He looked around, realizing he had fallen asleep.

"She's good. She not too thrilled about being on bed rest, but she understands what has to be done," Arianna told them.

"I'm going back to see her." Terrell stood up.

"Hold on, Terrell. She's not ready to see you right now. I told her you were out here, but she doesn't care. I'm sorry, but you can't go back."

"What about when she comes home? Who's gonna take care of her? She's gonna need help," he told her.

"Don't worry about her. I'm quite capable of taking care of my sister. She'll be in good hands," Gary said.

"No way. You don't—"

"I'm gonna stay with Nicole while she's home, Terrell. I don't work at the clinic anymore, and it won't be a problem. I've already talked with Nicole about it. Don't worry. I'll keep you updated on her progress daily, and I promise if anything happens, you'll be the first person I'll call," Arianna told him. She must've noticed the distress in his face because she added, "Just give her a little time. I'm sure that she'll be calling you soon. I know she loves you, but her hormones are a little out of whack, and there's no reasoning with her right now. I'll give her the stuff you bought and tell her you're waiting for her call."

Terrell reluctantly took the items off the table and passed them to her. Gary was even giving him a look of sympathy. There was nothing left for him to do or say. He slowly turned and left.

He sat behind the wheel of his car in the parking lot, not knowing where to go or what to do. For the first time in his life, he felt alone. He cursed himself for letting his ego and sexual desires get the best of him. Trying to be a player had cost him his best friend and now his girlfriend, and now the one who always had the answers for everyone else didn't have any words of wisdom for himself.

Terrell threw himself into his work. He went in early and stayed late working on special projects and developing new procedures for the company. He became a mover and a shaker, causing management to take notice of his skills and abilities. He was offered positions on executive committees and staff councils by managers and department heads left and right. At work, he was the man.

His home life was a different story. He didn't hang out anymore. His social life consisted of calling Arianna and checking on Nicole. Once a week, he would go to the grocery store and buy everything he thought she would need make her stay in bed more comfortable. He bought her DVDs, novels, puzzle books, and he even bought her a laptop and computer games. He purchased things for the baby in her favorite color, yellow. She still hadn't told him whether it was a girl or boy, and he didn't know if she knew or not, because he hadn't talked to her. When he questioned Arianna about the baby's sex, she would say she didn't know.

He was still determined to be faithful to her and a good father to his child, no matter what it took. Working with CJ made it a challenge for him. She was constantly in his office, leaning on his desk, propositioning him every chance she got. He was going over some notes one afternoon when she walked in without knocking.

"What are you doing, sweetheart? Working on something new to wow the powers that be?" She walked around his desk, looking at his computer.

He frowned at her, wondering what she was up to. "What can I do for you, CJ?"

"I tried calling you, but your voicemail kept picking up, so I came to see what you were doing." Her eyes scanned the computer screen. He was tempted to turn it off while she was standing there being nosy, but didn't.

"Just going over some notes, that's all. I must've forgotten to turn my voicemail off when we got back from the meeting earlier, that's all. You act like I'm in here sending out company secrets or something."

"You never can tell these days, and the way you've been moving up the corporate ladder, I'm trying to learn some secrets from you." She turned and looked out his window, which gave a full view of the parking lot. "So, do you have big plans for next weekend? I heard your brother has a huge party that is off the chain. Think I can tag along?"

"He's not having one this year, so no, I'm not doing anything special."

"We could always have our own private party. You could come over and I could throw some steaks on the grill, open a bottle of Dom P." She winked at him.

"I don't think so. I have to finish decorating my baby's room, which I've been putting off for a while."

"How is your girlfriend? I saw an invitation to her baby shower on Kayla's desk."

He didn't even know when her shower was. No one had even mentioned it to him—not even Kayla. Even though they weren't speaking beyond a polite hello when they passed in the hallway, he knew that she was aware of his and Nicole's situation.

"She's fine. Doing great. We're excited about the baby." He nodded.

"Speaking of Kayla, looks like she's got some excitement of her own in the parking lot." CJ laughed.

Terrell got up to see what she was talking about. He looked out the window to see Kayla screaming angrily at Craig, who was standing nearby. He hurried out of his office and down the staircase, praying he got there before anyone else saw them.

"Yo, what's going on peeps?" he called to them as he rushed out the door.

"Get the hell away from me, Craig. If you don't, I'm calling the police to come and haul your ass away from here, and you know your dope dealing behind is already skating on thin ice!" Kayla yelled.

"Call them. I don't give a damn! I don't understand why you're tripping. All I want to do is spend time with my daughter. Is that too much to ask?"

"Nope, it sure isn't. You can come by the house and see her whenever you want to. I told you that."

"See how unreasonable she's being, Terrell? I'm paying daycare and taking damn good care of my daughter, but I can only see her at the house."

Terrell looked over at Kayla, who was daring him to say something. He decided to take the neutral approach. "Where is it that you want to take Day, Craig? I mean, why can't you see her at the house?"

"Man, next weekend is my family reunion. I want her to meet my people, which is her people, since she is my child."

"She's not even a year old! How the hell is she gonna meet somebody, Craig? No, I'm not letting my child go with you, and that's the end of that. Now, leave!"

Terrell still didn't understand what was going on, so he quietly asked, "Kayla, why can't she go? It's only his family reunion."

Kayla looked at him like he was speaking some language she didn't understand. "How about because his *wife* is a fucking retard? Do you know how often she calls my house at two and three o'clock in the morning talking about how she hates me, and her son will always be the king of the family? Do you know how many messages she leaves talking about how I got her fired from her job and had food taken from her son's mouth? How about how she called and asked me why I didn't let Day call her son and wish him a happy birthday or send him a card? Day can't talk! And you know what? I really don't care about her son's birthday!"

Terrell pulled Kayla away from Craig and told her, "You're wrong, Kayla."

"What?"

"You're wrong. I love you and you're my dog, but you're wrong. Despite what went down between you and Avis, and no matter how stupid and psycho she may be, that boy is still Day's brother."

"Half-brother," she corrected him.

"Whatever. They still come from the same father. You should let her go and be with her people some time. Craig takes care of her. He should be allowed time to spend with her."

"Whose side are you on, Terrell? Mine or Craig's?" she snapped.

"Day's," he told her. "I take it you don't want to go to the reunion?"

"Hell no! Avis' fat ghetto behind will be there!"

"Okay, okay. Are you still cool with his parents?"

"I don't have a problem with them. It's her psycho self."

"I don't have nothing to do with her. All I do is take care of my son the same way I take care of my daughter. I don't hear you complaining about that."

"Do I need to call security?" They turned around to see CJ standing in the doorway.

"Does it look like we need security?" Kayla snapped.

"Well, being that this is a place of business and not the parking lot of the projects . . . " CJ began.

"No, we don't need security, CJ. We're just out here talking. You can go back inside," Terrell told her. She hesitated, kissed her teeth then went back inside.

"She makes me sick. Who does she think she's talking to? Old Amazonian-looking hussy."

"Let it go, Kayla." Terrell thought for a minute and then yelled, "Craig!"

"Yeah?"

"Kayla's gonna let Day come to the family reunion," Terrell informed him.

"Word?" Craig looked at Kayla to see if she was in agreement, which she obviously was not.

She started to object, but Terrell stopped her.

"But she's gonna be with your parents. And you'd better keep your ignorant wife—"

"Ex-wife," Craig corrected.

"You ain't filed no divorce papers, so she's still your wife. I don't care what you wanna call her, but you'd better keep her away from my goddaughter. If I hear about her even breathing on her, I'm coming after you. And I mean that. We may be cool and all, but I don't play when it comes to Day."

"That's my daughter, Terrell, man. I'ma make sure don't nothing happen to her. Is it all right if I come by later and see her, Kayla?" Craig asked.

"I don't care, Craig."

"Thanks, Terrell. I 'preciate it, man." He shook Terrell's hand and went to hug Kayla, but she rolled her eyes at him. "I'll call before I come."

"Whatever," she said, and watched as he got into his black Honda and drove off. "I guess I should thank you for coming out here and mediating?"

"You don't owe me an apology. I was just trying to stop things from getting out of hand, that's all. It's all good." He turned and walked toward the building.

"Terrell, wait a minute. I'm sorry. Look, thanks anyway. I'm glad you came out here when you did. You know how emotional I can get." She smiled and gave him a hug.

"Naw, for real? Not you, Kayla Hopkins."

"Shut up. I haven't forgotten that I'm not talking to you. Don't push it."

"A'ight, a'ight. But seriously, Kayla, you've got to start thinking about things. You're blessed enough to have a man that takes responsibility for his child. You know how many women out here would kill for a guy to *want* to take their child to a family reunion? That's a good thing."

"I know, Terrell, but I still don't feel comfortable with my child being around Avis," she told him.

"That girl may act crazy, but she's not stupid. She knows that she'd better not lay a finger on that baby to harm her, and she won't. She'll have to answer to you, Craig, me, *and* Geno!" He laughed.

"You're right about that," she told him. "I know I should have told you this a while ago, but I am really proud of the way you're doing things around here. You are really making a change and handling your business in the office."

"Thanks, Kayla. Coming from you, that means a lot. I know how you hate to give compliments."

"Yeah, I really had to struggle to get that one out."

"So, Nicole is having a baby shower? Can you tell me when?"

"The fifth of July, that Saturday. I heard what went on between you two, and I'm sorry. But what you're doing is a good thing, and it doesn't go unnoticed."

"She still ain't talking to a brother, though. Think you can sneak me in to see her?"

"Past Arianna the warden? That's gonna be a hard one. I had to convince her I wasn't going to talk loudly in the room before she let me in."

"I can believe you. When I drop stuff off for Nicole, I only get as far as the doorway, and that's on a good day. Most of the time she meets me in the parking lot of Nicole's building when I pull up."

"I like her, though. The fact that she's so cool took me by surprise. And she don't play, either."

"Terrell, Mr. Phillips needs to see you in his office," CJ walked up and announced.

Kayla scowled and opened her car door. "I'll talk to you later, Terrell."

"Do that, and please give Day a kiss for me. Oh, and tell Geno I said what's up. He ain't hung out with me in a minute."

"That's probably why we're still together. The only person he needs to be hanging out with is me." She laughed as she got in. She waved good-bye and cut her eyes at CJ as she pulled away, honking her horn.

"What does Mr. Phillips need to see me for?" Terrell asked as they re-entered his office.

"He doesn't want you for real. I just decided to rescue you from the likes of her. You all had been out there talking for a while, and I thought you needed an excuse to get away."

He couldn't believe the nerve of her. He could see now why the females disliked her so much. She was catty, and in a matter of a few seconds, she seemed less attractive to him.

"I didn't need you to do that. Kayla is my best friend, not to mention the mother of my godchild. There was nothing to rescue me from."

"Well, I don't like her. She's disrespectful to me and thinks she's all that. When we do the department cutbacks next month, hers is gonna be one of the top names on the list." CJ sat down and crossed her legs. She began examining her nails as if she was pondering what color she should polish them next.

"What are you talking about, CJ? Kayla is one of the best reps we have at this company, not to mention one of the brightest."

"That may be one of her problems. She's too smart for her own good. And you see what almost happened in the parking lot. You and I work too hard around here disproving stereotypes and breaking through glass ceilings for our people, and here she comes like she knows every damn thing and someone owes her something."

"Kayla's not like that at all. I will admit she has the tendency to get dramatic every now and then, but when it comes to intelligence and hard work, I would put her up against you and myself any day of the week. And I'm not just saying that because she's my friend, either. You have no reason to fire her." Terrell was furious. To think that CJ was actually considering letting Kayla go because she was intimidated by her was unthinkable.

"Well, I'll say this because she *is* your *friend* . . . Looks like you just found a reason to make my Fourth of July a little bit hotter." CJ stood up and smoothed down her skirt.

"What are you saying, CJ?" he asked, trying to control his tone. Never in his life had a female given him an ultimatum, and he wasn't about to take one from CJ, of all people. He didn't care how fine she was. *This trick has lost her damn mind. I know she's not about to do what I think she is.*

"I'm saying that if you want—your goddaughter, is it?—to continue to have benefits with this company, you'll make our little rendezvous on the Fourth happen. It's not that difficult, Terrell. What's the big deal? It's only one date."

Terrell knew she was serious. He had been putting her off for several weeks, and now she had the leverage she needed to do whatever she wanted. She was the puppet master and he was damn Pinocchio. *And the strings are tied around my balls.*

Chapter 24

"So, you mean to tell me that we ain't doing nothing for the Fourth of July?" Jermaine asked Toby as they installed the security camera. This was the sixth job they had done together, and another one based on a referral from Stanley, their favorite customer.

"I mean, we can throw something on the grill and have some drinks in the backyard, but no, I'm not having a huge cookout."

"Damn, man. Anjelica and I were hyped up about it and everything. We went to the mall last week and got our outfits."

Toby stopped what he was doing and looked at his best friend.

"I was gonna be clean, too. We were gonna wear all white. That was gon' be fly." Jermaine actually sounded disappointed and Toby shook his head.

"Tell me you're playing, right?"

"Naw, I ain't playing. You can call her and ask. And I told Meeko I was chillin' over here when she called wanting to do something for Isis's birthday."

"Isis's birthday? When is her birthday and why didn't Meeko call me?"

"Her birthday is on the fourth. And duh, why would she call you if I already told her I was coming to your bash? By the way, she is mad that you didn't invite her. Pass me those wire cutters."

Toby passed him the tool and said, "How am I gonna invite her to a party that I'm not even having? I can't believe I forgot about Isis's birthday."

"That's messed up, Toby. And you see her every day, too. I can't believe I bought new gear and you're not having a cookout," Jermaine said through clenched teeth holding the wire he was cutting. "Are we at least gonna go to a club or something?"

"No. If I step into a club, they're gonna be calling for me to come into that booth. I definitely ain't going to a club," Toby told him. "Tell you what. I'll call Meeko and we can have a small get together at the crib. That way we can celebrate Isis's birthday and all hang out."

"That's cool with me. Anjelica and I can wear our new gear." He winked.

"You're about as bad as a woman. And the operative word is *small*—you, Anjelica, Meeko, me and maybe Terrell. That's all."

"What about Isis? I mean it is her birthday, after all."

"You're not funny. And Isis."

They finished up the installation and were loading up the truck when an Infiniti SUV pulled behind them.

"Hey there, fellas! I see you guys are working hard today," Stanley called from the driver's side.

"What's up, Stan? Looks like you're the one that's been working hard. I like your new ride," Toby said as they walked over to him.

"See, Toby, I told you we were in the wrong line of business. The drug game is definitely where it's at." Jermaine nudged him and they all laughed.

"I bet you get all the ladies with this, huh, Stan?" Toby joked. "Don't lie, either."

"Aw, come on, guys." Stan shook his head bashfully and pushed his glasses up on his nose. "It's not even like that. I got this for tax purposes. Besides, I've been too busy to get with the women these days."

"Come on, Stan. You always gotta make time for the ladies. All work and no play makes life dull," Jermaine said.

"Look, I have someone you might be interested in. What are you doing next Friday?"

"Next Friday, that's Independence Day, right?" Stan asked.

"Yeah. You got plans?"

Toby looked at Jermaine, wondering where he was going with this inquisition and who he was talking about.

"No. I was gonna hang out by the pool and catch up on some reading. That's about it." Stan shrugged.

Jermaine raised his eyebrows at Toby then looked back at Stan. "Well, Toby is having a get together Friday evening and she'll be there. Why don't you drop by? Toby and I will introduce you."

"Really? That would be great. I mean, what's she like? Is she cute? Not that it matters. Is she smart? Now, that matters more than her looks. Well, as long as she can hold up her end of a conversation. What does—"

"Just show up Friday and you'll see for yourself. Now, we're not promising that you're gonna marry this girl, just that we'll introduce you. That's it, nothing more," Jermaine clarified.

"That's all I need. I really appreciate this, you guys. Man, I heard about your parties, Toby, and now I'll get to be at one. I gotta go find something to wear. I'll see you guys Friday." Stanley jumped into his SUV and started it up. He was about to drive off when he slammed on the brakes, startling them. "Hey, you guys didn't tell me what time to be there."

Jermaine looked at Toby, who was still confused by what his boy was doing. "What time you kicking things off, T?"

"Five o'clock," Toby said, slowly shaking his head at Jermaine.

"Five it is. You need me to bring anything? I'll bring something anyway. Thanks again," he yelled and took off.

"Jermaine, man, what are you doing? Didn't I say a *small* get together? Here you go inviting people already. And how the hell are you gonna hook Stanley up with Isis? She ain't gonna be interested in him," Toby said.

"What are you talking about? Stan is only one person, and he's our best customer. That's why I invited him to hang out. You know he's cool. I didn't think you'd mind. It ain't like I told him to bring his brother. And I plan on introducing him to Meeko, not Isis."

"Meeko?" Toby asked, surprised. He started laughing when he thought about Meeko and Stanley. "Meeko. Terrell thinks Meeko is trying to get with you."

"Please, Meeko is trying to get me to hook her up with any single man that owns a house out here. That's the only reason she's been on my back these past few months. Besides, she knows I'm with Anjelica."

"Meeko and Stanley. That's hilarious." Toby was laughing so hard that he was crying. "She is gonna curse you out next Friday. This get together may not be so bad after all."

Since Jermaine was the one who thought having a party was such a great idea, Toby made him come over early Friday morning to help get everything prepared. They went to Sam's and bought plenty of food, drinks and a birthday cake for Isis, then went to Party City and picked up balloons, decorations and paper products for the event.

"You didn't invite anyone else, did you?" he made sure to ask Jermaine while they were unpacking everything.

"I haven't told a soul, Toby. I swear. The only person I'm responsible for is me, Anjelica and Stanley. That's it. You talked to Meeko, Terry and Isis, right?"

"Yeah."

"So they're *your* guests."

By 2:30 they had everything ready and Jermaine left to get dressed and pick up Anjelica. Toby lay across his bed, thinking he would get some rest before everyone arrived. The phone rang, preventing that from happening.

"Hello."

"Hey, Toby, were you 'sleep?" Roni asked.

"Not really. What's up, Ron?" He rolled over onto his back, not really wanting to talk to her. Their last few conversations had led to arguments, and he wasn't in the mood to argue today.

"I just wanted to wish you a happy anniversary, that's all," she said with a sigh.

"Huh?"

"We met a year ago today, at your house."

"That's right. Happy anniversary to you too. You hanging out today?"

"Not really. My mother is having a little something over at her shop. That's why I'm calling. She wants you to come. You feel like rolling over there with me?"

"Sounds like fun, but I can't. I already have plans. I'm sorry. Tell her I'll be there next time."

"Plans? What are you doing today?" Roni asked.

"Jermaine and Anjelica are coming over in a little while." He regretted telling her the moment the words came from his mouth. He started to lie and tell her he had to work, but didn't feel the need to.

"I thought you said you weren't having a party, Toby," she retorted. He knew she was mad. *I should've just lied*, he thought.

"I'm not having a party, Veronica, just Jermaine and Anjelica."

"I can't believe he's still dating that girl."

He really wasn't up to having this conversation with her, so he told her, "Give your mom and everyone my love and tell everyone I said hello. I'll talk to you later."

"Fine, I will. And Toby?"

"Yo?"

"I love you."

He tried to think of a correct response, not wanting her to read into anything. "You too, Roni."

His answer must have satisfied her because she hung up the phone. He sat up on the side of the bed, trying to get his thoughts together. He was so confused. He loved Roni, no doubt about that, but he still didn't feel ready to pick up where they left off like she wanted to do. There was something still preventing him from making that move.

And then there was Isis. He smiled at the thought of her. She was so special to him, always had been. There were times when they were together he wanted her so bad he could taste it. But it wasn't going to happen. He had accepted the fact that they would be no more than friends—good friends, special friends, but friends nonetheless. And for right now, he was cool with that. *For right now.*

He decided to get up and get dressed. There were some last minute details he needed to take care of.

He was in the backyard making sure his bar was stocked when he heard his doorbell ring. He looked at his watch and saw that it was only 4:30. He hurried to the door and opened it.

"Uncle Jay?"

"What's up, Toby? Am I the first one here?" His uncle brushed past him. He was dressed in a pair of white shorts and tank top, a pair of white sandals on his feet and a white hat. He was carrying a plastic bag in each hand.

"Uh, yeah. What are you doing here, Uncle Jay?"

"I came for the cookout. What do you think I'm doing here? I got some fresh catfish for you to fry. I already battered it up. You want it in the kitchen or the backyard?"

"I, uh, you . . . put it in the kitchen." Toby closed the door and followed him into the kitchen.

"This all the food you got, Toby? I know you got more food than this," Uncle Jay said, looking into the refrigerator.

"That's all the food I'm gonna need. I'm not having a big party this year. Just a little get together."

"So, I bought a new outfit for nothing. You like it, though? I look nice, huh?" He started dancing like he was a long lost member of the Temptations.

"You look good, Uncle Jay." Toby laughed. The doorbell rang again and he told his uncle to hang out in the backyard while he went to answer it. Jermaine and Anjelica were kissing on the doorstep.

"Uh, y'all might wanna get a room instead of coming here," he told them.

"Don't hate because I got the flyest female in town on my arm tonight, Toby. Ain't that right, boo?"

"No, I have the finest brother by my side," she told him. "But you come in as a close second, Toby."

"Come on in before the flies start buzzing with all that crap both of you are talking." Toby laughed. They made a great couple and they looked good dressed in their white attire. He didn't know whether Jermaine brought out a different side of Anjelica or maybe he had just never noticed it before, but Terrell was right. She was as funny and down to earth as her sister, and he liked her.

"You start the grill yet?" Jermaine asked.

"No, not yet. I was about to when Uncle Jay showed up."

"Uncle Jay? He's here?"

"In the backyard. Go on back. I'm gonna put some music on."

"Please don't let it be Bobby Womack. You know how your uncle is."

The doorbell rang again. "Shut up and go in the backyard. This is probably Meeko and Isis."

It wasn't. Decked out in an all-white linen suit, complete with a derby on his head, was Stanley. He was even carrying a huge bouquet of white roses and a bottle of champagne.

"Hey, Toby. Is she here?"

"Naw, Stan. She's not here yet. Come on in. You got clean for this one, huh?" Toby couldn't help laughing.

Stanley brushed the front of his shirt and adjusted the flowers. "I wanted to make a good first impression. You think she'll like the flowers?"

Toby thought about Meeko and nodded. "I'm sure she'll be impressed. Come on out to the back."

Toby took the flowers and champagne from him and directed him to the backyard. He was introducing Stanley to everyone when once again the doorbell beckoned him.

"I'll get it," Jermaine told him. "It's probably your date, Stanley. You ready?"

Stanley looked at Toby, who gave him a pat on the back. "Let them in, Jermaine. He's ready."

Jermaine went back into the house and Toby lit the grill. He was about to get the meat that was marinating in the fridge when Jermaine came back out. Instead of Isis and Meeko, he was followed by Tia, Theo, Kayla and Geno.

"What's up, Toby? Hey DJ Terror. Player, player, where's the food?" They all greeted him.

Jermaine rushed over and told him, "I didn't know what to do. I couldn't just turn them away. I swear I didn't invite them."

"Then why are they all wearing white?"

"I don't know." He shrugged.

Before Toby could respond, Isis and Meeko came through the side gate and entered the yard. He walked over and hugged both of them. Isis looked stunning in an all-white strapless halter dress with silver accessories. Her hair was beginning to grow back, and was held off her face by a silver studded headband. Her partner in crime, Meeko, was also decked out in the color of the evening.

"You look beautiful," Toby whispered into Isis's ear as he held her close to him. "Happy birthday."

"You don't look so bad yourself, and thank you." She hugged him back.

"Ahem." Meeko interrupted their moment. "Why is everyone dressed in all white but you? Aren't you the host of the party?"

"No one told me there was a theme, I guess," he answered, looking down at the yellow Nautica shirt he was wearing along with his jean shorts and yellow-and-white Air Force Ones. "And I didn't know I was having a party until all these people showed up."

"Oh." Meeko looked over at Jermaine, who was serving drinks at the bar. "Well, Jermaine told us he was wearing all white like we were all supposed to. Let me go curse him out right quick."

"Wait!" Toby stopped her, remembering her date was already present. "There's someone here that's been waiting to meet you. Sit over there at the umbrella table and I'll bring him over."

"For real? Don't play with me, Toby. Where is he?"

"Just go sit down and I'll bring him over. Isis, you want something to drink?" he asked. "How about a Slow Comfortable Screw?"

"How about a bottle of water? We'll discuss the other thing later." She winked at him. He smiled at her, hoping that she wasn't talking about the drink. He rushed off to get her water and find Stanley.

He found him near the back of the yard, talking to Uncle Jay, who had started frying fish in the deep fryer.

"I found this here deep fryer in the kitchen closet. Good thing I remembered to bring some cooking oil," Uncle

Jay told him. "And I see you done stole some of my Jasper's aprons, too."

"Yeah, Uncle Jay," Toby admitted. "Hey, Stanley, there's someone looking for you."

"Uh, okay, Toby. Where?" he asked nervously.

"Right over there, sitting at the table with the umbrella. I told her you would come over."

"God, she's beautiful. She looks like Janet Jackson! You guys didn't tell me she was *fine*! Not that I care," he added. "Oh God, I can't wait to meet her. What did you do with the flowers?"

"Hold up, man. I think you're looking at the wrong one. The one sitting at the table across from Janet is the one waiting to meet you. Let's go into the kitchen and get the flowers." He gestured toward the house. *And pray that we can scrounge up some more food for these people,* he thought, looking around at the crowd of people that was now in his backyard.

Chapter 25

Terrell sat on the side of the bed, rubbing his throbbing temples. He looked over at his clock and saw that it was close to 6:00. He was supposed to pick her up an hour ago, but he didn't care that he was late. His head was pounding and he didn't want to go pick her up at all.

"So, what are you going to do?" Anjelica had asked when he told her what CJ had threatened.

"I don't know. I really don't have a choice. If I don't take her out, your sister is gonna lose her job."

"Can't you just report her to human resources or something? There has to be something you can do. That's sexual harassment."

"I know, but I'm just gonna bring her to Toby's house, stay for about an hour, then tell her I have to leave."

"Okay, I can go in the house for a minute then come back out and say you have an emergency phone call. You go to the phone then pretend that you have to leave."

It sounded like a damn good plan when Anjelica said it, and he agreed that it was foolproof. But even with a plan, he still didn't want to go. Unfortunately, he had no choice, so when CJ called his cell phone for the ninety-ninth time, instead of letting his voicemail pick up, he answered it.

"Where the hell are you? You were supposed to be here an hour ago," she yelled in his ear, making his head hurt worse.

"Man, stop yelling. I had a headache and laid across my bed. I fell asleep. Damn, you act like we gotta be there *at* five. It's a cookout, not the job. We can be late."

"When you tell me you're gonna pick me up at a certain time, I expect that. Now, what time do you think that'll be, because it definitely ain't gonna be at five now, is it?"

"I'll be there in thirty minutes."

"You'd better be," she said and hung up the phone in his ear. He looked over at the white shorts set hanging in the doorway of his closet along with his brand new white Classics. For the first time that day, he smiled.

"You're wearing all white to a cookout?" she asked when she opened the door to her townhouse.

"You know how I do," was his only response. She leaned over and gave him a kiss on the cheek. He recognized the strong scent of Fendi, which she usually wore. He was beginning to hate it.

"Come on in. You want me to make you a drink?" She smiled. He smiled back when he noticed she was wearing an all-red Capri set and red sandals. Her micro-braided hair was hanging to the middle of her back.

"No thanks. We'd better get going," he told her.

"I thought you said there was no rush. You can come in for a minute. I have to get my purse anyway." She pulled him inside.

He looked around in her nicely decorated living room while he waited. She had a lot of African paintings and statues. There was also a bookshelf full of books, mostly about Black history, and also quite a few books on beauty and makeup. Her furniture was red, and the room accented with black lacquer tables.

"Nice place," he called out.

"Thanks. I haven't really done what I wanted to do with it, but it's home," she replied. "You ready?"

"Yep, let's be out."

Their conversation in the car was mostly about music and movies. Terrell tried to keep the topics light, anything not to add to his stress level. He was surprised at the

number of cars parked in front of his brother's house wher
they got there. Toby assured him that this was going to be a
small barbecue, no more than ten people. There were at leas
ten cars parked outside the house.

"I thought you told me that he wasn't having his usua
big party this year." CJ looked at him.

He shrugged in reply and said, "He told me he wasn't
And believe me, if he was, we wouldn't even be able to turr
down the street it would be so crowded."

They got out and walked inside without knocking.

"Wow, he has a lot of CDs!" CJ commented as they
walked past Toby's living room. "This place is nice."

"Yeah," Terrell said and continued to the kitchen. He
was surprised to see Uncle Jay inside making potato salad.
"Uncle Jay, what are you doing here?"

"What does it look like I'm doing? Your brother got al
these people that just showed up, and we're trying to figure
out how to feed them all. You know the club is closed
tonight, so I rode over there and got some stuff out the
freezer."

"It's that many people here, Unc?"

"You'll see when you get out there. How you doing
there? I'm James Jasper Sims, Terrell's uncle. But you can
call me JJ." He wiped his hands on his apron and held one
out for CJ.

"I'm Cora Ware, Terrell's co-worker, but you can call
me CJ." She laughed.

"Come on, CJ. Let's see if Uncle Jay is exaggerating as
usual," Terrell said, opening the back door. He noticed that
his uncle had a strange look on his face as he went back to
stirring the big bowl of salad.

Uncle Jay wasn't exaggerating. The yard was full of
people. Some were dancing; others were at the bar where
Terrell noticed Jermaine was mixing drinks. He spotted Toby
behind the grill, decked out in yellow, unlike all the rest of

his guests who were dressed in all white—with the exception of CJ, of course.

"Everyone has on white," she hissed. "This is an all-white party and you didn't tell me."

"I didn't know. And Toby doesn't even have on white; he has on yellow."

"I am so embarrassed. I can't believe this." She grabbed his arm and squeezed it.

Hoping this was his way out, he offered, "You want to just go ahead and leave? We can go."

She looked around and saw the good time everyone was having and hurriedly told him, "No, I'm fine. Just get me a drink."

Terrell directed CJ to a seat he spotted at an empty table toward the back of the yard, and told her he would bring her drink to her. He didn't even ask what she wanted, thinking that if she was thirsty enough, she would drink whatever.

"What's up, Terry?" Jermaine greeted him. "I see you brought your date from work."

"Your girlfriend has a big mouth," Terrell responded.

"Hey, don't talk about my woman. You wouldn't want me to say anything about yours now, would you, Anita Hill?" He cracked up and then noticed Terrell wasn't laughing. "Just kidding, bro. What can I get ya?"

"Man, I don't care. As long as her ass can drink it and she won't be thirsty no more."

"How about a Margarita?"

"Fine. Just hurry up before she comes over here and someone sees her."

"Man, you can't miss her. How tall is she, 'bout six feet? And she got on all red. How could you not see her?" Jermaine passed him the drink.

"Thanks, Jermaine. If I wasn't already feeling bad about this situation, I definitely would be feeling that way now," he told him as he turned to walk away.

"No problem, Terry." Jermaine snickered.

Terrell had just made it back to the table when he saw Kayla dancing with Geno. Toby had thrown on one of his line dance CDs and everyone was up doing the Bus Stop to a mix of Teddy Pendergrass's "Get Down" and Michael Jackson's "Don't Stop 'til you Get Enough". Even Meeko was dancing with some corny-looking dude wearing glasses.

"Come on, Terrell, let's dance!" CJ pulled at his arm.

There's no way I'm dancing with her so everyone can see us, he thought.

"I hate line dances," he lied. "They remind me of square dancing we had to do in high school."

CJ finished her drink and stood up. "Well, I'm going out there and join them. You sit here and be a spoil sport all you want. You've had a stank attitude all day. If I were you, I'd change it. After all, your girl's job depends on it. Isn't that her over there? I think I'll go and speak."

It took all he could not to curse CJ out right then and there. He took a few deep breaths and told her, "Wait. You want to dance, we can dance."

They joined the bunch dancing in the middle of the yard and began sliding with the music. Terrell started to relax and told himself that he needed to loosen up if he wanted the evening to go off smoothly. After a while, the crowd of dancers thinned out as people went to eat the food that Uncle Jay was spreading on the table. It wasn't Toby's usual smorgasbord, but they had hooked it up the best they could.

Terrell told CJ he was hungry, and they went to stand in line to make their plates. He was trying to make eye contact with Anjelica to give her the signal, but she was too busy yapping with Isis. He excused himself and scurried over to where they were talking near the bar.

"Uh, are we gonna do this or what?" he asked her.

"Do what?" Isis looked at him like he was crazy.

"Not you. I'm not talking to you."

"I don't know what you're talking about either." Anjelica smirked.

"Come on, Anjelica. Don't play with me."

"All right, all right. Calm down. You ready for me to do it now?" she asked. Isis looked at both of them, trying to figure out what scheme they were about to perform.

"Not right now. We're about to eat. But as soon as you see me taking our plates, you come and get me. Okay?"

"Okay." She nodded.

"What's going on here?" Isis squinted her eyes at him.

"She'll fill you in later. I gotta go," he said, noticing CJ had started fixing her plate. Terrell was on his way back to her side when the goofy guy Meeko was dancing with earlier started screaming. He was standing right in front of CJ.

"What the hell are you doing here? Someone call the cops! Now! Toby! Jermaine, call the police!"

Toby came flying from behind the grill and Jermaine from behind the bar.

"What's going on?" Jermaine yelled.

"Stan, calm down!" Toby told him.

"I told you he was stalking me! How did you know I was going to be here? You'd better get away from here! I have a restraining order against you!" Stanley yelled.

"I had no idea you were going to be here. Terrell brought me here as his date. I suggest you leave if there's a problem. I am an invited guest, the same as you." CJ popped her neck and put her hands on her hips. As much as she talked about Kayla acting ghetto in the parking lot that day, she was doing a good job herself, Terrell observed.

"Stanley, she's my brother's date. She came with him, Toby explained calmly.

"Do you know who that is? That's the *guy* that's been stalking me for the past six months."

"Oh hell!" Jermaine's eyes widened. "This is *him*?"

"What are you talking about, *him*?" Terrell asked confused by everything they were saying. "What the hell is going on, CJ? What the fuck is he talking about?"

"I am very much a woman, Terrell. I don't know what they're talking about," CJ responded. "This man is obviously crazy, and I can't believe you're asking me this, especially in front of these people."

"Tell her to prove it!" Anjelica yelled from where she was standing.

He turned and looked at CJ. She had a pleading look in her eyes, and he didn't know if it was from the embarrassment of the situation or because she knew Stanley was telling the truth. "Prove it, CJ."

"I will do no such thing. How dare you!"

"She can't prove it. She's a pre-operative transsexual. A man, living as a woman, who plans on having the surgery one day. A man who fools people into believing he's a real woman," Stanley announced, cutting his eyes at CJ.

"I don't have to take this from you. I'm leaving." She ran out the gate leaving everyone at the party stunned.

"I knew it! I knew there was something about her! I told you, Terrell! A man!" Kayla laughed out loud. Terrell looked at her, his eyes filled with anger.

"Chill, Kay. This ain't funny right about now." Geno told her. "It may be later, but right now, it's not."

"Damn, Terry. I know you ain't one of those DL brothers, are you?" someone cried out.

"You never can tell these days. Maybe that's why he tries so hard to be a mack anyway," another guy said, laughing.

"Fuck all of y'all!" Terrell yelled, still baffled by what had just happened.

His brother patted him on the back then called out, "What happened to the music? And Uncle Jay, we need some more fish. Y'all wanted me to have a party, so hell, let's party."

"I ain't even realize the music stopped," Terrell looked over and told Toby.

"The music always stops when the drama goes down. You know that, baby brother. But the party always starts up again. Always remember that."

"Now you giving out words of wisdom?" Terrell laughed.

"I learned from the best," his brother told him, looking over at Isis, who was talking to Uncle Jay. She looked over at the two brothers and blew them a kiss. "Was that for you or me?"

"I think that one was for me, Toby. She knows I need some feminine affection right about now. I can't believe CJ is a dude. I knew she was tall, but she ain't even look like a dude. Am I losing my ability to screen them out? Am I giving out a signal or something?"

"No, man. It was just one of those things that just happened. It has nothing to do with your manhood. And don't let this mess with your head, either," he told him. "I gotta get back to this grill before Geno burns my crib down. You gonna be all right? I need to call Nicole and get her over here so you can feel better?"

Terrell laughed. "I wish she could, then I wouldn't be in this mess, for real. I miss her."

"I know you do, but time heals all wounds. Believe me, I know."

"More words of wisdom?"

"I got plenty if you need them. I'll check on you in a minute." Toby rushed back to the grill where it looked like

Geno had started a small fire. "Geno, man, what are you doing to my meat? Don't you know this is steak?"

Terrell sat at the table, still in a state of disbelief.

"You mind if I talk to you for a second?" Stanley asked.

"Naw, have a seat." He sighed.

Stanley sat across from him and took off the white derby he had been sporting all evening. "I think that I'm the only one out here that can relate to what just happened, and I feel the need to tell you that it's not your fault. That was the first issue I had to deal with myself when he did the same thing to me. Just because you didn't know, or even the fact that you were attracted to her, doesn't make you a punk—or shall I say a homosexual? These guys nowadays look just as good if not better than most of the females out here.

"But what they're doing is deceitful, and they don't understand that they could easily wind up hurt. I commend you for not snapping on her and taking a swing." Stanley laughed.

"I ain't the one to talk about anyone's lifestyle," he continued, "but when you try to infringe on mine and be deceitful about it, that's just wrong. That's all I wanted to tell you."

"I appreciate that, Stanley. I really do."

"Now, I have a new lady I'm trying to impress myself, so I'd better get back over there before someone scoops her up from under me." He stood and put his hat back on.

Terrell gave him a handshake, and as Stanley walked away he told him, "Hey, Stanley, the lady you're trying to impress, she loves poetry. Oh, and walks on the pier."

"Thanks, man. Good looking out."

The vibration of his cell phone caught him off guard and Terrell nearly jumped out of his skin. He didn't recognize the number and hesitated as he answered it, thinking it might be CJ stalking him now. "Hello."

"Terrell Sims?"

"Uh, who's calling?"

"This is Leah. I'm a nurse in labor and delivery over at County Hospital. Your girlfriend has just been admitted and she wanted us to call you," a snotty voice told him.

"Very funny, Anjelica. You know I ain't in a playing mood," he uttered.

"I'm sorry, sir. This isn't a joke," the woman replied.

He looked over at the bar and saw Anjelica feeding watermelon to Jermaine. She looked over at him and waved.

"Uh, I . . . I'm on my way!" He closed the phone and rushed out, ignoring his brother and Kayla, who were calling behind him. *I've got to get to my wife and my child,* was all he could think about as he raced to his car. As he turned the corner, he saw CJ climbing into the back seat of a cab. *Please, God,* he thought, *no more drama.*

Chapter 26

"He should have never invited her over here to begin with," Kayla told her friends as she grabbed a Pepsi from the cooler. "I told Terrell a long time ago that there was something wrong with that woman—I mean man. Well, whatever it is. But he didn't want to listen to me. He's gonna mess around and Nicole is gonna leave him for good if he doesn't get his act together."

"I can't believe she found out about him and your sister. And she has the nerve to be here all up in Jermaine's face," Yvonne added.

Toby was still flipping burgers and hot dogs on the grill, glad that they hadn't mentioned his name. But when he saw Anjelica standing behind them, he knew it was about to get ugly and the music was about to stop again.

"That's right. I'm here all in his face because he is *my* man. And you know what? He ain't got no complaints. You barely got a man yourself, Yvonne. And you, Ms. Hopkins, let me tell you a thing or two. The reason Terrell brought CJ was because she threatened to fire you if he didn't. So to save your ass—again—he did what he had to do."

"What?" The two sisters stood face to face.

"She was going to fire you when they did the departmental cut backs next month. Now, you know and I know that you haven't done anything to be fired because Ma and Daddy would kick your behind. But you were about to be let go, sweetie, until your boy stepped in. So, while you're talking about him behind his back, you need to be thanking him."

Anjelica turned, walked over to Jermaine and placed a passionate kiss on lips. She smiled and called out, "Sweetie, think you know all about my past and what went down with a few people here tonight, don't you? There are no secrets between us."

"You're right." Jermaine nodded then gave Geno a wave. Yvonne and Kayla looked appalled.

"Now, since he doesn't have a problem with it, that's all that matters. Anybody got any questions?"

No one made a sound as she looked around. Satisfied, she called out, "What happened to the music? Y'all wanted to have a party, so hell, let's party!"

The music came on again, and people began dancing. Meeko beckoned for Toby to come inside, and he followed her. Uncle Jay was placing candles on the birthday cake.

"I know you got a lighter somewhere around here, Tobias."

"Should be one in this drawer right here. Here it is." He passed his uncle the lighter then said to Meeko, "I see you and Stanley looking cozy over there. What's up?"

"I mean, he's cool. A little corny, but he's a sweetheart." Meeko smiled and sniffed her roses, which were sitting on the counter.

"I bet you he is. Brought all them flowers like it was a funeral or something," Toby teased.

"Don't hate because he's a romantic. There's nothing wrong with that, is there, Uncle Jay?"

"Nothing at all. Matter of fact, I can get real romantic myself. Get some candles and some baby oil . . . "

"Okay, Uncle Jay. We get the idea. Let's take the cake out. The candles are melting." Toby opened the door and held it while his uncle and Meeko walked out. Everyone started singing, and he grabbed the microphone next to the stereo.

"Happy birthday, Isis. I know you thought we forgot, but we didn't. We love you," he told her. She looked at him and he saw the tears in her eyes. Meeko ran to her side and gave her a big hug. "Now, may I have this dance, birthday girl?"

She nodded and met him in the part of the yard tha was the designated dance floor. He took her hand in his and held her close. The music began to play, and he looked down to see her reaction. People had to be wondering why he chose that song, but he knew why and so did she. They smiled a each other as they rocked to Klyymaxx singing "I'd Still Say Yes." It was the one CD that he didn't have in his collection but he searched on Amazon and had it rushed out to him sc he would have it in time for this night. It was the best idea he'd had in a long time.

"Thank you," she whispered to him.

"For what?" he asked.

"Just being you." She laid her head on his shoulder.

He had no doubt that her friends were watching, but he didn't care. Isis was his friend, and she deserved everything he was doing and more. She had been there for him when he was at his lowest and taught him a lot about himself.

The song went off and they began jamming to "The Men All Pause." Everyone was having a ball, and Uncle Jay began putting away the food.

"Having fun at your party?" Toby asked.

She looked up at him and smiled. "Don't even try it. This isn't *my* party. This is your annual bash. It's just a coincidence that my birthday is today. But I am having fun. Is it always this excitement-filled?"

"Yeah, it is," he admitted. "Let me go help Uncle Jay before he calls me out. After all, it is *my* house."

"I'll help out too. After all, it is *my* party." She hit him playfully on his chest.

They began carrying trays of leftover food into the kitchen to put away. It had gotten dark and Toby said they needed to hurry because the fireworks were about to start.

"I think I've seen enough fireworks for tonight," Uncle Jay told them. "I knew something wasn't right about that woman when she shook my hand. I tried to give Terry the look, but he didn't see it, I guess."

Isis cracked up. "What look is that, Uncle Jay?"

"You know; the look." Uncle Jay's eyes widened and he gestured with his head as he grimaced, demonstrating the look he gave Terrell.

"How was he supposed to know what that meant, Uncle Jay? You just made the same face when you wanted me to open the fridge for you." Toby shook his head. Isis laughed even harder.

"That was this look, not that one. And he should have known something was up when I made it. Shut up and hand me that foil!" Uncle Jay snatched the box out of his hand.

They finished just as the fireworks began. Toby grabbed Isis by the hand; she grabbed Uncle Jay, and they returned to the backyard. Toby put on some mellow music then sat close to Isis on a picnic table, away from the rest of the crowd.

"I thought you said you weren't having a party."

Toby turned and was shocked to see Roni standing behind them.

"Hey, Roni. Believe it or not, I didn't plan on having a party. All of these folks just showed up. I think it was a set up, though, because as you can see, they're all dressed in white." He jumped off the table and stood up. He looked at Isis, who excused herself. He reached out his hand and helped her off the table.

"She didn't have to leave. Obviously she was an invited guest, unlike me. I can't believe this. I'm walking around here wearing your ring and you have a party, don't invite me, and when I do show up, I catch you hugged up with some chick." Roni folded her arms in disgust.

"Hold up. I told you I ain't plan to have a party. You know you would've been invited if I did. And I wasn't hugged up wit' nobody. Don't even come here with that bull. We've had enough drama for the night," he warned. She looked at him and he saw the look on her face soften. He couldn't help smiling at her. "You want something to drink? We got strawberry daiquiris."

"With whipped cream?"

"Always a diva, huh? But I think we can make that happen. How was your mom's?" They strolled over to the bar where Jermaine was holding Anjelica in his arms.

"It would have been better if all of my friends had shown up there instead of here."

"Well, they're right over there. Go over and I'll bring your drink to you." He pointed toward Kayla and the rest of the crew. She swept past him to join her girls, ready to hear about everything she missed.

He walked over to the bar and began fixing her drink. He looked up and saw Isis standing next to Uncle Jay. Her head was tilted up to the sky and he could tell that she was laughing. As if she could sense him staring, she turned around and waved. He gave her a nod and took Roni her drink.

"Thank you, baby." Roni put her arm through his and leaned on him. "So, who is the girl you were with?"

"That's my friend, Isis."

"Your friend? Wasn't she the girl that sang that night at Jasper's?"

"Yeah," he answered.

"I've never met her before. How long have you known her?"

"About three years. And she just moved back in town. That's why you've never met her." Toby began to be irritated by Roni's line of questioning. "What's with the third degree?"

"Don't get loud out here, Tobias."

"I'm not loud. You are, Veronica."

Toby had struck a nerve and he knew it. People around them turned and stared. Roni's face turned red and she looked as if she wanted to kill him. "Can I see you inside for a moment?"

He wasted no time following her into the house. They climbed the steps and went into his bedroom. He sat down on his bed, not even in the mood to argue. His day, although filled with unexpected events, had been pretty good until she showed up and started grilling him about Isis.

"What's going on with you, Toby? Even if you didn't plan to have a party, when people started coming, you could have called me. But it's obvious that you're not happy to see me anyway. I get no kiss, no hug, no affection period."

Toby listened to what she was saying, wanting to answer her, but couldn't. It was true, he loved Roni. She hurt him, but he was healing. And there was still the possibility that they would wind up together. That's why he didn't mind that she wore his ring. He did still love her.

"I love you, Roni, but you are the one that got caught wit' another dude. Or has that incident slipped your mind? And now you're here making an issue over nothing. I ain't even trying to hear that."

"I know, but isn't part of loving someone forgiving them? I've apologized time and time again. I love you, Toby, but I feel like you're going to let this hang over my head forever. Do you love me enough to forgive me? If so, then we've got to move past this. If not, take your ring back and let me go on with my life. I can't keep living in limbo like this," she cried.

He hated seeing her like this. He reached out and held her close. "Don't do this to me, Roni. Please, don't. I love you, I do." Not knowing what else to do, he grabbed her and kissed her passionately on the mouth. His mouth explored hers for several minutes until he pulled away.

"I missed you so much," she told him as she ran her fingers along his back.

"We need to get back downstairs." He turned and opened the door.

"I told Mama that I would help clean up after everyone left. You want me to come back when I finish?" She offered when they made it down the steps. Toby was hesitant in his answer, so she added, "We still need to talk.

"It's cool. I'll be here." He kissed her once again as she got in her car. *It's just to talk, that's it,* he reminded himself.

People began leaving, and Toby was glad that the bash he didn't even know he was hosting was over. Instead of going inside the house, he walked back into the yard to make sure everything was put away and in order. He picked up two bags of trash and took them to the large garbage can located on the side of the house. When he got inside, he was surprised to find Isis washing the remaining dishes.

"Where's Meeko?"

"She left with Stanley. He offered to give her a ride in his truck. I'm taking her car home. Everybody else gone?" she asked.

"Yeah, the party is over. I think everyone had a good time, though. Anybody heard from Terrell?"

"No, he rushed outta here without saying a word to anyone. Pass me that dishtowel."

"You know you don't have to do this, right? I could have finished all of this myself." He handed her the towel. "I'm glad you did, though."

"So, you and Roni made up? That's good." She smiled at him.

"How do you know that?" Toby leaned against the counter.

"Okay, I need to be honest with you." She folded the towel and laid it on the side of the sink. Toby's heart began to beat rapidly as he prepared himself for what she was about to tell him. "I didn't stay here just to wash the dishes. I stayed for something else."

She walked up to him and seductively ran her hands under his shirt.

"What's that?" he asked. She looked up at him and licked her lips. *This can't be happening to me. I've wanted this woman for months and she rejected me. Now that I've reconciled with Roni, she's coming on to me. What am I supposed to do?*

"I stayed to tell you . . . " Her hands moved to his back and she ran her fingers along his spine. He shifted his weight so she could reach farther.

"Tell me what, Ice?" he whispered.

"I told you so! I knew you were gonna get back with her!" She laughed. "I knew you were getting back together, especially when she walked up and saw me with you. That was it right there."

"You're crazy. If I didn't know it then, I definitely know it now. Why you playing with me like that?" He snatched her arms from around him, laughing.

"What did you think I was gonna say, Toby?" She raised her eyebrows at him.

"I thought you were gonna discuss your Slow Comfortable Screw that you didn't get earlier," he confessed.

"You can give it to Roni when she comes back. She is coming back later, isn't she? And don't lie."

Toby looked at her. He couldn't lie. "Yeah, she says she's coming back."

"I guess I'd better get outta here, then. I ain't trying to get you in no trouble."

"Wait a minute, Isis. I got something to give you before you leave." He rushed up the steps and into his room. He opened the drawer and took out the small box. He was glad that he had left it in the bottom of his drawer instead of on top of his dresser where it had lain all week. Jermaine had ordered it for him from an exclusive jeweler he had done some work for in the mall. He hoped Isis would like it.

She was waiting at the bottom of the steps when he got there. "This is for you. Happy birthday."

"Toby, you didn't have to do this. The party was enough." She hugged him. "Thank you."

"Come over here and open it." He pulled her to the sofa.

She slowly unwrapped it then looked up, her eyes filled with tears. "It's beautiful, but I can't accept this."

"Yes, you can. Let me put it on you. You know I had to get some ice for my Ice." He reached into the box and removed the platinum necklace holding the heavy platinum charm. It read *True Love*, and was encrusted with diamonds.

He reached around her neck and fastened it. "It's perfect. This is the one true love you have to be willing to accept. You are such a special woman, and deserve everything your heart desires, but you've got to stop pushing people away and let them in. Part of learning to love is learning to trust."

"Now look who's the one giving advice on love. You've been back with Roni how long, thirty minutes, and now you're giving out Tobyisms? Thank you, Toby. I'm glad that you've found your way back to that person that you believe in and trust enough to love unconditionally."

She stood up and walked to the door. "Does this mean I have to find another workout partner?"

"Be there Monday, same time. Meet you at the treadmills." He hugged her, enjoying the feel of having her in his arms. She was the most beautiful, intelligent, humorous, talented person he knew. *Whoever winds up with her is damn lucky, and I'll be the first to admit it.* Isis Adams was truly a gem, and he knew it.

Chapter 27

Terrell made the forty-minute ride to the hospital in twenty minutes flat. He didn't care that it was a holiday weekend and state troopers were on the lookout. All he cared about was making it to Nicole's side. He skipped taking the slow elevator and climbed the five flights of steps to labor and delivery. He could barely talk when he got to the nurses' station.

"I'm loo . . . looking for . . . my girlfriend. Some . . . someone called and . . . told me she was . . . here," he managed to say as he struggled to catch his breath.

"Are you okay? Calm down. Breathe. Do we need to get you some oxygen?" the nurse asked him. He shook his head at her. She was a young girl and her nametag read PEACHES. "Okay, now, what's your girlfriend's name?"

"Nicole. Nicole Matthews."

Peaches' fingers ran quickly along the keyboard and she told him, "We don't have a Nicole Matthews, sir. Are you sure she's here at County?"

"Yeah, I'm sure. That's who called me. Some nurse named Leah called and said she was in labor!"

"Calm down. Let me page Leah and we'll see what's going on. She could have been here and we released her."

"That was less than forty minutes ago. I don't understand why she came to County anyway."

"Well, this is a county hospital. Does she have insurance? If she doesn't, we would be where she would come." Peaches picked up the phone and paged Leah to the reception area.

"She works at Mercy Memorial in labor and delivery. This is crazy!" He exhaled loudly. His nerves were already shot from the entire CJ fiasco, and now someone was playing games on his phone. He took his phone out of his pocket and was about to call Arianna when a short, plump brunette came through the doors. He could hear screams coming from one of the rooms and he shuddered.

"Hey, Peaches, you paged me?" she asked.

"Yeah, did you call this gentleman about his girlfriend?" Peaches asked.

"I called quite a few gentlemen this evening. Did you look her up? What's your girlfriend's name?" Leah questioned him.

"Nicole Matthews," Terrell answered. "She looked but couldn't find her."

"We don't have any Nicole or Matthews, I don't think. What's your name?"

"Terrell Sims."

"Oh, okay. I remember calling you. You got here fast. Come on back. You're just in time." She smiled.

He looked back at Peaches, who just shrugged at him, then he followed Leah through the doors. As they walked down the hall, the screaming became louder. They entered the room where the howls originated and as he realized what was going on, the blood rushed from his head. His worst nightmare was coming true right before his eyes. Instead of Nicole, the love of his life, lying with her legs in the stirrups, there was Darla. Her hands were gripping the sides of the bed, and she was shaking her head back and forth like she was possessed, her hair standing on top of her head. A masked doctor was posted between her legs, ready to catch whatever was about to come out.

"What the hell is going on? Is this some kind of a joke? It has to be!" Terrell growled.

Darla's eyes grew wide and she reached for him. "Oh, Terrell, you're here, baby. I knew you would make it!"

"You need to get over there and hold her hand so we can coach her through this, sir. She's been refusing to push until you got here," the doctor told him.

"I'm not holding her hand. You've lost your damn mind, and so has she!" he snapped.

"Mr. Sims, if you're not going to help the situation, then you need to leave. You can have a seat in the waiting room and we'll come and get you when your baby is born. You would think you would be a little more concerned and sensitive at a time like this," Leah huffed at him. She pointed to the door and he turned to leave.

"No, Terrell! Please don't leave me! I need you here! This is our baby and you should be in here. Just stay in here, please!" Darla howled.

"She's crowning. Okay, we're gonna need you to push, Darla. Come on."

"Just stay right there, please!" She begged him.

Terrell looked over at the doctor and the nurse, who was trying to calm her down and get her to cooperate.

"Can you just stand over there in the corner where she can see you?" Leah asked.

He quietly walked over to the corner of the room farthest away from the action. He tried to ignore them completely by looking around at the small, cramped area, which not only held the bed Darla was in, but a chair, some monitors, a small TV and what he knew was a warming bed. He had learned that term from Nicole. There was another small door, which he assumed led to the bathroom.

This has got to be some kind of set up. I can't believe I am in here while she's over there having a kid— my kid, which I already paid for her to get rid of. She hasn't called, come by, wrote me a note to tell me shit, but she wants me to be here to hold her hand. There's no way.

Why, God? I've started living right; I don't hang out, I don't party, I work hard. I even started going back to church.

All I wanted to do was marry Nicole, be a good father, a good employee, and a good person. Now here it is I got transvestites on the job harassing me, the woman I'm in love with won't even see me, and now a girl I can't stand the sight of is about to deliver my baby. Life can't get any worse.

At that very thought, Terrell's phone began ringing.

"You need to cut that off in here!" Leah yelled so she could be heard over Darla's squelches.

He looked at his caller ID and saw Nicole's number. He looked from his phone to what was going on in the room then back at his phone. It soon stopped and the screen read 1 MISSED CALL. Just as he was about to turn it off, it began ringing again.

"Turn it off!" the doctor yelled.

Instead of turning it off, he walked into the hallway and answered it.

"Terrell, its Arianna."

"What's up, Ari? How's Nicole?" he whispered. The door was closed, but Darla's screams could still be heard. He saw a sign for the waiting room and he headed toward it.

"Her water broke and her contractions are steady. We're leaving for the hospital in about fifteen minutes," she said.

If ever Terrell wanted to crawl in a hole and hide from the rest of the world, it was at that very moment. He hated the fact that God had a sense of humor and had proven his last thought untrue. He tried not to panic, and to focus on what had to be done.

"Is she okay? Does she need anything?"

"She's in labor, Terrell. She doesn't have the flu," Arianna replied. "I don't know where the hell Gary is. I can't find him anywhere. I need for you to get here!"

"I can't," he confessed weakly.

"What do you mean, you can't? Where are you, and what's all that crying in the background?"

Terrell thought quickly. *God, I know what I'm about to ask you is wrong, but please help me come up with a lie and make it a good one,* he prayed.

"I'm across town at County. One of my friends had a little mishap, and I came to try to help out," he blurted.

"Oh, okay. Well, get to the hospital as soon as you can," Arianna told him.

"I will," he assured her.

"And Terrell?"

"Yeah?"

"She's asking for you. Please hurry up."

"I'll be there in twenty minutes," he told her and put his phone back in his pocket. Leah was coming out of the room when he walked back down the hallway.

"Well, it's a boy. Nine pounds, four ounces," she announced.

"A boy," he said to himself. *I have a son.* "Can I see him?"

"Sure," she said with a confused look on her face. "I didn't think you'd wanna come back inside."

They walked into the room where the doctor was still with Darla. She was no longer screaming, but she was still moaning something terrible. Terrell focused his attention away from her and on the tiny creature lying on the warming bed, wrapped in a blanket. Terrell just stared, waiting to see if he would feel that instant bond he had heard so many fathers brag about when they tell of the first time they laid eyes on their children. There was none for him. No tingling sensations, no overwhelming emotions; all he saw was a kid he didn't want.

"Wanna hold him?" Leah asked, picking up the small bundle.

"No, that's okay. I gotta go. Nine pounds. That's pretty big for a preemie, huh?" He looked at Leah.

"Preemie? This kid definitely isn't a preemie. As a matter of fact, she was two weeks past her due date."

Terrell began to calculate. He counted months and days, and remembered the two times he had slept with Darla. Both times were in early December, before he was committed to Nicole. There was no way that this baby was his. As a matter of fact, she had to already be pregnant while she was sleeping with him.

She set him up. It took all the strength he had not to walk over to her and push her fat, yellow behind out of the bed. Instead, he looked up at the ceiling and gave God thumbs up. Without saying anything, he walked out of the room and never looked back.

Chapter 28

Toby had just stepped out of the shower when he heard the doorbell. Hoping it was Roni, who never showed up the night before, he threw on a pair of shorts and went to open the door. He prepared himself for the pitiful excuse he knew she'd have. But instead of his fiancée, Stanley was standing in his doorway.

"Oh, I'm sorry, Toby. I thought you'd be up by now. I left my hat and I came back to get it. I guess I should've called," he said, clearly embarrassed.

"No, it's no problem, Stanley. Come on in. Where did you leave it?"

"It was on the bar. That was the last place I had it. I can get it later, really."

Toby unlocked the back door and cut on the porch light. He looked down at his feet and told him, "You go ahead."

"Okay," Stanley said and walked outside. "I don't see it. You think someone picked it up?"

Toby went to the hall closet and slipped on a pair of old K-Swiss he wore whenever he cut grass. He joined his friend in the backyard in an effort to find his missing hat. While they were searching, Stan's phone rang.

"Must be Meeko. I told her to call me when she got up." He smiled and flipped the state of the art device open. "Hello."

Toby walked away to give him some privacy and continued the search. He reached behind some tables that were stacked near the bar and found that what he thought was a paper plate was Stanley's hat. He tried to smooth it out as best he could. "Yo, Stan. I found it, but it's a little messed up."

Stanley was sitting on one of the picnic tables, rocking back and forth. Toby eased up to him, noticing something was very wrong.

"You okay, Stan? What did Meeko say?" he asked.

"It wasn't Meeko. It was the police. Someone set my house on fire," Stan mumbled.

"What? When?" Toby was stunned.

"A little while ago. I have to get to the hospital."

"The hospital? For what?"

"My brother was inside when the fire was set. He's pretty messed up." Stan continued to rock. Toby could see that he was in shock and in no condition to drive. He pulled him up and led him to his car, which was parked behind Toby's.

"Where are your keys?" Toby asked him.

"On your kitchen counter."

Toby ran to the door and turned the knob. It was locked. He ran around to the back of the house and went through the door that was still slightly ajar. While inside, he grabbed a We Secure U T-shirt and threw it on. He found the keys and rushed back outside. Stanley was leaning up against the truck. He unlocked the doors and commanded him to get in.

"What hospital, Stan?"

"Mercy."

Toby kicked the truck into gear and high-tailed it to Mercy Memorial.

"My brother is all I got in this world, Toby. You know that? We don't have any parents. It's just me and him. If he dies, what am I gonna do?" Stanley asked.

Toby's heart went out to him. He knew exactly how Stan felt. With the exception of Uncle Jay, Terry was all Toby had for family. He couldn't imagine life without his younger brother. "Don't worry, Stan. Your brother is going to be all right. You have to stay positive, though."

Stanley wasn't in any better shape when they made it to the emergency room. Toby had to ask for Sean, because Stan couldn't even say his name, he was so broke down. The nurse had to practically carry him to the back so he could see Sean. Toby told him he would be waiting for him when he came out.

He was leaving a message for Roni, letting her know that he had an emergency and wouldn't be home if she stopped by, when another call came in. Recognizing the number, he answered.

"Yo. You a'ight? I was worried about you," Toby said as he paced down the hall.

"I'm cool, man, but have I got some stuff to tell you. I had a hell of a night," Terrell replied.

"Naw, I bet it don't compare to what I gotta tell you. You're not gonna believe where I'm at."

"You ain't gonna believe where I'm at. Nicole has been in labor since last night. We're at the hospital now."

"Stop playing. I'm at the hospital too!"

Toby heard Nicole let out a yell for Terrell to get off the phone before she threw it across the room, and his brother told him he had to go.

"Let me know what happens. And Terry?"

"Yeah?"

"I love you, bro. Congrats."

"Love you too, Uncle T."

"You're talking to Toby? I'm dying over here and you're talking to Toby of all people?" he heard Nicole squeal.

"I had to call him and tell him we were at the hospital, baby."

The phone went dead and Toby walked back down to the waiting area. He had just taken a seat when he saw Ms. Ernestine coming in, wiping tears from her eyes.

"Ms. Ernestine," he called to her.

"Oh, Toby," she cried as she embraced him. "I'm so glad you made it. I knew you'd be here soon enough. I just knew it."

"Ms. Ernestine, what's wrong? What are you doing here?" He was confused.

"What do you mean what am I doing here? This is where they brought Roni."

"Roni? What happened? Where is she?" Toby was distraught.

"She was in an accident, Toby. No one called you? I'm so sorry." Ms. Ernestine began crying harder.

"Accident? Where?" Tears began to form in his eyes now. He knew she was upset, but he needed to know what happened.

A few moments later, Kayla, Geno, Tia and Yvonne all arrived. They began to comfort Ms. Ernestine and he slipped out to the receptionist to see if he could find out some more information.

"Excuse me. I'm Veronica Black's fiancé. Is there anyone that can give me an idea of what happened to her and how she is?" he asked.

The nurse recognized him from earlier and nodded. She told him to stand there and wait a few moments while she found someone to talk to him. He stood, expecting a doctor rather than the police officer who approached him.

"You're here for Veronica Black?" the man asked.

"Yes, I am. I'm Tobias Sims, her fiancé. I understand she was in an accident, but no one is giving me any information. Where was she driving?"

"Driving? She wasn't driving. Your fiancée was in a fire in a home located in Wheatland Heights. She's received some serious burns and she's in stable condition. All in all, she's lucky to be alive. So is the friend she was with."

"Roni?" Toby called her name softly. She looked so fragile, lying in bed with all the tubes and monitors attached to her. He walked a little closer. "Roni?"

There was a nurse at the foot of her bed, writing something on her chart. She looked at Toby and told him, "She's pretty out of it because of the drugs, but she can hear you. Just talk to her."

"Ron, can you hear me? It's me, baby. Open your eyes for me."

Her face was dark and bruised. The doctors said that she had suffered several first- and second-degree burns, but she would be fine. He had spent all day at the hospital along with everyone else, waiting to see her. Her mother told him he could go in first, alone. He thought seeing her would be hard, but it wasn't. He needed to see her; he wanted her to be awake so she could explain why she was inside Stanley's house, asleep with Sean when the fire was set. There had to be a reasonable explanation for it. Just hours before, she had assured him that she loved him and he could trust her.

God, just let her wake up and tell me something, anything to make me understand how she could do this to me. Could she really betray me like this again?

"Can I kiss her?" he asked the nurse.

"Gently, just on her forehead."

He leaned over and kissed her lightly, whispering her name again. "Roni, I love you."

Her eyes fluttered open and she blinked. He smiled at her, elated that she was finally conscious. The feeling of anger with her seemed to subside when he saw that she was alive.

"Hey, sweetie." He grinned. An overwhelming feeling of love came over him as the fear of losing her gripped his heart.

"Sean?" was the name that escaped from her lips. Her eyes closed once again and she drifted back to sleep.

Devastated, Toby looked down at her hand, which he was holding. As he slipped the ring off her finger, a tear rolled down his cheek.

Chapter 29

Tyler Alexander Sims was born at five minutes after 7:00 on the fifth day of the seventh month. He only weighed five pounds, seven ounces, and although he was born premature, he was healthy. For that reason, his father felt he should be named Seven Cinque Sims, which would be a tight name should his son want to embark on a future career in hip-hop. His mother, who already had plans for her son to be either a biochemist or a heart surgeon, instinctively said no to such a ridiculous name. They did, however, agree that he was the most adorable baby they had ever seen.

Not only was Terrell present for the delivery, he even cut the cord. And when he looked into his son's eyes for the first time, he wept like he had never done before. He looked over at Nicole, who was crying as well, and told her, "Thank you. You have always been a remarkable woman, but this is the most remarkable thing I have ever seen. Thank you for letting me be here with you."

"You were there with me the entire time, Terrell. I love and appreciate everything you've done over the past few months. Now you're ready to be a father *and* my husband."

He took his son into his arms and carried him over to his mother. He had never felt so complete in all of his life. He was glad that he had made the changes he did, because having Nicole and his son in his life made it well worth it.

The nurse came in and said that she was going to take Tyler and let Nicole get some rest. Terrell kissed Nicole and told her he would be back by the time she woke up, then followed his son, making sure he got to the nursery safely.

"You did good, Terrell," Arianna said as she walked up to him.

"You did good too, Ari. You held it down for my girl, and we have a healthy son. I don't know how I can ever repay you." He hugged her.

"Oh, I'm sure you'll think of something. How about something big and expensive, like oh, let's say a Benz?" She laughed.

"Sure. After my son's first album goes platinum, I got you." He nodded. "Where's Gary? I'm surprised he hasn't shown up yet to regulate."

"Well, you know we're not together since he can't regulate what time to come home at night. He thought that just because I was staying with Nicole he could go out and do whatever."

"Take it from someone that knows firsthand, that's the easiest way to lose your woman," Terrell told her.

She went inside to see Nicole and he went off to find Toby, who hadn't shown up yet.

As he was headed to his car, Terrell found his brother sitting outside the front of the hospital. "What are you doing out here, Toby? I thought you would've been up to check out your new nephew."

Toby nodded. There was something about the way he looked that worried Terrell.

He walked over and sat beside Toby on the curb. "What's going on?" he asked.

"Too much to tell. Where do I even begin?" Toby shrugged and looked down.

"You been here all day?"

"Yep." Toby nodded. He picked up a pebble that was next to his foot and threw it.

"Come on. You can treat me to breakfast and tell me all about what happened."

Terrell held his hand out. Toby looked at him then grabbed it, pulling himself up. They went into the hospital cafeteria and each got a cup of coffee. Finding a table in the far corner, they sat and Terrell listened as his brother recounted everything that happened after he left the cookout. At the end of his story, he reached into his beat up sneaker and pulled out the ring he took back from Roni. It was then that Terrell truly saw how hurt his brother was.

"I'm sorry about all of this, Toby. I'll be the first one to tell you that what happened last night was messed up. I mean, I never would've thought that Roni would even cheat on you."

"Join the club. But she did—not only once, but twice, and with the same guy, at that. I guess I must be real stupid, huh? I wonder what he had that I ain't have."

"Don't be stupid. That's Roni's loss, not yours. You have a lot. She just threw it away. Just like I did with Nicole, but I was blessed enough to get it back, and I am not losing it again. I think when you lose it, it makes you appreciate it more, because then you realize how you really fucked up after it's too late. And then, if you're ever given that second chance, you'll do whatever you can to make it even better than when you first got it, if it's true love."

"Terry, what the hell are you talking about?" Toby asked with a frown.

"Man, who cares? All I know is that I been up all night, my girl took me back, I got a new son, and life is good. Yesterday my life was at the worst possible point I thought it could be, but today it's at its best. What a difference a day makes, huh? Come on. Let's go buy some *It's a Boy* stuff for little Seven."

"You named him Seven?"

"No, Nicole made me name him Tyler Alexander Sims, but Seven would've been a tight name, huh?"

"You gave him my middle name?" Toby beamed.

"Yeah, I wanted the middle name to be Cinque, but let me explain why . . . " Terrell put his arm around his brother as they walked out of the cafeteria and he explained the method to his madness.

Chapter 30

Toby stepped out of his truck and looked at the mirrored glass building. He looked down at the card and made sure he was at the right address. The sign on the front door confirmed that he was. It looked more like a finely decorated doctor's office than the atmosphere he expected. There were several women sitting in the lobby, chatting softly as they waited.

"Can I help you?" a beautiful Puerto Rican woman asked him. She was dressed in what he thought was a lab coat, but he could see she had on a dress underneath.

"Um, yes. I'd like to get a massage," he told her.

She stared at him with a look that let him know that a massage would be all that he was getting. "Full body?"

"Uh, yes." He nodded.

"Let me see if we have anything available. Weekends are always busy, and it's the holiday weekend, which makes it even worse." She looked down at her schedule. "I think I can squeeze you in. Marguerite can take you if you can wait twenty minutes."

"No, I want Isis to do it," he said quickly.

"Excuse me?" She frowned.

"I prefer Isis. That's who I need an appointment with."

"I'm sorry, sir. Isis is our busiest masseuse. She's been booked up for months. I can get you in with Marguerite today, and then let you have Isis's next available, which is two weeks from Thursday. How about that?"

"That won't work. I need to see her today. I'll pay double."

She gave Toby a startled look. The women who were waiting became silent as he waited for her answer.

"That's very generous of you, sir, but I'm sorry. There's nothing I can do. She's really booked up."

"Please, ma'am. I have had the worst night of my life. I am tense to the point that if I don't get a massage by the best in the business, I am going to snap. There has to be something that can be done." Toby threw his hands up in exasperation.

"Lisa, let him have my appointment with Isis and I'll go to Marguerite," a woman approached and said.

"Why, Mrs. Taylor, that's very generous of you," she said. "You should thank her, sir."

"Thank you, Mrs. Taylor. I appreciate it." Toby nodded.

"You're welcome." The woman went back and took her seat.

"Let's see. That one hour with Isis, that'll be $300."

"What?" he shrieked.

"You said you'd pay double, and you know we're gonna have to compensate Mrs. Taylor, as well."

Toby took out his credit card and passed it to her. After giving him his receipt, she told him to follow her, and led him further into the office.

There was soothing jazz playing and the aroma of lavender in the air. He found himself relaxing with each step. She opened a door and gave him a robe, a towel and some slippers, telling him to get undressed and lie on the table. "Isis will be here momentarily."

He obliged, and after fighting the sudden wave of sleep that overcame him when he lay face down on the table, he heard the door open. He buried his head into his arms, which were crossed in front of him.

"Hello, I'm Isis. I heard you requested me personally. I'm flattered. Did someone recommend me?" she asked him softly. He could hear her moving around.

"Yes. A friend of mine," he said without lifting his head.

"Well, you be sure to thank your friend for me. Is this your first time?"

"Yes," he told her. He moaned as her hands began to knead into his back.

"Then I'll have to keep that in mind and be gentle." Isis laughed, and he giggled along with her.

She remained fairly quiet as she pushed and rubbed his shoulders and then his legs. Her stroke was strong yet her touch was light, and he thoroughly enjoyed it. He was grateful that his tattoo was on the front of his chest and she couldn't see it.

"It's okay if you fall asleep. That happens quite a bit. But I can always wake you up with a hand job—I mean a manicure."

He lifted his head and looked at her. "You knew it was me!"

"Of course! How could I not? You think guys come in here every day and pay three hundred dollars for me?" She slapped him on his shoulder.

"I would've paid more, believe that," he confessed, noticing that she was still wearing the chain and charm he gave her.

"What are you doing here?"

"Meeko told me you had to work all day, and I had to see you. Your cell isn't on."

"Because I'm at work." She sighed.

"So, I figured I'd buy an hour of your time. Didn't know it would be three hundred dollars, though."

"You would've paid more, though. What's going on, Toby?"

He sat up and told her about Stanley and his house being burned down, and Roni getting caught in the blaze with Sean. She climbed on the table next to him and laid her head on his shoulder as he confided everything.

"You're gonna be okay," she told him when he finished. "I know you will. You're a strong man."

"Ice, please don't. Just let me say something before you go off on one of these encouraging tangents, please. I know that I'm gonna be fine. I found true love and someone I can love unconditionally. I didn't know that before, but I have."

"I know what I said earlier, but Toby, don't be stupid. I mean, unless she has a really good excuse, which I'm not saying she can't have, then I think it's time to let it go. I like Roni and all, but—"

"I'm not talking about Roni, Ice. I'm talking about you. I love you. You are my true love."

"Toby, you're talking out of hurt and anger because of what happened."

"No, I'm not. I'm talking out of frustration of being in love with you, but you won't forgive yourself for what happened that night and just allow me to love you. Loving someone is not beating yourself up over something you had no control over. You've got to love yourself enough, Ice, to let someone love you. And that someone is me, baby."

Toby didn't stop the tears from falling, and this time there was more than one. He stood up and looked at Isis so she could see that he was serious and this was real. He reached into his pocket and pulled out the ring.

"I know that's not what I think it is, Toby."

"What is that?" He smiled through the tears.

"You took the ring back?"

"I took it back. Now I can pawn it and pay off my three hundred dollar credit card bill for this massage that I'm not even getting."

He pulled her to him and kissed her on the mouth. As her tongue met his, he thought this was what perfection must feel like. She stroked his back, and he felt himself getting aroused. When they separated, they looked down at the towel he was wearing. "Looks like I need a manicure, huh?"

"You'll get it when I get the drink I never got at the party," she teased and kissed him again.

"Let me ask you this question," he said then paused. "How do you feel about having kids?"

"Depends on if I'm having them with a man who loves me enough to make some." She winked and his heart leapt.

Epilogue

T'was the night before Christmas, and the church was standing room only as everyone prepared for the entrance of the bride. The bridal party was fairly small, consisting of two bridesmaids and two best men. The maid of honor, Meeko, who had recently become engaged to Stanley, proceeded down the aisle first. The matron of honor, Kayla, who had wed a month before, was next. The bride was escorted by her father, who beamed with pride as he walked down the aisle with a daughter on his arm for the second time. And as happy as he was that both his daughters were now married, he knew he would still be working for a long time to pay off the debt of their weddings.

The bride looked lovingly at her husband-to-be, who now, with the help of his partner and best friend, owned one of the fastest growing security installation firms in the state. The groom looked over at his best men, knowing that this day would not be complete without them.

As the couple took their place at the altar, Toby, along with his fiancée, Isis, came before them and performed "The Closer I Get to You." Before they even finished, there wasn't a dry eye in the church. The wedding went off without a hitch.

Uncle Jay hosted the reception at Jasper's. While everyone ate, drank, and partied to "This Christmas" by the Temptations, he passed out cigars.

"What's this for, Uncle Jay? Anjelica, is there something you and Jermaine need to tell us?" Toby asked.

"He's passing out cigars, I'm not." Jermaine laughed.

"And you won't be passing any out until after we buy that house in Wheatland Heights, either." Anjelica kissed him on the nose.

"You all ain't hear?" Uncle Jay asked. "I found out I'm a father. Got the call on Friday."

"What? When did you have a baby?" Isis laughed.

"Well, the baby was born Fourth of July, but the mama just moved back into town last week and called me. You all may remember her. Darla. Yes sir, got me a big old fine boy!"

Everyone groaned as he began singing along with the Temptations, happy with the news he'd just shared.

After toasting the new couple, Terrell went and sat next to his best friend who was now his supervisor. Cora Ware had been convicted of first-degree arson and sentenced to thirteen years in prison. Kayla now had her job and was doing fine.

"What's up, DQ?"

"Not anymore, Terrell, not anymore. I haven't had any drama in a while, so you have to find a new name for me." She smiled.

"I have to find something else to call you since you've relinquished your title as the queen of drama. You're growing up. You were there for Anjelica on her big day, and I'm proud of you," he told her.

"I mean, she is my sister. Nothing can ever change that. You can't pick your family."

"You're right about that," Terrell looked over at Uncle Jay, "but you can always pick your friends."

"I'm glad I picked you," she told him.

"What are you talking about? I picked you."

"You did not, Terrell. I remember that day we were in the break room and you came in sitting by yourself. I invited you over there to sit at our table!" Kayla yelled.

They went back and forth with each other until he noticed a couple walking in. She looked over and stopped mid-sentence. All eyes seemed to be on Roni and Sean as they walked into the room, hand in hand.

"I'm going over there before something jumps off," she told him.

"And I thought you said there wouldn't be no more drama." He stood. "Man, this stuff is just getting started."